Ball Buster

Ball Buster

The Playbook Series

KARA SHERIDAN

FOREVER
YOURS

New York   Boston

Copyright © 2018 by Kara Sheridan
Excerpt from *Tight End* Copyright © 2018 by Kara Sheridan
Cover design by Claire Brown. Cover copyright © 2018 by Hachette Book Group, Inc.

Forever Yours
Hachette Book Group
1290 Avenue of the Americas, New York, NY 10104
forever-romance.com
twitter.com/foreverromance

First published as an ebook and as a print on demand: May 2018

Forever Yours is an imprint of Grand Central Publishing. The Forever Yours name and logo are trademarks of Hachette Book Group, Inc.

The publisher is not responsible for websites (or their content) that are not owned by the publisher.

The Hachette Speakers Bureau provides a wide range of authors for speaking events. To find out more, go to www.hachettespeakersbureau.com or call (866) 376-6591.

ISBNs: 978-1-5387-2718-8 (print on demand edition), 978-1-5387-2716-4 (ebook)

To my sister, Michele,
thanks for being here again.

And to my Philadelphia Eagles for providing
decades of on-the-edge-of-my-seat excitement.
I'll bleed green forever. And thank you for the
Super Bowl win!!!

ACKNOWLEDGMENTS

Thanks to the greatest agent in the world, Jill Marsal—we love football, right?

Hugs to my street team, Violetta's Valkyries, especially Barbi Davis.

And a big thank you to my editor Lexi Smail for holding my hand through our first book together.

Ball Buster

CHAPTER ONE

Savage," Coach Rangall called from across the locker room, hovering in the doorway of his office. "Get in here. Now."

Carson Savage buttoned his jeans and slipped on his boots before he threw his wet towel on the floor in front of his locker. Then he took a second look at the newspaper on his bench. He wondered if that's what Coach wanted to see him about—the *Mobile Tribune*'s latest headlines.

Truth no longer mattered to the media. Whatever increased sales ended up on the front page, making the once respected newspaper read like a gossip rag. And that gossip usually featured Carson or one of his teammates. Today, they called Carson a playboy. He quickly read the small print: *At 6'4" and 235 pounds, Carson Savage lives up to his name on and off the field. Local fans call the blond behemoth Apollo, the sun god, with his tan skin and perfect physique. We know what naughty gods like to do best... and we're not talking about completing passes or avoiding sacks on the field. As long as she's wearing a skirt and heels, Apollo will go down willingly…*

A photo of him climbing out of the swimming pool at his friend's party last weekend was also featured. The next shot showed his arms draped across the shoulders of two French supermodels. What the journalist failed to mention was Carson made an appearance at the party to help raise money for an international cancer nonprofit.

He crumpled up the paper and threw it in the garbage can. His teammates on either side of him laughed and looked away. That didn't make Carson feel any better. The dressing room was supposed to serve as a haven away from the media and crazy-ass fans—but over the last couple of years it seemed everyone was disposable. Veterans were traded or retired to make room for new talent. And that new talent usually liked to start trouble. Carson shot a suspicious look at the rookie getting dressed next to him. Trust and respect was earned. The Warriors jersey hanging over Jag Patera's locker didn't qualify him as a superhero. In Carson's eyes, that jersey should motivate the twenty-year-old jock to work that much harder.

The team had been plagued with problems last season and, of course, since Carson was a captain, it didn't matter who screwed up or why—he had to answer for it. And the shit-eating grin on Patera's face told Carson everything he needed to know.

"What the hell, Jag?" Carson asked.

"What?"

"Did you do something I should know about? Preferably *before* I end up on the hot seat with Coach?"

Patera lifted his arm and applied his deodorant, ignoring Carson's questions. *Sonofabitch.*

"Baxley?" Maybe his best friend would shine some light on what exactly they were so entertained by.

"Nothing, bro. Can't blame me for the Apollo tag. That's something you're gonna have to live with."

Carson smirked. "Any idea what they call *you* in private?"

"Big."

Carson rolled his eyes. Was Baxley referring to a certain body part or his stats? With 1,865 total yards, twenty touchdowns, and forty-eight receptions during the regular season last year, Tyrone Baxley was definitely big—larger than life, really. And he didn't have a problem letting the world know it.

"Save it for the ladies."

Tyrone laughed. "Is that what you think I do? Recite my personal stats while I'm…"

"Pretty sure I don't want to know."

"Carson. Now," Coach growled.

Carson did a quick check in the mirror hanging in his locker. Nothing looked out of place; his hair was damp and his face freshly shaven.

They had just kicked the shit out of the Florida Heat in a special exhibition game, 28-7. But that wouldn't save him from Coach. Not even a championship ring could do that. Coach Rangall expected the best from his players, even during the off season. "Nice passing today," Sam said as Carson walked past.

"Thanks, man. We still on for Sullivan's tonight? A couple beers and steaks?"

"Sure." Sam glanced in the direction of the coach's office. "If you don't get sent to bed without dinner."

Yeah…

Coach Rangall stepped aside as Carson entered his office and then slammed the door shut. "It's days like this I wish I was still a college coach."

Carson claimed one of the leather guest chairs in front of Coach's desk and waited for him to sit down.

"While you ladies are busy primping and scratching your asses, I had to deal with the front office about this crap…"

Coach shoved a stack of photocopied images in front of Carson.

"Take a look, *sweetheart.*"

Almost afraid to, Carson stared down at the first paper. What the…definitely someone's lily-white ass. He gazed at the second photo, recognizing his own muscular posterior. But…how? He flipped the papers over so he didn't have to see more, then met Rangall's angry eyes.

"Care to tell me how your ass ended up on Twitter, Facebook, Instagram, Google, Snapchat, and Tumblr within forty-five minutes after the game ended?"

Carson had to think about it, because he didn't have any answers *or* excuses.

"I almost forgot." Coach turned his laptop around so Carson could see the screen. "The first picture is also available on Shutterstock for four ninety-nine."

Carson studied the crisp color image. Yep. No mistaking the partial view of the black and gold serpent tattoo that curled around his lower back. That confirmed it.

"If you think I'm taking selfies in the showers, Coach, and posting them…"

"What else am I supposed to think? It wouldn't be the first

time one of you narcissistic assholes sent lewd photos to someone."

Carson had to admit his coach had every reason to be upset. NFL players weren't exactly known as altar boys. Just last year, one of his former teammates had texted dick pics to his girlfriend. They broke up a week later and she plastered the X-rated shots everywhere. The media went crazy. Hell, the fans did, too.

But if Coach thought about it, he'd realize Carson wouldn't do this. Sure, he maintained his bad boy image to keep the fans guessing, but the truth was, he preferred anonymity. Unlike most players, Carson spent most of his time out of town at the three-hundred-acre farm he purchased over a year ago.

He folded his hands on top of the desk, hoping Coach would believe him. "I'm not into this sort of trash, Coach. But I'm pretty sure I know who is."

"Yeah?" William Rangall asked. "Who?"

Two names came to mind, but Carson wouldn't expose them. He'd deal with Patera and Baxley his own way. "I can't share that information."

"*Can't*, or *won't*?"

"Does it matter, sir?"

Coach rubbed the back of his neck and sighed. "It does if you lose your starting position with this team. Do you think I want my daughter exposed to this kind of shit, Carson? What about your mother and sisters? This is Alabama, not New York. We're in the Bible Belt."

"I understand."

"Do you?" Coach inclined his head. "I know you didn't do

it, Savage. But it's your job to make sure this kind of thing doesn't happen. You've got to separate yourself from the clowns. The commissioner already slapped us with a dozen fines for violations last year. We can't afford another PR nightmare."

"The game sold out today."

Rangall chuckled. "To see you play great ball or to watch the circus freaks?"

That hurt, and Carson frowned. "Honestly? Probably a little bit of both."

"Yeah. That's what I'm afraid of."

Carson leaned back, extending his long legs. "What do you want me to do? Accept responsibility for something I didn't know about? Check my file, Coach. The worst thing I've ever done is get caught with a girl in the men's bathroom at Sullivan's."

"Not one of your best moments."

"No." He was too drunk that night, his mind and heart twisted up in memories from the past that still haunted him. Memories of a girl he should have never let get away. "It never happened again. And won't."

Coach nodded, and his tense jaw relaxed some. "You know who the troublemakers are, Carson. I get the whole brotherhood thing, believe me. But it's not going to work anymore. There are thousands of starry-eyed athletes salivating to get a chance to play pro ball here. The front office would rather pay off contracts and trade offenders to a new team than risk further damaging our reputation. The Alabama Warriors aren't supposed to be the bad boys of the NFL."

Carson wanted better for his team, he really did. But wanting and getting were two different things. He still partied occasionally, soaking up the attention and enjoying the women who chased after him. "Don't you read the gossip rags? Reporters keep a solid record of who's doing what."

"Don't need to. I have four teenage daughters. They give me daily updates."

With his own sixteen-year-old sister to worry about surfing the web, Carson knew what Coach meant. "I'll handle it."

"Not good enough. Fix it. *Now.*"

"I'll work on it, but while I'm here, most of the team wants to know why we've been called in early. Vacations were canceled. Plans changed at the last minute. It's June, Coach. I know the game was for charity, but an extra camp? Why?"

Rangall rubbed the back of his neck. "You're perceptive, Carson. Why do you think half the team has been ordered to camp early?"

"You want me to speculate?"

"I want you to use that good judgment I know you have."

"All I know is the front office is staying hush-hush."

"Yeah, they like staying employed," Coach said.

"Garrett and Ness aren't here anymore." The offensive coordinator and his assistant hadn't reported to camp as expected. And the rumors were flying in the locker room already. "The owner is cleaning house, isn't he?"

Coach Rangall drummed his fingers on the edge of the desk. "Yep. And if you think the coaches and staff are the only ones being looked at, think again."

Rangall motioned at the pictures. "Winning games isn't good enough anymore. The fans expect more out of you, from the team, and from the league."

"What happened to just playing ball?" Carson sighed. He hated the controversy and had never liked being in the spotlight. But if you wanted to stay in the NFL, you had to play the part of a superstar.

"That's a great question. One you'll never get an answer to. Here's the facts. If you can't accept the responsibility of a franchise quarterback, the owner will find someone who can."

Carson's jaw clenched. He'd never expected to hear those words. The Warriors had traded two draft picks, players, and cash to get Carson on the team. Would they be willing to part with him so easily? "Should I call my agent?" He eyed his coach. Maybe Rangall was making empty threats to get his attention.

"Call the damned commissioner if you think it will help keep you on the team." Coach shot up from his chair and began pacing. "I'm on your side, Carson. I know who the culprits are." Coach looked in the general direction of the locker room. "But the public doesn't differentiate between players so easily. One bad choice translates into everyone suffering the consequences."

"I get it."

"Do you?"

"Yeah. And I'll do whatever I can to help."

"Good. Now get out of my office."

Carson stood, feeling very much like Atlas with the weight of the world resting on his shoulders. "How much time do I have?"

"Six weeks. Before team-wide camp starts. I want to see press coverage of you and whoever else it takes to convince the public you've suddenly found God. Public appearances at charitable events. Visit hospitals and schools. Go shovel horse shit at the animal shelter if that's what turns you on."

Carson already spent a substantial amount of time volunteering at the local hospitals and mentoring troubled teens during a weekend sports camp every month. "Got it. Anything else, Coach?"

"Yeah." Rangall looked up. "We're bringing in a professional to train you heathens on how to use social media to your advantage."

"What?"

"You heard me, Carson."

"I manage my own accounts just fine."

"That may be," Coach said. "But someone needs to rebrand all of the accounts." He looked over Carson's shoulder, staring out the big picture window into the locker room. "Damn internet is a blessing and a curse. Wouldn't surprise me if the front office instructs us to scrub all your profiles."

"But I have two million followers just on…"

"Save it for Monday, Savage." He held his hand up.

Carson nodded. "Goodnight, Coach."

"'Night."

Carson exited Rangall's office and headed back to the locker room.

"That bad?" Ty asked.

Carson slumped onto one of the benches and looked around to make sure no one was listening. "Did you have anything to do with that ass shot?"

"Me?" Ty smirked. "I see enough of that ass in here."

"But you know who did it?"

"I might."

Carson knew what his captain responsibilities were, and sacrificing his career to keep his teammates safe wasn't part of it. Not when the stakes were so high. But he would protect Ty at all costs, their friendship ran that deep. "I need you to pass along a message for me."

Ty crossed his arms over his chest. "I'm listening."

"Tell the prick if he does anything like that again, his ass is mine first, then Coach's."

"What happened in there, Carson?"

"None of us are safe, Ty. The front office is bringing in a social media expert to rebrand us."

"Shit. Really?"

"Yeah. And if we don't cooperate, there will be some big changes around here. Coach is talking trades and contract buyouts."

"Jesus Christ." Ty sat next to Carson, obviously taking the news seriously. "Did my name get mentioned?"

"No. But everyone who was called in for early camp is under the microscope. We have six weeks to get our shit together. I need your help."

"Anything."

"Nothing specific right now, but I'll need you to back me up whenever I need it."

Ty fist-bumped Carson. "I've got your back, bro."

Carson nodded and stood. "I'm stopping by the house before I go to Sullivan's."

"OK, I'll see you there."

Carson watched his best friend walk out of the locker room. They'd been through some shit together. And if Carson had anything to say about where his team was headed, he and Ty would still be standing in the Warriors' locker room this time next year.

He grabbed his duffel bag from his locker and started for the parking lot. Not the way he'd hoped to start the weekend, but at least Coach Rangall had given him fair warning of what to expect on Monday. And no matter what it took, Carson would make it work, because nothing or no one was going to take him away from this team or this town.

CHAPTER TWO

Sadie Reynolds looked at her best friends, Barbi and Erika, then back at the itinerary in her hand. She'd reluctantly agreed to attend a three-day life skill building workshop at the Red Horse Inn in Landrum, South Carolina, because she'd been told she had trust and control issues. Her friends also believed she'd never gotten over her first love—Carson Savage—and, as a result, continued to self-sabotage her dating life.

Surrounded by the Blue Ridge Mountains and rolling hills, Sadie could think of better things to do, like hiking or horse-back riding. She'd even settle for a taste tour at the local winery. Not to mention enjoying the sheer luxury of their accommodations, which included a spa and a five-star restaurant.

"Zip lining." Barbi said. "We're in the first group."

"And just how is that supposed to build trust?" Erika asked.

"Didn't you read the itinerary?" Sadie asked. "We're partnered with a life buddy for this exercise. We'll be suspended three hundred feet above the river on wire no thicker than a clothesline. By crossing the canyon together, we'll successfully demonstrate complete trust and, in my case, how to let go of that control thing."

"I don't like your ominous tone, Sadie." Barbi snatched the paper out of her hand. "This isn't just about trust and control, you know. We're also supposed to leave behind any negative feelings."

"About what? Men?" Erika giggled like a little girl.

"Since I don't have negative feelings about anything, I'm pretty sure that excludes me from this event." Sadie turned to go.

"Wait a second." Erika grabbed her arm. "I forgot you're afraid of heights."

"No."

"Yes," Barbi confirmed. "That's why you never climbed the cherry trees when we were kids. You always stood below with the basket."

"I fly all over the country," Sadie countered.

"After you pop a Valium." Barbi crossed her arms over her chest. "I know this isn't your thing, sweetie, but let's be honest. If you don't face your demons now, you're never going to get over the past. So why not try to have some fun while dealing with your issues?"

"What issues?" Sadie asked, knowing perfectly well what they were. Carson Savage. Blond hair, bright blue eyes. And judging by the latest photos all over the media, hotter than ever.

"General trust issues and the fact that you refuse to date someone for longer than a month," Erika said.

"The latest one asked me for my address," Sadie countered, trying to sound reasonable.

"That's normal, Sadie. Especially if he wants to send you flowers."

Sadie gazed at Barbi for support.

"Chad was a nice guy," she said.

"His head was too big for his body!"

"Whatever." Barbi rolled her eyes. "He had a buzz cut. That always makes a guy's head look too big. You're just picky."

"I liked his blond hair and blue eyes. It's your favorite combo, Sadie," Erika said.

"Erika!" Barbi gave her a little push. "We're not supposed to mention anything that reminds Sadie of…"

"What?"

"Him."

"Who?" Erika looked confused.

"Carson," Barbi blurted, then covered her mouth.

"You really don't know what you're talking about. None of my issues have anything to do with Carson." Sadie scanned the footpath ahead. Every man who expressed interest in her fell short of Carson's superior physique and Southern boy charm. Unfortunately, no one lived up to her high school sweetheart.

But right now, she needed to focus on the freaking zip line, which would probably cause that aneurysm that was definitely in her brain to finally burst. "What if I get a blood clot in my lung from being so high up?"

Barbi gave her a what-the-hell-are-you-talking-about look. "Stop making shit up."

"I'm not!"

"You just had a physical last month," Barbi reminded her.

"I have high blood pressure."

"Nope; one-oh-five over seventy is excellent," Erika said.

They were supposed to meet their crew leader at the trailhead in thirty minutes and then hike a mile up the hillside to the staging point for the zip line exercise. "The last time I rode a Ferris wheel I threw up, remember?" This was *kind of* pushing her boundaries.

"Everything makes you throw up, Sadie," Barbi teased. "Heights, men, spicy food…"

"That's not true!"

"Didn't I get a call at one in the morning after you blew Chad off?" Erika asked. "I believe your exact words were 'I think I need to throw up.'"

Sadie laughed. "He was giving me those I-want-to-fuck-you eyes."

"That's normal," Barbi offered. "Your reaction wasn't."

"I didn't want to sleep with Chad."

"Who do you want to sleep with?" Barbi asked.

"I don't know."

"Here…" Erika looked around. "What about him?" She pointed to a random guy—tall with dark hair, athletic, and twenty-something.

"Nice legs," Sadie admitted. "But his hair is too long."

"Wait a second." Barbi smiled. "The blond. Look at that. He screams Carson, doesn't he, Erika?"

Erika watched the man walk by. "Shorter, but definitely similar. So…" She turned to Sadie. "Your type. Period. Let's get his number."

Sadie hadn't talked to Carson Savage in seven years…since she broke up with him at their high school graduation party. And just because she dated men who looked similar to her first love—okay, near genetic copies—didn't mean anything. She had a checklist of attributes the perfect guy would have. It just so happened that all the men she'd dated since moving to South Carolina four years ago lacked something in the personality department. On top of that, she was married to her job, so anything too complicated didn't work for her.

Erika started to lead Sadie in the guy's direction, but Sadie gripped her arm. "Wait! I'm not here to pick up men."

"No?" Barbi asked. "All right. Then you're here to challenge yourself. So, we're going zip lining, then?"

"How about a manicure and afternoon tea?" Sadie asked.

"No, Sadie. And the only way this workshop is going to make a difference to us is to work as a team," Erika said. "Remember that trust exercise we did our senior year in psychology class?"

"Oh, God," Barbi said.

"The one where you folded your arms across your chest, turned around, and trusted your team would catch you?" Sadie rolled her eyes. "Bad example. Don't you remember how that worked out, Erika?"

"You sneezed!" Erika said.

"I didn't plan it!" Sadie said.

"I fell," Erika wheezed out. "On the floor!"

Barbi laughed. "You had to go to the nurse."

"I had a lump on the back of my head the size of an egg."

All three of them laughed so hard it hurt.

Once they pulled themselves together, Barbi inched closer to Sadie. "Give me a hug, girlfriend."

Whenever Barbi asked for a hug like that, she was up to something. However, it had been too long since she'd seen her best friends. If she were being honest, Sadie missed Barbi's antics and Erika's matter-of-fact attitude. She stepped into Barbi's embrace.

"I have a wager to make," Barbi said, giving Sadie a good squeeze.

"Here we go." Sadie stepped back and stared at her.

"Complete the zip line challenge and Erika and I will stop harassing you about men for the rest of the weekend."

Sadie liked the sound of that. "And if I fail?"

"We get to pick the guy you have dinner with."

Barbi had a way of making things seem easier than they really were. Sadie gazed up the hillside, wondering if she'd be able to complete the hike without hyperventilating. Heights scared the crap out of her more than anything. "I'm raising the stakes."

Barbi arched a sculpted brow.

"If I do this, I don't want to hear anything from the two of you about finding Mr. Perfect for six months—unless I bring it up first."

Barbi looked at Erika, who nodded in agreement.

"Okay. We accept your terms, girlfriend. And if you lose, you have to invite Chad to dinner at your condo."

"What?"

"You upped the ante," Barbi reminded her.

"Fine. Pinkie promise." All three locked fingers. "Let's get this over with." Sadie started up the path.

They arrived to find a long line at the trailhead, but the scenery alone made it well worth the hassle of dealing with the big crowd.

"Ready?" Barbi squeezed her hand.

"Why not?"

The expansive grounds of the inn were postcard perfect—with the equestrian club and endless pasture land and a botanical garden filled with colorful exotic flowers and plants. Pair that with a cloudless sky and warm sunshine…and she couldn't believe the beauty was real.

"Sadie Reynolds, Barbi Smith, and Erika Zane?" a twenty-something-year-old guy with a clipboard called.

"Right here." Sadie raised her hand.

"Great." He joined them at the back of the line. "I'm Matthew, your crew leader for the weekend. Did you eat breakfast?"

"Sure did," Barbi said in a flirtatious manner.

Matthew smiled at her. "Let me guess, you're Barbi?"

"How'd you know?" she asked.

"I read your personality profiles in the paperwork you filled out to get accepted to the workshop. You're listed as the gregarious one."

"Personality profiles?" Sadie didn't know anything about that and she definitely hadn't filled anything out. She threw Barbi an accusing look. "Do you have a copy of my profile, Matthew? I'm Sadie."

"Sure do." He flipped through a couple of pages on his clipboard, then offered her a piece of paper. "We have a few minutes to spare, take your time."

Sadie scanned the page, recognizing Barbi's handwriting. The first question asked what the participant hoped to gain from the workshop. Barbi wrote: *inspiration, skills on how to be a team player, general trust, confidence, and how to let go of the past.*

Well, apparently her best friend knew Sadie *too* well.

The second question asked what bad habits or addictions she had. Barbi put one thing: *control freak. Ha!* Barbi and Erika still lived in Sadie's small hometown and didn't understand how the corporate world worked. Barbi owned a flower shop and Erika was a mother of two and married to a plumber. They had simpler lives. Sadie, on the other hand, had left Alabama to pursue an Ivy League education in New England, then moved to South Carolina, where she accepted a job at Charles Longley Publicity. It was the perfect place for her to work. She taught people how to micromanage their own lives—which fit with Sadie's controlling personality.

There wasn't much more to tell. Her profile kind of depressed her. She did everything precisely and for a reason. She blamed that on her past. Growing up with economically challenged parents gave her the initiative to become her high school salutatorian. The resulting scholarship to college gave her an excuse to leave Fairhope, Alabama.

Breaking up with Carson gave her a reason to never go back.

"Ready, Sadie?" Matthew asked.

They hiked the last part of the trail together and arrived at a platform manned by two employees wearing Red Horse Inn jerseys.

"Take a look over the edge," Matthew suggested.

Sadie stepped to the railing and looked down. A waterfall and raging river cut through the limestone below. Beautiful and wild, it was the kind of view Sadie usually admired…at a safe distance in travel magazines or on TV.

"All right, ladies, let's gather round and discuss the basics of the zip line." Matthew waited for them to join him. "Our zip lines are accredited by the Professional Ropes Course Association and inspected regularly. We utilize a simple pulley and harness system, which ensures a safe and comfortable experience. You'll also wear a helmet and thick gloves." He showed them a yellow hard hat and leather gloves. "Zip lines operate on gravity and inertia, so there's no smoke and mirrors here. You can see the angle of the wires, how this side is the highest point. Once you reach the other side, Jamie is waiting for us and will drive us back to the inn. Do you have any questions or concerns?"

Sadie raised her hand. "Do you have a last will and testament worksheet?"

Matthew chuckled. "We've had zero safety violations and no injuries since we opened three years ago. I know it can be intimidating looking over the edge of the ravine, but this is easy. And fun. It also teaches you to let go a little, to give up some control and trust your inner voice that craves adventure."

"Or premature death," Sadie murmured just loud enough for Barbi to hear.

Her best friend snickered.

"Do I have a volunteer to go first?" Matthew asked.

No one moved.

"In order to pass the workshop, you have to do the zip line. Still no takers?" Matthew looked disappointed.

Barbi gave Sadie a little shove in his direction. "She'll do it."

"What?" Sadie preferred to go last, after she was assured Barbi and Erika were still alive after crossing.

Matthew smiled. "Let's get you fitted, then."

Sadie closed her eyes while the two employees buckled the harness around her legs and hips. Once she was strapped in, Matthew put the helmet on her head, handed her a pair of gloves, and then offered her safety glasses.

He then led her to a mini zip line rigged between two trees. "Since this is your first time, we need to go over the safety procedures and how your body should be positioned during the ride. Then we'll try out the test line. Okay?"

Why hadn't he told them about the test line earlier?

After spending ten minutes learning how to grip and clip herself to the line, Matthew showed her how to hold on to the pulley, sit down, lean back in the harness, and then raise her legs so she achieved an optimal ride. Once he was confident she understood, she took a test ride.

"Well?" Matthew asked. "Did you like it?"

"If this was the only thing I had to do, hell yeah." She turned to the platform. "That's the problem."

He waved her off. "You're a natural, Sadie. Trust your instincts. You can do this."

Sadie returned to the platform and prepared for the monster ride. Pretty sure her heart was in tachycardia, she sucked in a breath, whispered Psalm 23, and when one of the workers yelled for her to get ready, she pushed herself off the platform and headed straight for the other side of the ravine. Holy shit! Now she knew what it felt like to be in a horror movie two seconds before the psycho killer slashed his latest victim with a machete.

She yelped as she picked up speed, and she had reached the halfway point when her cell phone vibrated over and over again in her pocket. Common sense told her to ignore it, but whoever was calling wouldn't give up. She let go of the pulley with one hand, unzipped her jacket pocket, and retrieved her phone. It was her manager and friend, Leonard.

Why would he call? He knew she was on vacation for a long weekend. The phone went quiet and then started vibrating again.

She quickly accepted the call. "Leonard? Everything okay?"

Before he could answer, she shifted awkwardly and started to spin. Sadie screamed and her phone slipped through her fingers as she reached for the pulley again, holding on for dear life.

She landed on the other side, where the other instructor was waiting. As he unclipped her from the line she shoved her way forward, bent over, and hurled.

Hours later in her suite, showered and still feeling queasy from her near-death experience, Sadie accepted a cup of herbal tea from Barbi. "Thanks."

"I can't believe you," she said. "How do you fail a self-improvement workshop in the first hour?"

"I'm sorry, Barbi. Leonard never calls me on the weekend."

"You violated every safety rule Matthew taught you. I'm glad your smartphone is gone."

"Is Matthew mad at me?"

"He practically shit his pants when you screamed. But he's not upset."

"Oh yeah? How do you know?"

"We're having dinner later."

"Isn't he a little young for you?" Sadie winked.

"We were born in the same decade."

"He's not too young?"

Barbi merely shrugged and gave her typical confident smile. "Men peak younger than women. What's three years?"

"In what? Their income? IQs?"

Barbi rolled her blue eyes. "Sexually."

Sadie didn't want to think about or talk about sex. How long had it been since she'd orgasmed from something other than her hand or a battery-powered toy? Being unable to remember an exact date meant it had been too long. But she was glad something positive had come out of her the zip line nightmare. She gave her best friend a hug. "I'm happy one of us is making gains this weekend. Can I borrow your cell phone?"

"Let me guess…work. Not a chance."

Sadie took a sip of tea, then set the cup on the nightstand. "I need to call Leonard back."

"No you don't, Sadie. You just think you do. Why don't you climb out of bed and get dressed? There's a bar full of eligible professionals downstairs, just waiting to meet someone as talented and beautiful as you. Change starts here." Barbi tapped her fingers against her temple. "Please?"

"Nope. I'm going to stay here and watch a movie after I call Leonard on the hotel phone."

"Fine." Barbi crossed the room and dug her cell out of her purse. She tossed it on the end of the queen-sized bed. "Keep it. I won't need it tonight." She winked at Sadie.

Sadie tossed one of the fluffy pillows off her bed at her. "Have fun, and don't do anything I wouldn't do."

Barbi turned on her way out of the room. "You mean do everything you wouldn't do."

As the automatic lock clicked on her door, she wondered if Barbi was right. Everyone but Sadie was having a great time. Shrugging it off, she immediately dialed Leonard's number and got him on the second ring.

"Hello," he said.

"Lenny, it's Sadie."

"Thank God." He sighed. "I've been trying to reach you for two hours."

"Yeah, I'll tell you about my little adventure later. What's going on?"

"We have an emergency in Mobile."

"Alabama?"

He chuckled. "Where else?"

"I'm listening."

"It involves the Warriors. And from what I've been told, their PR nightmare has reached critical level." As he explained the situation, Sadie could hardly believe her ears.

"Let me get this right," she said, finding it hard to breathe all of a sudden. "You want me to fly to Mobile because the owner of the Warriors is having a meltdown and a couple overpaid jockstraps got caught posting lewd content on social media? Tell me a better story, Leonard. Give me a real reason to care."

"Sadie…It's the NFL."

"I know."

She gazed out the closest window. "I can't blow off Barbi and Erika. I haven't seen them in ten months. What will I tell them?"

"The same thing I just told you. Charles made it abundantly clear what I would be forced to do if you refuse to go."

"Really?" She arched a brow, always ready to counter her boss, the stubborn owner of Longley Publicity. "What did he say this time?"

"I'd rather not repeat it."

"Why not?"

"It involved shoving something in a few orifices."

She couldn't resist laughing. Charles had a way with words—filthy ones, anyway. "So he's on the rampage, again? Singling me out because I refused to work with the most well-known misogynist on the east coast last week? I don't have to succumb to that kind of pressure to keep my job. I have a proven record…"

She had a successful work history in South Carolina, but a pathetic past in Alabama. The kind you kept hidden away in a locked diary. The last thing Sadie wanted to do was go home. She'd do whatever it took to avoid the situation. "This is a job better suited for someone who has experience with professional athletes."

"I know." Leonard sounded genuinely sympathetic. "But Charles has certain expectations for this new account and he thinks his best bet is sending you to take care of things."

Disappointment flooded her mind. "I won't let Charles bully me."

"This isn't personal, Sadie, it's about money."

She huffed out a frustrated breath. "How much money?"

"I don't have exact figures, but if you nail this assignment, we could get a long-term contract with the NFL. With all the PR nightmares going on in the league over social justice, domestic violence, substance abuse, and traumatic brain injuries, this is our chance to show them what a company like ours can do to improve public relations."

"You mean exploit an unfortunate situation for money?" she whispered.

"On Charles's terms, yeah. But for you, Sadie, I can't think of a better image consultant to entrust this account to. You care about our clients. And these guys need real guidance, possibly a miracle to turn the team's reputation around."

"Damn." She liked to make a comfortable living as much as the next person. But Lenny was right. She put her heart and soul behind every project, actually kept in touch with many of her past customers, loving to hear their happily-ever-after stories once they completed training with her.

But this assignment wasn't worth the cost of her pride and confidence. Her job required getting personal on every level, invading a client's professional and private life, dissecting everything about them, from the way they dressed to who they socialized with. Though her official title was a marketing and image consultant she was really a marketing spin doctor.

But even the temptation of working with an NFL team—which would definitely boost her resume to the next level—didn't negate the negative history she had in Alabama. Though she visited her parents every Christmas, they'd moved to

Huntsville five years ago, hundreds of miles away from her hometown, she still avoided the place like the plague. "What do I get out of it?"

"Bonus potential."

All right, she'd play along just to see how much Charles was willing to pay. "What percentage?"

"One percent."

"Not worth the energy to pack my suitcase."

"Come on, Sadie."

"I'm one of the best in the business, Leonard, not a babysitter," she said, knowing how hard it would be to get a team of egomaniacs to cooperate.

"That's what we want you to do."

"Really? Playing mom isn't in my job description. And if you don't already know, the reason I've had such success in the past is because our clients actually *wanted* to change."

"I get it. You don't like wasting time on ungracious people. But this is the NFL. Think about it. Let that sink in for a moment."

She already had. Carson Savage would be her client. And that scared her.

"Seriously, Sadie. I ran some analytics on the team, it's not good. We're talking a complete makeover."

"Are you telling me the Warriors don't have an in-house staff capable of launching new brand campaigns?"

Leonard snorted. "Haven't you heard the latest news? All the major networks are talking about it. The owner of the Warriors, Jack Menzies, fired half his front office today. Several people walked out, too. If the staff had even been doing a half-ass job before, the team wouldn't be where it is now."

"And where is that exactly?" She meant it more as an after-thought, but said it out loud.

"In the goddamned toilet."

She sighed. Why now? Why here, on the one holiday she'd taken with her best friends—the very trip meant to help her forget Carson? She laughed—*karma*. Maybe she'd thought about Carson a little too much and denied her unresolved feelings for him a little too often. This was the universe's way of getting back at her for lying.

"I don't want to miss out on time with my friends," she said.

"Reschedule."

Not what she wanted to hear. Leonard should know better. "You know my history."

"I do," Lenny admitted. "So does Charles."

"What? How?" Only a handful of people in the office were privy to her relationship with Carson, and none of them would discuss it with Charles.

"Leslie."

"Oh, God." She gritted her teeth. Leslie Callahan hated Sadie. They'd competed for a promotion last year and Sadie landed it. Apparently, Leslie had waited for the right moment to pay her back.

"Charles wants you to reconnect with Carson. We believe he's the key to reaching the rest of the team. I have paperwork waiting for you at the office. A file as thick as a technical manual covering the demographics of all the players."

"I'm not crazy about the idea."

"I know you're a football fan," Lenny said.

"A long time ago," she lied, fantasizing about a certain broad-shouldered, quarterback with a devastatingly handsome face. Carson's smile alone could make her forget her own name.

How could she ever top that first kiss behind the bleachers their sophomore year? The only reason she waited for him after the Friday night game was to prove her best friend wrong—that she, indeed, had the courage to confess how hot she thought Carson was to his face.

And how did that turn out for you? she asked herself.

It turned into a three-year relationship full of ups and downs, unbelievable passion, and the pressure associated with being the darlings of a small Southern town. When she broke off their engagement after graduation, half of Fairhope turned their backs on her. She even received death threats. *That's* how seriously some people took their football in Alabama.

She'd secretly followed Carson's professional career, though. He'd won the Heisman Trophy and was the number one draft pick four years ago. Time had been generous to Carson, that boyish face had grown more rugged and savage, just like his name. They should stay as far away from each other as possible, because their insatiable attraction would just get them in trouble. Big trouble.

"You there, Sadie? What just happened?"

"Sorry, I can't do it," she said, feeling unpredictable. "I didn't part on good terms with Carson. I can't go back there, Lenny."

Not parting on good terms was an understatement. She broke their engagement because Carson actually believed that she'd give up her dreams, marry him, and have half a dozen kids. Another symptom of growing up in the South.

Sadie had ambition and a need to get away from outdated traditions.

"You were kids."

"I was eighteen," she said. "That's not really a kid."

"For you, maybe not, Sadie. But Carson has moved on, trust me."

Yeah, she didn't like being reminded about his womanizing. All the media outlets covered his activities on *and* off the field. The very areas of concern she'd be expected to fix. "Revisiting the past isn't something I'm good at, Leonard. Pick someone else."

"Damn it, Sadie…"

"What?" she asked.

"I don't want to fire you."

"Fire me?"

She heard Lenny suck in a frustrated breath. "Charles's words, not mine."

"I'm that replaceable?"

"I believe his exact words were, 'she's replaceable, don't forget it.'"

"Which makes me replaceable *and* predictable. Not sure which is worse."

"Don't be so hard on yourself," he said. "And as for Carson, show him how far you've come, girlie. I'm taking off my managerial hat. This is Teddy Bear Lenny talking now, okay?"

She couldn't hold in the laughter. Leonard meant the world to her. "You make everything sound so easy."

"Well…" He started. "Stop overthinking everything. You are a control freak. Self-admitted, right?"

"Yes."

"This is uncomfortable territory for you. I get that. Your fight-or-flight instinct probably kicked in a few minutes ago."

It had.

"Fight this time, Sadie. Don't let a guy keep you from fulfilling your potential. The Warriors would be lucky to get you. I know it. You know it. And obviously douchebag Charles knows it, or he wouldn't have tapped you for the job."

"He's taking advantage of my past."

"Yes. But spin it back on him. Take advantage of Charles."

"How?" she asked. Sadie was a black and white person—everything had a proper place and a logical explanation. She didn't do gray area well—not at all, really.

"Accept the assignment and go down to Alabama and blow everyone away. Earn that bonus and then some. Show Charles you don't need him, but that his company sure as hell needs you."

Sadie rubbed the back of her neck, in deep thought. Leonard had a way with words, a way of making a shit-covered stick look appetizing. "Fine."

"Excuse me?" he asked. "I didn't hear you clearly."

"I'll go. On one condition."

"Name it."

"If I need help…"

"I'm your man. Promise."

"I'll hold you to that, Lenny."

"Good. I'll be waiting for your arrival tonight." The trace of desperation in his voice suggested he'd say anything to get her to leave right away.

"Remember what it's like in the field?" she asked.

She could hear him smile. "I miss it."

"We're a fantastic team," she said.

"Someone has to stay here, Sadie. Charles has been in and out lately, he's unreliable. And besides…you don't need a security blanket to face Carson. Just walk in there Monday morning and do what you do best. Seize control of the situation. Make those guys beg for mercy like you always do."

"Yeah…" Sadie typically worked with corporate types, vice presidents of accounting firms, the occasional Wall Street outfit, and maybe some engineers. Not football players. "Two percent," she blurted.

"For what?"

"My bonus."

"Are you worth it, Sadie girl?"

She tucked a stray hair behind her ear. "Every zero."

"If you can turn the Warriors around and get a long-term contract, I'll give you three percent of the signing fee."

Sadie considered it compensation for pain and suffering, because it wasn't going to be easy facing that old heartbreak again. "I'll catch a flight back to home tonight." She disconnected, hoping she'd made the right choice.

CHAPTER THREE

Carson reported for the usual team meeting on Monday morning. Dressed in jeans and a team T-shirt, he rubbed his eyes and took a swig of coffee. He'd spent a contemplative weekend alone, preparing for today, knowing he'd have to bust some heads to get things done the right way. Unwilling to sacrifice his career for the actions of a few careless players, he'd decided late last night to do as Coach had insisted, separate himself from the clowns.

It might not make him the most popular player in the locker room, but it would ensure his future with the team, the one thing he loved almost as much as his family.

"Mornin," Tyrone croaked, looking like he hadn't slept all weekend.

"Hey." Carson eyeballed him. "What the hell, Ty? Your eyes are swollen and bloodshot. Can you see two feet in front of yourself?"

"I could catch one of your balls blindfolded."

"Really?"

"Maybe not today."

"While I have you cornered," Carson started.

Ty pursed his lips and tried to kiss him. "Come here, baby."

Carson rolled his eyes. "Joking aside," he said. "I really need you to follow through on what you promised Friday. Did you deliver my message?"

"Yeah." Ty instantly sobered. "There won't be any more unauthorized photographs posted."

"I want to believe that, Ty."

"Short of beating the guy senseless, I made it clear that if anything else shows up on social media that damages the team's reputation, he'll answer to me first, you, then Coach."

Carson nodded. "I appreciate the effort."

"If things are as bad as you say…"

"It is." Coach hadn't given Carson permission to share the details about the marketing expert coming in, but Ty and his other teammates would find out soon enough. As if coming to an early camp wasn't punishment enough, Carson could only guess what the front office had in store for the team.

"One good thing did come from that ass shot, though."

"What?"

Ty waggled his eyebrows. "Did you read some of the comments? I counted thirty-six marriage proposals on Twitter alone. Not a bad thing, bro. Variety is the…"

Before Carson could respond, the media room door opened and Coach Rangall stepped into the hallway. "Listen up. Check the list on the far wall. If your name is there, grab a seat inside. If not, report for drills outside."

Carson scanned the paper, he was number five on the list of twenty-some players. Reluctantly, he entered the media room and chose a seat in the back. Once the space filled up, Coach closed the door and walked to the front.

"I'm going to make this short," Rangall said. "The fact that we're even here makes me sick." His penetrating stare zigzagged across the room. "After thirteen arrests, two suspensions, and over four hundred thousand dollars in personal fines last season, the commissioner gave us an ultimatum. If you don't cooperate, you'll spend the season on the bench, be cut from the roster, or even traded. Understand? We've hired the best marketing firm in the country to help clean this franchise up. I'm ashamed of all of you. Jack's too embarrassed to even come downstairs and be spotted with you asshats."

A few murmurs sounded from the tables in front of Carson. He could only guess what his teammates were thinking and saying. Accountability would now be the name of the game, since Coach threatened to take away their million-dollar paychecks.

Coach opened the door and made gestured for someone on the other side to come in. "Welcome Ms. Sadie Reynolds from Charles Longley Publicity."

Time seemed to stop after Carson heard *Sadie Reynolds*. The name triggered a chemical reaction, because his mouth immediately went dry and he got hard. But how could it happen if he hadn't seen her in seven years? He didn't even know what she looked like or sounded like anymore. Apparently, it didn't matter. The beast inside him still wanted to touch and taste her—to remember her the way she'd always been...*his*.

He closed his eyes, the image in his mind as real as anything.

A hint of her delicate perfume made him smile. Was that part fantasy or reality? He opened his eyes just in time…

She entered the room from the side door, wearing a fitted black skirt suit and three-inch heels.

Holy shit. Seven years had aged her like a fine wine—softening her features, giving her time to fill out a skirt like a supermodel. She wore her silky hair mid-length now, just over the shoulders. In high school, her braid almost reached the top of her butt.

Bottled waters had been set up on the tables. He forced the cap off and took a deep drink, his gaze never leaving Sadie. Not ready for her to see him yet, he made sure to slump down in his chair.

The room had grown disturbingly quiet, leaving Carson with only one thought: he wasn't the only man wishing he could take Sadie home tonight. And that realization made him growl out loud with unspoken possessiveness. Though he lost any right to her, something primal and raw boiled below the surface from just one look at her. Carson didn't know what to think about his feelings. Unresolved issues remained between them, but he had moved on—or at least he'd thought so.

"Good morning, gentlemen," Sadie said. "My name is Sadie Reynolds. I'm a senior marketing and image consultant with Charles Longley Publicity." She gazed around the room. "All of you were handpicked to work with me. I'm here to teach you how to engage with the public on a more professional level—to guide you through the process of fostering trust and admiration from your fans. We're going to spend the next two months together. In case you don't know what my job entails, I've put together a little presentation to demonstrate the kind of work I do. Could you dim the lights, Coach Rangall?"

Carson wet his lips and sat up in his chair. Was Sadie indifferent to him? Or had she just not seen him yet? *One look— just one…* Carson begged silently, praying Sadie would meet his gaze before the lights went out.

But she didn't see him, *not yet*. Or she was avoiding his hungry eyes on purpose. As the big screen lit up, Sadie clicked the controller and a collage featuring team members appeared. Pictures from the nightclub in downtown Mobile they frequented after the games. Some of the guys were holding beers, others were holding women in various stages of undress.

"When the average person in Alabama thinks about a player from the Warriors, this is what they describe the most. Partiers. Players. Bad boys. That's not what we want, gentlemen."

She clicked the controller again. More pictures from around the city appeared. "Two hundred people from random locations in Mobile, Columbus, Montgomery, Birmingham, and Huntsville were surveyed recently. Eighty-six percent agreed that they had negative views on pro athletes. That football players were as corrupt as politicians."

"Shit," someone commented.

"Not shit," Sadie shot back. "Simple truth. Congress has a better approval rating than the Alabama Warriors. Why, you ask?"

The next slide nearly made Carson fall out of his chair—his exposed flesh filled the screen.

Laughter exploded.

Sadie cleared her throat. "Clothing isn't optional, gentlemen, it's mandatory. And if you think this is acceptable behavior, let me remind you of something. Many states would deem this an arrestable offense if you didn't have permission to take this picture." She turned to the screen, the light haloing her beautiful profile.

Did she just smile? Was she ogling Carson's ass shot? He leaned forward. There's no way she didn't recognize his body; he had that tattoo in high school. And if he remembered anything about Sadie, she had always loved his butt. Practically drooled on it whenever they got naked.

She faced the crowd again. "Social media is a powerful tool. It can make or break your career. Can you think of a couple examples of people who paid the ultimate price for posting risqué photos of themselves?"

She waited patiently for someone to answer, but no one did.

"Okay," she continued. "Does Brett Favre ring a bell? Anthony Weiner? Remember one thing: anything you post becomes part of the public record. You can delete all you want. It might disappear from your account, but trust me, it's out there, forever."

More laughter followed.

"I'm glad you all have senses of humor," she said, "because it will take an equal balance of sincerity and good old-fashioned humor to admit you've made mistakes and need to start over, to rebrand yourself. I'm familiar with your personal data, gentlemen. All of you have very different profiles and backgrounds. This week, we'll spend a little time one-on-one getting to know each other, discussing what we need to do to help reverse some of this negative publicity. Coach Rangall mentioned something about interest in community service. You can turn the lights up, Coach."

Once the lights were on again, Coach stood at the front of the room. "All right. I expect you all to do your best with Ms. Reynolds. I have meetings scheduled for the next three days. But I'm always available if you have any questions." He excused himself, leaving Carson one man closer to being alone with the woman he'd always wanted.

Even after she graduated high school and moved to New England for college, he never forgot her. How could he? That face. That body. That sass. All the memories they'd built together. Yeah, they lived separate lives now, but Sadie wasn't the kind of woman any man could get over, not completely.

"Mr. Savage?"

Carson flinched. She'd finally acknowledged him. "Back here."

"Yes," Sadie said, capturing his heart with her smoldering gaze. "You're a co-captain of the team?"

"Yes," he said. "And the one called on the most when it comes to situations like this."

"I understand you're the victim of the unfortunate photo I shared just now."

"Which one?" he whispered sardonically, not expecting her to hear him.

"The back shot," she said politely.

God, he knew that face so well. Even after all this time he could tell when she was laughing on the inside, at his expense, of course. "Yeah," he said. "That's my ass."

"Yes," she said again, a slight tremor in her voice. "How did it make you feel to find out your friend posted it without your permission?"

He shrugged. "A little pissed. But I expect it."

"Oh?" She arched a perfectly sculpted brow. "How so?"

"It's part of the game," he said. "Part of being a football player. If you want to join the brotherhood, you look the other way a lot. Learn to blow crap off."

Their gazes locked and her million-dollar smile faded, replaced by a sad expression. "Thank you for your honesty, Mr. Savage."

"Call me Carson," he said, needing to hear her say his name.

"I prefer Mr. Savage."

"No one calls me Mr. Savage, *Ms. Reynolds.*"

She clicked her tongue, then raised her chin. "Here's a learning moment, gentlemen. Part of the problem is we've lost that formality between each other. It's been replaced by false familiarity with people we don't really know. Manners mean something." She gazed at Carson again. "So this is a good start. Using formality to address each other. Right, Mr. Savage?"

"Sure," he said. "If I didn't know you. But I do, Sadie, and we're the same age. Let's try something else, because there's no way I'm calling you Ms. Reynolds."

Her mouth dropped open, and Carson immediately regretted what he'd said in front of his teammates without thinking. Never let emotions get the best of you, on or off the field. But it was too late to take it back.

"Will you join me in the hallway, Mr. Savage?" she asked.

Similar to a high school classroom, his teammates taunted him as he made his way to the door, following Sadie. Dear God, her ass looked even better close up. He shut the door behind them and waited.

She crossed her arms over her chest and stared up at him, her green eyes full of brimstone and fire. "Just what are you trying to accomplish, Carson?"

In the past, whenever Sadie got mad, he'd kiss her happy again. The temptation to do so now nearly overpowered his restraint. "Keeping it real."

"Real?" she asked. "What's that supposed to mean? I think you're trying to show off or undermine me."

"And why would I do that, Kitty Kat?"

She went dead still at the sound of her old nickname. "Don't you ever call me that again." She poked him in the chest with one of her long, blood-red fingernails. "I don't want anyone to know about our past. No one."

"Might be a little too late for that."

"Why?" She chewed on her bottom lip, making him think about things he shouldn't.

"A couple of the guys already know who you are."

"Everything?"

"We're friends, Sadie. They know I had a life back home."

"Did you know I was coming?"

Carson shifted on his feet. "Of course not. Do you think this is how I wanted us to see each other again?"

Sadie shook her head. "If you're anything like me, you never expected to see me. There's no reason for us to be in each other's lives. Anything we had to say has been said a long time ago."

His shoulders stiffened at those words. Did she really dislike him that much? Had she forgotten everything they'd been through together? Or how she up and left without explanation, without even a goodbye? In his opinion they hadn't said all that they needed to. But he tried to shake it off. "We're obviously adults now, Sadie. Capable of working together." But Carson had ulterior motives already. He never turned down a chance for a rematch, especially when someone had kicked his ass before. And Sadie had left him down and desperate. Getting her to go out with him would be a victory for him.

She nodded. "Can I rely on you to help me get through today without any more resistance?"

He leaned against the wall, his gaze drifting lazily up her body. "Sure thing, Kitty Kat, but it will cost you."

"You haven't changed a bit."

"Nope."

"What do you want, Carson?"

"Dinner. Tomorrow night."

"Do I have a choice?"

Technically, she did, but if Carson guessed correctly, she needed his help with this whole social media rehab thing. He was more open to change than most of the men sitting in that classroom.

"Not really," he said. She clearly still possessed the same stubborn streak because that same adorable pout appeared. The one that usually made him give in to anything she wanted. But not this time. He had one chance to get her alone, one chance to sit her down and tell her how wrong he'd been all those years ago. Not that it would change anything, but maybe he'd feel better afterward. Maybe he'd stop dreaming about her gorgeous face. It was worth a shot.

"Fine. Pick me up at my hotel at seven. The Royale, on…"

"I know where it's at."

She sighed and turned away. He opened the door for her, and she stepped inside the media room. It quieted down as Carson made his way to his seat in the back. Fate had brought them back together; he'd put money on it. And Carson didn't believe in coincidence. Everything happened for a reason. Touchdowns and interceptions. Wins and losses. And second chances.

CHAPTER FOUR

Sadie poured herself a glass of red wine, then sat on the king-sized hotel bed with her laptop. Seeing Carson again had brought up a whirlwind of emotions. Nothing could have prepared her for the moment they first made eye contact. The look on his ruggedly handsome face made her want to run back to South Carolina. Fat chance of that happening now. She'd agreed to take this assignment. Failure was *not* an option.

Besides, she'd never let Carson Savage have the satisfaction of scaring her off, even though he was more intimidating than ever. Sexier. More successful. She could already tell he was determined to challenge her every move…which made him more of an asshole. Taking a gulp of wine, she opened Skype and called Barbi.

Her best friend's pretty face always made her smile. "Thought you forgot about me, girl."

"Sorry I'm late, Barbi. I took a long bath and had a glass of wine after work." She held up her half empty glass. "Wish you were here."

"Me, too."

In reality, Sadie's hometown of Fairhope was only a thirty-minute drive away. There was no excuse for *not* inviting Barbi and Erika up for a visit this upcoming weekend. Barbi was just too good-natured to say anything, which made Sadie feel like crap. "Maybe after everything settles down you can take a drive this way."

Barbi nodded with understanding. "Must have been a hell of a reunion."

"If you call Carson embarrassing me in front of his team members and then cornering me in the hallway and demanding I have dinner with him tomorrow night a reunion, then yeah." She set her wine glass on the nightstand, then repositioned herself on the bed, lying on her stomach and propping her head up on her hands. "These guys get paid millions of dollars and act like juvenile delinquents." She reached for one of the files Coach Rangall had given her earlier. "Look at this." She held up one of the pics. "Recognize anything?"

Barbi's eyes widened. "Can you tilt the photo some?"

Sadie could do better than that, she held it in front of her face, filling her friend's computer screen with the image.

"Oh. My. God! That's Carson's ass, isn't it? I remember when he got that tat, after winning the state championship his sophomore year. How many times did our team moon everyone—didn't Harp, Jonathan, Georgie, and Miguel get matching tattoos to commemorate that season?"

Sadie cringed. Their high school football team was the

Fairhope Vipers. Carson, Harp, Jonathan, Georgie, and Miguel were known as the Front Five—comprising four of Carson's offensive linemen and him. They were as cliquey as the characters from *Mean Girls*.

"Yes." She lowered the picture and stared at Barbi. "Do you know how hard it was keeping a straight face in that classroom when I shared his pic?"

Barbi took a sip of her Red Bull. "I think his ass is a little more muscular though."

Sadie couldn't hold in the snort. "You always were an ass woman."

"So are you!"

Having already committed Carson's great posterior to memory, Sadie couldn't disagree. But she wanted to talk about something else. Something to get her mind off the danger of falling apart over Carson, over being back in Alabama. "How did dinner go with Matthew?"

"No…you're doing it again. Changing subjects because you're uncomfortable."

"What are you talking about?"

"I don't know, Sadie. If you stayed at the retreat and completed the classes, you might know exactly what I mean. By the way, I rescheduled our holiday."

"Excuse me?"

"In four months, we're going back to the Red Horse Inn and finishing what we started."

Not likely! If everything worked out in Alabama and Sadie landed the long-term contract for her company, she planned on rewarding herself with a long vacation in Europe—maybe touring Scotland and Ireland. "I'll leave that to you and Erika."

Barbi frowned.

"Now, are you going to tell me about Matthew?" Just because Sadie didn't have a love life worth talking about, she could still live vicariously through her best friend, who never seemed to have a problem hooking up with quality men.

"We skipped dinner and ordered dessert in my room."

"Dessert, huh?"

"Yeah—fondue—chocolate syrup and strawberries. You should have seen the look I got from the maid the next day when she showed up to change the sheets."

"Let me guess, you didn't exactly eat the strawberries?"

"Melted chocolate is great for finger painting. And Matthew's body is quite the canvas."

"Is that it?" Another thing Sadie had a hard time with—hooking up with a stranger for a one-night stand. Not that she hadn't tried before. It just never worked out. The minute a man stuck his fingers under her panties or in her bra, she freaked out.

"No, he's flying down next weekend."

Sadie clapped her hands. "Finally!"

"Nothing serious—we're just friends."

"Okay. Friends. Like us." Before Barbi could reply, Sadie's hotel phone rang, startling the shit out of her. "I better get that."

"Okay, girlfriend. Night." Barbi blew her a kiss.

Sadie made it to the phone by the sixth ring. "Hello?"

"Hello, gorgeous."

Carson. Her whole body went rigid. "What can I do for you, Mr. Savage?"

His deep-throated laughter made her skin prickle with angst and desire. "We're still wrapped up in formalities, Kitty Kat?"

That nickname had been buried with their failed relationship. "Stop calling me Kitty Kat."

"Why? It's the only thing I have left of you, sweetheart."

Frustrated by his persistence to not honor her request, she decided to simply end the conversation. "Goodnight, Carson."

"Wait!"

"What?"

"I'm in the lobby."

"Good for you." She lowered the handset.

"Sadie. Don't hang up."

Weighing her options carefully, she'd give him a last chance to make his point. "I'm exhausted, Carson. We have an early morning, remember?"

"Give me five minutes."

"Fine. I'm in room…" The line went dead.

Two minutes later, Carson knocked on the door. Forgetting to grab her robe, Sadie opened it. The intensity of his roving gaze reminded her of what she was wearing—or what she wasn't wearing. Dressed in a silky camisole and matching shorts, she probably looked like she was ready to seduce him.

"Christ, Kitty Kat, is this your way of making up for lost time?"

Her cheeks flushed. "Go away, Carson."

He shook his head and proceeded to invite himself inside the room.

If she caused a scene, someone might call security. She closed the door. "Make it quick, Carson."

He groaned with satisfaction as he studied her again, then looked around the room. "This is a nice hotel."

"Adequate accommodations," she agreed, trying to sound detached. "Why are you here?"

"To make a friendly offer. Staying in a hotel can be uncomfortable, and my house is closer to the stadium, Sadie. I have a guesthouse." Carson seemed to read her dark thoughts because he quickly added, "No expectations, sweetheart. Just seemed like the neighborly thing to do, since we're old friends."

She stared up at him. Those blue eyes were uncomfortably observant. Soul-reading eyes that had always made her feel like she was under constant scrutiny. "Old friends?" She snorted. "Honestly, thanks but no thanks, Carson. We need to establish boundaries."

He raised a brow. "What kind of boundaries?"

"The kind where you respect me as a professional and quit trying to blur the lines between the past and present. If I could have avoided coming here, I would have."

He rubbed his stubbled chin. "You expect me to pretend like we don't have a long history? To treat you like a stranger?"

"Absolutely."

"I don't think I can do that, Kitty Kat."

Having reached her limit, she swatted his chest. "I'm twenty-five, Carson, not fifteen! Stop calling me Kitty Kat."

He leaned forward and brushed a stray hair off her face. "I don't care if you're sixty, Sadie. All I can remember when I look at you is the day we met. How you got stuck in that magnolia tree in front of the school trying to rescue the stray kitten. Turned out you needed saving, not the damn cat."

She licked her lips. Why was he insisting on reliving the past? Highlighting what embarrassed her the most? Yes, she'd always been afraid of heights but decided to forget that fear in order to save a little orange kitten. She shook her head. "Someone called 911 before you got there," she whispered.

"But I beat the fire truck, didn't I?" he asked.

Yes, he had. At least fifty people had surrounded the tree by then, including half the football team. Carson ambled up the branches with little effort, successfully handed down the kitten, and then focused on her. Once they were safely on the ground, she nearly fainted. But he wrapped a steadying arm about her waist, then asked her on a date.

With his teammates in earshot, how could she refuse? When she accepted his invitation, the crowd cheered. In the span of five minutes, she went from being a nobody to being Carson's girl. That's how Kitty Kat was born.

"Stop focusing on the past, Carson. It makes my job harder."

"Why? I think it should have the opposite effect. Knowing someone on the team will help get things done. Think of me as an anchor."

"Anchor?" she repeated skeptically and laughed. "If anything, you're a sore reminder of what I don't want to deal with."

"Ouch. Guess I deserved that."

"You guess?"

"Correction. I deserved it."

"Good. Now leave. Please."

"Sadie."

"Carson." She thrust her hand on her hip.

"Tell me there's a smidgen of hope for us to be friends."

Sadie rolled her eyes. "Exes don't make reliable friends."

"How many exes do you have?"

"None of your business."

He chuckled. "I like when you're mad."

"Have you been drinking, Carson?"

"I had a few beers." He looked over her shoulder. "How many glasses of wine have you had?"

"Two."

"Maybe we should head down to the hotel bar and have a cocktail, get reacquainted. Don't you know drinking alone is bad for the soul?"

Temptation surrounded her again—just like it had in the media room earlier today. "A risk I'm willing to take."

His smile faded. "How are you, Sadie? Happy?"

She had to think about it—which meant she wasn't. Though she had a great job and a tolerable routine, something was missing. "I'm good, Carson. What about you? Is playing for the Warriors everything you thought it would be?"

"Almost everything." He looked at her intently.

"I'm glad to hear it. So many people don't get to fulfill their dreams."

"We did," he observed.

"Yes."

"But not like Jack and Diane," he added, referring to the classic John Cougar song he would always play when they were together in his car—claiming it had been written for them.

She smiled at the memory. "But you are a football star."

"I'm something, Kitty Kat." He stepped closer, and she held her breath.

"I'm tired," she tossed out there hoping it would shield her from his overwhelming presence.

"Me, too," he said.

"We finally agree on something!"

"I bet there's a lot more we agree on, Kitty Kat. Maybe if you quit fighting it, stop being so defensive…we might have a chance of finding out." He stared at the big bed.

"No," she said flatly. "That's not going to happen."

"What?"

"You. Me. Us."

He was close enough for her to feel his warm breath on her face. "Thinking we'll have sex is a bit presumptuous, sweetheart. But if you insist."

She stiff-armed him in the chest. "That wasn't an invitation!"

He chuckled and backed up. "Can't blame me for trying." He wound a strand of her hair around his finger. "I'd never hurt you, Sadie."

Their gazes met, and she felt like saying he already had. But that would only give him another reason to stay. Carson didn't like loose ends. Just like she always had to maintain control. Age had only deepened her need for order. Carson represented the opposite, too many unknowns and chaos.

"I know," she reluctantly admitted, knowing he wouldn't purposely set out to hurt her. Underneath that bad boy façade was a compassionate man—he always had been.

"Coffee instead?" he asked.

"Caffeine will keep me up all night."

"What are you talking about, Kitty Kat?" he asked innocently and winked at her. "Staying up never bothered you before. I remember you drank pots of coffee during finals and could never go to sleep after. How many days did you stay awake our senior year to study for the ACTs?"

"Three, I think."

"I could never do that. I'm strictly eight hours a night."

"Guess that's my superpower," she said.

"No. You have better ones."

She arched a brow. "Like what?"

He swallowed and shoved his hand in his jeans pocket. "Rather not say."

Admittedly, it wasn't so bad talking with Carson. But all the reminiscing made her vulnerable, desperate to reconnect with her past. Which went against everything she'd worked so hard to forget. "It's getting late…"

They moved at the same time, she for the door, Carson toward Sadie.

"I need to touch you, Kitty Kat." He tugged her against his body, enveloping her in a possessive hug.

The minute they touched, her traitorous body sparked to life. Even after all these years she felt right in his arms. She sighed heavily, realizing with one word she could have him naked and in her bed. Then she'd have something to tell Barbi. Carson had always been an amazing, considerate lover. He'd been her first. And a girl never forgets that. But her heart and mind strongly disagreed on what she should do next. Just because he made her wet, it didn't mean she could forget everything. She'd worked too hard to create a new life away from

Alabama—away from him. "Let me go, Carson." She tried to push him away.

"Sadie…"

"No," she admonished. "Please leave."

His fingers lingered over the back of her neck. "There's a lot I need to say."

"It can wait." He needed to go.

He pulled back far enough to gaze into her eyes. "You can't cheat fate, Sadie."

"Fate?" She clicked her tongue. "This is a coincidence, Carson. I work for the best PR firm in the Southeast. Your boss chose us because he wanted real solutions for his team."

He finally let go. "When did you become so jaded, Sadie?"

"The day I left Fairhope."

He nodded. "Goodnight, sweetheart." He opened the door and then paused with his back to her. "By the way, the next time I come to your room, might want to put my ass shot back in your folder."

CHAPTER FIVE

Carson stepped off the elevator and into the lobby. The hotel was a historic building with a Tiffany glass ceiling and whispering arches, and he appreciated the mix of traditional Southern architecture and contemporary luxury. How many nights had he spent here, skinny dipping in the private rooftop pool with random women he met after home games? He usually tried to meet women away from the stadium, hoping they wouldn't recognize him. But lately, everyone seemed to know who he was even though he did his best to stay out of the public eye.

"Carson Savage?" a teenage boy asked, a grin on his face.

Carson never avoided kids. They were the exception to the rule. "Sure am."

"Dad!" The boy turned around and searched for his father. "It's Carson Savage—the quarterback for the Warriors!"

A man in his forties joined them and extended his hand. "We're big fans."

Carson shook his hand enthusiastically. "Thanks. Do you play football?" he asked the kid.

"First year. I'm a tight end."

Always prepared, Carson reached inside his jacket pocket and pulled out a Moleskine notebook and pen. "From Alabama?"

"Texas," the teenager answered, eyeing the pad in his hand. "Can I have your autograph?"

"Sure can. What's your name?"

"Daniel Sullivan."

Carson wrote the kid a personalized note and signed his name. "Here. Keep your head in the game, okay?"

Daniel accepted the paper and stared at it with awe.

"Thanks, Carson," the dad said. "Can we get a picture?"

Posing with his arm draped over the kid's shoulders, Carson smiled and waited for the flash to go off. Once he was done, he shook hands with the father and son again and watched them amble off, chatting excitedly. That's what made the game worth it, starry-eyed kids with big dreams. Not the fame and fortune, or the endless stream of women he had access to.

"Mr. Savage?"

Carson found the concierge waiting for him. "Good evening, Blake."

Blake nodded. "Can I get you anything? A room? Perhaps a table in the restaurant?"

"Actually, I was just leaving. But now that I think about it, my friend is staying in room 802, Sadie Reynolds. Could you arrange for a Champagne breakfast and three dozen red roses to be delivered in the morning?"

"Of course."

"And I'd appreciate if you'd keep an eye out for her—she's been away from Alabama for a long time. Might not know her way around." Code for *She's mine and I don't want other men sniffing about.* Blake was an invaluable asset, used to making discreet arrangements for Carson and his teammates.

"I understand, Mr. Savage."

"If she needs anything, call me." Carson reached inside his back pocket and pulled out his wallet. He offered Blake a generous tip. "Keep an open charge on my account for her."

Satisfied his wishes would be carried out, he exited the hotel. Unlike most of his teammates, Carson didn't mind being out by himself. He didn't keep a driver or bodyguard because it would only draw more attention. His truck was parked around the block, and he walked casually down the street, the cool breeze off Mobile Bay a welcome relief from the high humidity.

He'd come to the hotel for a couple of reasons, to see Sadie and to offer her his guesthouse. He didn't like the idea of her staying in a hotel alone. The fact that she agreed to dinner revealed a lot. Sadie May Reynolds still wanted him. And though she acted hostile, her body gave off different signals, especially when he took her in his arms. Christ…those tiny shorts showcased her perfect ass, and that silky top gave him an eyeful of cleavage that practically made him drool. He bit his tongue, his blood boiling with desire. Seven years apart hadn't changed anything between them.

It made him want to bash his head against a wall for having been a fool when she ran away from Fairhope right after their breakup. Yeah, he'd called, written letters, and even talked to her parents. But pride had kept him from getting on a plane and flying to New England to get her back. Instead he partied all summer—drinking himself stupid to try to forget about her.

"How'd that work out?" he asked as he reached his vehicle.

Apparently not too good, because the minute he saw her again, he reverted back to the little asshole he used to be in high school.

Opening his truck door, he slid into the leather seat and started the engine. Air-conditioning blasted his face and he leaned back, closing his eyes, remembering what it felt like to hold her. Her pebble-hard nipples pressed against his chest, her toned stomach rubbing across his body. People couldn't buy that kind of chemistry. His heart ached for the past, for what they shared. That comfortable familiarity that only comes with time and love.

He opened his eyes and slammed his hands on the steering wheel, frustrated with himself. He'd deserved to lose her all those years ago. He was a selfish prick for not considering her dreams—for putting his own above hers. Football had invaded his mind and heart, blinding him to anything going on around him. Carson had made some big assumptions back then, like Sadie would follow him to Florida while he played ball on a full scholarship, and then marry him after he graduated.

One-sided dreams.

Merging with traffic, he headed for his house in the College Park neighborhood, west of downtown Mobile. The real reason he'd invited Sadie to stay in his guesthouse was so she could see the property he'd bought two years ago. It reflected her idea of the perfect Southern home, the kind of place she'd told him she'd love to raise a family. Well, he'd succeeded in getting the dream house, but not the family.

Surrounded by two acres of landscaped yard and gardens, the thousand-square-foot wraparound porch was a pleasant respite from the heat. Instead of going inside, Carson sat in one of the wicker rocking chairs and waited for his housekeeper to join him outside like she did every night. Tamera Collins was more like a mother to him. Employed by his parents for twenty years, when he landed a contract with the Warriors, she demanded to move to Mobile with him. She had lost her only child in a car accident fifteen years ago, so Carson told her she could do whatever she wanted. She didn't have to work. But Tamera liked to be needed, so she mothered him, and Carson loved her for it.

The screen door opened, and Carson hid his smile behind his hand.

"Carson?"

"I'm here, Tamera."

She carried a tray to the nearby table and set it down. There was a small bucket of ice with four beer bottles in it. Two for him and two for her.

"Trying to get me drunk?" he teased.

She chuckled. "You look out of sorts."

Gazing up at her, he found instant comfort in her sincere, dark eyes. When he was in town, their nightly ritual was to drink and shoot the shit. "Sadie is in town."

Tamera gaped at him. "Sadie Reynolds?"

He nodded.

"Good Lord in heaven."

"I stopped by her hotel tonight."

Tamera sat in the rocking chair opposite his and helped herself to one of the Coronas. "How did you know she was here?" She twisted the cap off the bottle and took a sip.

"Jack Menzies is on the warpath and hired Sadie's PR firm to revamp our social media profiles and improve public relations."

"Well…" Tamera rocked back and forth. "Did you guys give Jack a reason to get mad? I know how you feel about watching the news, but there always seems to be negative coverage of the team. Boys behaving badly, if you know what I mean."

Carson appreciated that Tamera was too much of a lady to give more details. "Yes," he said taking a swig of beer. "Jack's actions are justifiable."

A moment of silence passed between them before she spoke again. "I bet Sadie is as pretty as ever."

Carson swallowed the emotions building up in his throat. "She's beautiful, Tamera. Not the beanstalk we remember."

"Beanstalk? Long and lean, maybe."

Yeah, long and lean and curvy in all the right places. The kind of curves Carson wanted to run his hands over again and again. "She wasn't too happy to see me tonight."

"Gentlemen don't make unannounced visits."

"Are you chastising me, Tamera?"

"Maybe," she admitted. "Depends on why you went to see her."

There were too many reasons, really. "I offered her a place to stay."

Tamera emitted another soft chuckle. "I might be an old woman, Carson, but I'm not stupid."

Carson considered his housekeeper. At fifty-eight, she had more energy than most thirty-year-old women. She also had a keen sense of right or wrong, never compromising to make Carson feel better. If he acted like an idiot, she called him on it. "All right." He raised his hands in mock surrender. "After spending the morning with her in the classroom, I wanted a chance to talk to her alone."

"That's better."

"For who?"

She raised an eyebrow. "The truth will set you free."

"Or make you miserable." He finished off his first beer and reached for another. "Regardless of my motivation, it seems she's not interested in me outside of a professional relationship."

"What did you expect? The two of you parted on bad terms, Carson, broke each other's hearts. You were kids. Be patient and kind if you really want to win her trust back."

Carson set his bottle aside and folded his hands on his lap, feeling more restless. Knowing Sadie was a twenty-minute drive away made him want to get back in his truck and speed to the hotel. He wanted to apologize for being an asshole. He wanted to listen to her rattle on about her life—to hold her in his arms—to just be a friend. And in the back of his mind, to seduce her...

"Give her time."

"Doesn't seven years count for anything?"

Tamera held his gaze. "It's a start."

CHAPTER SIX

The next morning, Sadie went for a run, took a quick shower, and then checked her email. Beyond work-related updates, there was nothing. Nothing from Barbi or Erika, and nothing from Carson—which surprised her. Before she dismissed the team yesterday, each player had received a folder containing materials they'd need for the first half of their class, including her resume and contact information.

After the way he left her hotel suite last night, she expected him to ramp up his efforts to reconnect with her. At least dinner tonight was a chance to share her timeline for what she expected to accomplish with the team. She'd need Carson's help as a captain to get the rest of the guys on board with the program. Football players were a different breed altogether, unlike the beta males she usually worked with.

She opened the closet and looked through her clothes. Today required something bold. After Carson's visit, she needed to make a statement, to let him know he couldn't just show up and seize control. Though she nearly lost it in his arms, she had to admit it felt right, like they'd never been apart. But that feeling passed as soon as he left. Out of sight, out of mind. *Yeah, in my wildest dreams.*

Choosing a red Rag & Bone Windsor blazer and matching fitted pants, she dressed quickly and then checked the time. At home, she got up at six thirty, ran for a half hour on her treadmill, made coffee, showered, dressed, and then headed to the office. There wasn't any reason why she couldn't keep her routine here—if Carson hadn't kept her up late.

Just as she buttoned her blazer, someone knocked on the door.

"Good morning, Ms. Reynolds," the hotel server said, ushering in a wheeled cart. He set it up in the sitting room, in front of the French doors that opened up to a private balcony.

Stunned by the extravagance of a crystal vase containing at least three dozen long-stemmed roses and a bottle of Champagne, she hardly noticed when the server lifted the polished stainless steel dome cover from her breakfast plate. Until she smelled bacon and pancakes, her favorite morning food.

"I didn't order room service," she informed the man dressed in a blue uniform.

"You are Ms. Sadie Reynolds?"

"I am."

The server pulled a guest receipt from his jacket pocket and scanned it. "Everything is in order, ma'am." He smiled and headed for the door.

"Wait." She followed him, confused. "I honestly didn't order breakfast, and I certainly wouldn't pick flowers and Champagne for myself."

He turned in the open doorway. "I believe everything is compliments of the hotel." He gave her a final nod and hurried down the hallway.

She stepped back inside and closed the door. What in the world was going on? Did Leonard do this to make up for cutting her holiday short? It seemed like the kind of thing he'd do to make her feel better. Though she received a generous per diem on the road, the roses and Champagne were too much. Convinced Leonard was being sweet, she grabbed her cell phone before she sat down at the table to eat.

She fired off a quick text, thanking Leonard for his generosity.

Champagne? Flowers? What—or who—have you been doing, Sadie? The winking emoji in his reply made her wiggle in her chair. His text confused her. Now he thought she was fraternizing with a player?

Honestly, nothing. And no one.

You're slacking off, woman. If I was surrounded by all that man flesh, I'd do someone.

Sadie rolled her eyes. Leonard appreciated men and women equally. *So, you didn't send the breakfast and flowers?*

No.

Unable to resist the aroma of bacon any longer, she snagged a piece off the plate and took a bite. She closed her eyes, chewing slowly, appreciating the burst of maple flavor. As for the pancakes…She poured a generous amount of syrup over the short stack and ate several bites before she eyed the Champagne flute containing strawberries and raspberries. Okay. Leonard wouldn't do that. It was too thoughtful, too romantic.

Carson.

This had his name all over it.

Suddenly the bite of pancakes in her mouth felt gravelly as she struggled to swallow it down. The unexpected visit was one thing, but making arrangements like this—spending a ridiculous amount of money and infringing on her privacy, well, it was unacceptable. She set the fork aside and stared at the beautiful, plump roses. Fragrant and flawless, she reached for one, pulling it from the vase. She rolled it between her fingers and sniffed. The asshat had always known how to spoil a girl. Of course, it helped he came from a wealthy family.

She remembered their first prom. The limo, red roses, and the diamond bracelet he gave her to wear with the gown he'd bought her because her parents were too broke to buy her one. The only way to show Carson she wasn't going to swoon over a fancy breakfast was to just act like nothing had happened this morning.

When she finished eating, she pushed the cart back into the hallway, minus the flowers. Those, she'd keep. The suite already smelled like her patio garden back home in South Carolina. She'd always had a weak spot for roses.

It took a few minutes to brush her teeth and style her hair. Then she put on some black eyeliner, mascara, and red lipstick. Checking herself a last time in the vanity mirror, she smiled. A woman in a red power suit smiled back. She was ready to deflate his infuriating ego and set him straight.

Typically, during training camp, Carson's day started at six thirty sharp. However, since he was required to attend Sadie's session after breakfast, his regular schedule wouldn't resume until ten thirty. He waited in the hallway outside the classroom for Sadie to arrive. Every few minutes one of his teammates shuffled into the room, looking unhappy about having to attend class.

Carson shoved a hand through his hair as Sadie entered the hallway looking well-rested and completely edible in her red suit. It pissed him off that she didn't even acknowledge him as she started to walk into the classroom.

"Sadie," he called out.

She paused and turned. "Good morning, Mr. Savage."

"Really?"

"I prefer to be punctual, Carson. I have three minutes to set up. Are you joining us today?"

Scared he could completely push her away by pressing her about last night, Carson decided to let it go for now. She obviously wasn't in the mood to discuss anything personal. The only hope he had? Dinner, tonight. He followed her inside the classroom and shut the door, then took a seat.

After a few minutes, she was ready to go. "Good morning, gentlemen," she said. "Zachary Abate, a journalist, wrote a piece last year about the five reasons fans are losing interest in the NFL. Number four on the list is the no cameras allowed policy. Are you familiar with it?"

Several guys nodded, including Carson.

"I'm glad to see at least half of you know about what many owners, players, fans, and analysts consider a Draconian policy. For those of you who aren't acquainted, I'll give you a brief intro. The rule simply states that players can't take video

footage or photos between kickoff and an hour after the game.
This makes league-controlled content off limits for every franchise. And just to demonstrate how serious it should be taken,
the punishment for a first-time offense is twenty-five thousand dollars."

"How does this affect us?" Ty asked

"To put it simply, Mr. Baxley, deeply. Those indiscreet photos taken in the locker room or on the sidelines fall under the
no cameras allowed rule—technically, anyway."

Ty turned in his chair and stared at Carson, mouthing *what
the hell?*

Carson shrugged and gestured for him to pay attention to
Sadie.

She grabbed a piece of paper off the desk and continued.
"Additionally, gentlemen, all of your contracts state that if a
player has engaged in personal conduct reasonably judged by
the club to adversely affect or reflect negatively on the club,
then the club may terminate your contract."

"Pretty sure that's a matter for our coach, the team owner,
and our agents to worry about," Sam, one of the tackles said,
sounding irritated.

"Mr. Gronig, I'm aware this is a very sensitive subject to
discuss with an outsider. But I've been given full authority
to review your individual profiles, records, and any other per-
tinent information. In essence, many of you have violated
league policy, team policy, and the moral clause in your
contracts."

"Jesus Christ." Solomon Webster shot up from his chair.
"Tight-assed little bitch. Do you know what's at stake here?"

Carson stood and quickly planted himself between his teammate and Sadie. "Knock it off, Solomon."

"Or what?" Solomon fisted his hands at his sides, then looked over Carson's shoulder at Sadie. "Tryin' to tap that?"

"Sit down," Carson gritted out, his patience waning. "This is a battle you're going to lose, really quick."

He gave his teammate a few seconds to consider his next move before Carson would physically remove him from the classroom. He sighed in relief when Solomon sat down and slammed his fist on the table.

Carson shot Sadie a concerned look, and she nodded in appreciation.

He returned to his seat.

"Mr. Webster, I'm aware what's at stake here—your reputations and livelihoods, for starters. That's why I want you to consider me an ally, not the enemy. I'm here to find solutions, not to condemn you."

"You have a jacked-up way of showing it," Solomon said.

"I'm on a very tight schedule, Mr. Webster. I have six weeks to rehabilitate twenty-three very public profiles."

"I'm not a goddamned drug addict or criminal," Ty said. "Find another word to use."

"All right," Sadie said calmly. "Do you prefer *rebuild* or *relaunch* over *rehabilitate*?"

Ty waved his hand. "You pick."

Sadie nodded and reached for a stack of papers on her desk, then offered it to the first player at the closest table. "Could you hand these back, please?"

Carson didn't like the tension in the room, especially who

it was aimed at. But somehow, Sadie had managed to keep her cool. She'd always been gracious under pressure—intelligent and fair-minded. It didn't surprise him that she'd found success early in her career. But he'd be damned if Solomon or anyone else threatened her again. That he couldn't allow.

Once the papers were distributed, Sadie addressed the group again. "The worksheet in your hands is a personal questionnaire. Please take your time and answer all of the questions honestly. Anything you share will be kept strictly confidential."

A couple of the players snickered.

"I intend to use these as guidance tools during our one-on-one sessions, which will begin tomorrow. Once we complete the exercise, the worksheets will be shredded." She cleared her throat. "The final topic we'll cover today focuses on regional publicity. National and international news outlets and larger social media resources will be discussed another day. The first step in reinventing a public profile is concentrating on local media—where your greatest fan base is located."

"Sweetheart," Haakon Wolfson said, "I'm an international sensation."

Sadie laughed along with everyone else.

"That may well be, Mr. Wolfson, but we need to start somewhere, right?"

"Makes sense to me," Haakon agreed.

"How many of you know Simon Fuentes?" she asked.

Every player in the room raised their hands.

"Simon owns and runs the most successful party gossip forum in the state of Alabama. Almost all of you have been featured on the Real Alabama website. Which brings us to an even bigger site, Southern Swank."

"Makes Girls Gone Wild look amateurish," Solomon offered.

"Yes," Sadie said. "If you like angry people submitting revenge pieces—like risqué pictures of half-naked, drunk women hanging off the arms of celebrities."

Sadie cocked her head after a few players mumbled their acknowledgment of the site. "Remember the first rule: the internet doesn't forget. No matter how many positive features on you are out there, it only takes one bad moment to destroy everything you've worked so hard to build."

"What's the point?" Carson asked.

"Simon Fuentes has agreed to visit us next week."

That made everyone pay attention.

"With the public outcry against violence and fake news, he's sincerely interested in launching a new project that highlights local heroes. I think it might be worth our time. A chance to feature some of you doing what you do best, playing football and giving back to the community. Please take the rest of the class time to complete the questionnaires and turn them into me before leaving."

Carson waited for everyone to fill out the sheet and then leave, staying in his chair until the room was empty.

"Thank you for earlier," Sadie finally spoke.

Carson gazed at her.

"Solomon Webster is a little intimidating."

Carson couldn't disagree, at 6'5" and 275 pounds, the man was a sonofabitch, on and off the field. "He has a hair-trigger temper, Kitty Kat."

She frowned.

Sadie's mere presence challenged him in every way—made him feel things he shouldn't, like wanting to beat the shit out of Webster for just looking at her wrong. But that was on Carson. He's the one who couldn't get over Sadie. From what he could see, she'd gotten over him—though their sexual chemistry was painfully still intact.

He rose and walked to the front of the room, standing a couple feet away from her. "I need to get to a meeting, sweetheart. But we're still on for dinner tonight, right?"

"Only if you promise that this dinner thing is about building our partnership to make my time here successful. It's a win-win for both of us, Carson."

He couldn't disagree about the win-win scenario, but he also couldn't tell her the truth behind his motivation. Before he dropped her off at the hotel tonight, he planned on kissing her thoroughly. Because Sadie had loved his kisses, and if anything remained of the couple they used to be together, then he needed to remind her.

CHAPTER SEVEN

I'm not sure which dress to wear, Barbi." Sadie held up a powder blue cocktail dress first, then a simple but elegant black one. She always packed the right kind of clothing for her business trips, but nothing could have prepared her for choosing the right I-want-to-show-Carson-how-sexy-I-am-still dress but not wanting to seduce him at the same time.

"I love Skype," Barbi said. "Let me see the blue one again."

This time Sadie rested it against her body. The crisscross bodice style would accentuate her breasts well.

"That one." Barbi smiled. "Black is too boring—give Carson a splash of color."

"What are you talking about?" Sadie had purposely left out the little detail about wanting to impress Carson.

"Sadie May Reynolds," her best friend tsked. "We've known each other since third grade, remember? I've watched you mature into a successful woman. However, some things never change. The only man that's ever made you question your fashion sense is Carson."

Sadie smiled inwardly, not ready to give her best friend the satisfaction of knowing how right she was. "I can see your point, Barbi." She laid the dress aside, then picked up her laptop and sat on the edge of the bed. "This dinner is purely professional."

"Then I'd have to say that little blue dress isn't an option. It's too revealing."

"Fine." Sadie gave up. "Maybe I want to tease him a little bit."

Barbi laughed. "Pretty sure you could wear a garbage bag with cutouts for your arms and he'd still trip over his tongue."

Sadie sighed. "It would be easier if you were here."

"Are you asking me to come to Mobile?"

"Yes."

"I have a better idea…"

"What?"

"Come down here."

At the mention of going home, Sadie's stomach knotted. There was nothing left for her in Fairhope. Yes, Barbi and Erika lived there. But they'd always agreed to meet on neutral ground to spare Sadie's anxiety.

"I…can't" Sadie finished lamely.

"Yes, you can. Even Matthew agrees you need to face your fears."

"You've been talking to Matthew about me?"

"Um, that started at the retreat, remember?"

Sadie felt like a case study. "Just talking about coming back makes me want to puke."

"I know, sweetheart," Barbi's tone softened. "Everyone has moved on, Sadie."

She wanted to believe it and didn't blame her best friend for not completely understanding. Sadie hadn't disclosed the depth of harassment she'd received after breaking up with Carson. The media had followed Carson's high school career, and senior year, when all the college scouts invaded Fairhope, she'd been forced to appear on television with him and had participated in several online interviews. Carson credited her for many things, including his 3.7 GPA.

The added pressure of being the hometown football star's "perfect" girlfriend had been a hard thing for her to live with. Not that she begrudged Carson his success. He'd earned every bit of it. She just couldn't handle the attention and wanted more privacy.

Admittedly, the timing of the breakup was horrible. She could have waited until they both reported for college at the end of summer. Instead, she let her emotions get the better of her when she overheard Carson discussing their futures with one of his coaches—how he didn't think she'd make it through four years of college in New England without him. How he hoped she'd quit school there and transfer to Florida. She'd had enough. And Carson vehemently refused to accept the breakup. Another reason she ran as far away as she could get. The man was relentless—even now.

In order to deal with the pain, Carson partied—drinking more and acting irresponsibly. When he nearly got a DUI a week after she broke up with him, Sadie ended up leaving Fairhope early, Carson's downward spiral more than she could handle.

"I hope everyone has moved on," Sadie replied nonchalantly.

"Except for you," Barbi added.

She shrugged, suddenly not knowing what to say. "Kind of hard to recover when everywhere I've looked these past seven years there's been constant reminders of Carson Savage. He's in the papers, on TV, online..."

"You knew he was meant for greater things when you started dating him, Sadie. Everyone did. He was born with a football in his right hand."

Sadie snorted. "Yeah, and a big ego and outdated expectations about women."

"He was raised by traditional Southern parents. And had single-minded focus back then, Sadie. Can you blame him?"

"Yeah, I can."

"Weren't you just as ambitious when it came to your studies and landing a full scholarship to a fancy college?"

Why was her best friend suddenly defending Carson? "Yes," she admitted.

"Well he was just as ambitious about football. And he's changed so much since then. Losing you and playing pro sports has opened up his mind. I think he now understands the importance of respecting your dreams as much as his own. And from what you're telling me, he still wants you. That's more than most women get!"

"I'm not complaining."

"And that ass shot..." Barbi made a silly face.

Sadie's cheeks heated. "Oh. My. God. Barbi. That's not helping."

Barbie only laughed. Sadie couldn't get upset with Barbi for being like every other hot-blooded woman. Carson was the all-American boy every father wanted for his son and every woman wanted in her bed. "I'll get over him, eventually. When I'm back home in South Carolina waiting for my next project. Preferably an assignment on another continent."

"Listen, girlie. Forget about all this stuff for the night. Have fun for once. Treat Carson like he's an old friend. Share a good meal, have a few drinks, and don't be afraid to reminisce about the old days. It's normal and healthy. If you feel uncomfortable, call a cab."

"Okay. Love you." Sadie blew her best friend a parting kiss.

Carson checked his watch for a third time in fifteen minutes. It wasn't like Sadie to be late, not even fashionably. Not in the mood to deal with the public, he chose a seat in the corner of the hotel lobby behind a potted fern where he could keep an eye on the elevators. If she didn't hurry up, he'd head upstairs and drag her out of her room.

Was Sadie testing him? Trying to drive him crazy? Or just letting him know on no uncertain terms that she didn't want anything to do with him?

Just then, the elevator doors opened and Sadie stepped into the lobby. He stood up abruptly, his gaze locking on her. As if sensing his presence, she looked in his direction. Those wide, green eyes and lush lips made him weak-kneed. And that blue dress, he bit down on his lip, stopping the animalistic growl he naturally wanted to make. Sadie had never looked more beautiful. And Carson couldn't remember a moment when he wanted her more.

Meeting her near the front doors, he greeted her with a smile. "You look gorgeous, Kitty Kat." Though she'd demanded he stop using her pet name, he refused to give up that right. How many men could say they fell in love with a girl stuck in a tree with a kitten? He chuckled out loud.

"Hello, Carson. What's so entertaining?"

Placing his hand on the small of her back, he didn't answer her question but guided her through the front doors, the sultry evening air made his skin tingle.

Within seconds, the valet delivered Carson's new black Dodge Viper VooDoo II Edition ACR, tossing Carson the keys with a shit-eating grin on his face. "How many of these were made, Mr. Savage?"

"Thirty-one. How'd she handle?"

"Tight," the valet answered.

Carson tipped the valet a twenty and then opened the passenger-side door for Sadie.

She gawked at the car before she slid inside. "Jesus, Carson, can't you drive something more practical?"

He rolled his eyes as he walked around to his side. "And what do you drive? Let me guess, a hybrid?" He revved the engine, all 645 horsepower, showing her exactly what he loved about it. "Some things aren't meant to be practical, Sadie." He peeled out of the parking lot, merging safely with traffic.

"Sorry to disappoint you. I drive a Mercedes-Benz GLA."

"Quite the utilitarian, aren't you?" he teased. "But can your little GLA do this?" He whipped into the far left lane, finding enough open road to speed up. He guessed it was accidental, but she smiled like she used to when he'd take her for long, fast rides in his Corvette after a Friday night game in Fairhope. "Some things never change, Kitty Kat." He gazed at her, hoping to keep that smile on her face.

Much to his surprise, it grew wider, and her eyes lit up. "I can't believe you own a Viper!"

"One of my little indulgences."

"Little?"

"Compared to my Lamborghini…"

"Now you're just showboating."

He held up his thumb and index finger, indicating an inch. "Maybe. But really, I consider my collection an investment."

"Do you still ride a motorcycle?"

"Every chance I get."

"I miss…" she stopped midsentence.

Unable to resist the chance to make a real connection with her, Carson rested his palm lightly on her exposed knee. Her skin was smooth and soft. "What do you miss, Kitty Kat?" he asked quietly.

"Nothing," she said, her body rigid.

Even though she acted like she didn't want to be touched, Carson could feel the electricity between them. He casually removed his hand and shifted gears. "Did you enjoy breakfast?"

Sadie huffed out a breath and stared out the passenger window. "Three dozen roses? Pancakes *and* bacon? Are you trying to get me fat, Carson?" She looked at him.

"Um…" He knew there was no right answer to that question.

She drummed her fingernails on the dashboard. "Kitty Kat got your tongue?" She arched a brow.

Sonofabitch. If she gave him a chance, she'd get more than his tongue.

Then she laughed, which made Carson chuckle, too. "Relax, superstar," she teased, using one of the many names she called him in high school. "Thank you for the flowers and the amazing food. But I don't usually eat breakfast during the week."

"Consider it the beginning of our new friendship," he said, knowing he intended to get that damned kiss before the night ended.

"Friends?" she asked, sounding doubtful.

"Why not?"

"Because I know you too well, Carson Savage."

He laughed and weaved in and out of traffic, burning off some of the building tension inside him by going faster. "You'll know a lot more before our date ends, Kitty Kat. That's a promise."

CHAPTER EIGHT

Sadie stood near the entrance of Wintzell's Oyster House while Carson parked the car. Damn, he was big and muscular, and his ass looked too good in those stonewashed jeans he was wearing. The classic, short-sleeved black Polo shirt hugged his broad chest. And his arms…Sadie had to look away before he caught her staring at his biceps. He'd always been well-built, but she guessed since the last time they'd seen each other he'd gained thirty pounds of sheer muscle.

As he approached, she said. "I can't believe you made a reservation for us here. I love this place."

Carson pointed to the funny and iconic sign by the front doors: OYSTERS—FRIED, STEWED, AND NUDE. "Who can resist their oysters?"

The restaurant was located on Dauphin Street, in an unremarkable part of Mobile, but Sadie knew how amazing the food was. She even heard something about Oprah endorsing the food here.

Carson opened the door for her, and she stepped inside—
the place was packed and noisy in a good way. Carson was immediately greeted by the manager.

"Good to see you, Carson." They shook hands.

"Hey, Randy."

"Loved that thirty-yard pass to Henry for a touchdown in
the fourth quarter last week. You were on fire, brother!"

"Thanks for supporting the team." Carson fist bumped his
friend. "Did my special request come through soon enough?"

Randy looked at Sadie, then back to Carson. "Anything for
you."

"Sadie." Carson placed his hand at the small of her back,
nudging her forward. "This is Randy DeLeon."

Sadie shook his hand enthusiastically. "It's nice to meet you.
I used to come here as a kid."

"So did I." Randy smiled. "Never thought I'd end up running
the place." The manager whispered something to the hostess
standing nearby, then returned his attention to Carson. "Everything is ready. Follow me."

As they maneuvered through the busy dining room, Sadie
was pleased to see nothing had changed. The sea-green paneled
walls decorated with local memorabilia made her feel at home.
Walking down a narrow hallway, Randy turned right through
an archway.

"Our private dining room," Randy announced, pulling out a
chair at a nicely appointed table.

Sadie set her clutch down on a nearby chair and then sat,
admiring the crisp white tablecloth and matching embroidered
linens. Though the room was small, the air of intimacy with the

oval-shaped stained-glass window and the nineteenth-century crystal chandelier overhead made it feel as if they were in a five-star restaurant. There was a white brick gas fireplace on the far wall, the yellow flames adding more charm to the space.

"Would you like to know what's for dinner?" Randy asked.

Sadie nodded, her stomach clamoring for a taste of oysters. Carson claimed the chair to her right.

"To start, four-dozen chargrilled oysters smothered in butter and cheese, served with Champagne. The main course is crab-stuffed flounder with steamed broccoli and rice pilaf. For dessert…"

Sadie held up her hand. "You're killing me, Randy. Surprise me with dessert."

Randy chuckled. "Anything for the lady." He left the room.

"Carson," she said, studying his face with renewed interest. "I can't believe you remembered how much this place means to me."

"Not just you, Sadie." He scooped her hand into his, massaging her knuckles with his thumb. "Remember our junior year state championship?"

She swallowed hard, her mind wandering back to a different place—a different lifetime, really. The Fairhope Vipers had just crushed the Huntsville Panthers 42-16, winning the state championship for a third consecutive year. Sadie had made a promise before kickoff—hugging Carson close and whispering in his ear, "Win this game for me and I'll give you whatever you want."

Instead of celebrating with the team, Carson and Sadie escaped to Mobile, had dinner at Wintzell's, then rented a hotel room, where she finally offered her body to Carson.

The memory made her insides sizzle. She squeezed Carson's hand. "How could I forget?"

His intense stare told her all she needed to know—he remembered it, too.

As Randy returned with a tray and a server in his wake, Sadie withdrew her hand from Carson's. This "business" dinner had suddenly taken on a new meaning. In fact, if she was forced to confess her sins in that moment, the first thing out of her mouth would be how good it felt to be with Carson again. How *right* it felt. How exciting it was to watch people react to his presence and then smile at her—like she was the luckiest woman in the world. But Sadie knew better: Carson didn't belong to her anymore.

And she definitely didn't belong to him.

Charleston, South Carolina, and Mobile, Alabama, were over six hundred miles apart—too far to maintain any kind of serious relationship with Carson. Even if that opportunity presented itself, she'd absolutely reject it on every level. Carson could charm a rattlesnake. That didn't make him boyfriend material. It didn't even qualify him for long-term friendship. When it came to her, Sadie didn't believe he could stay within the boundaries of what friendship meant. And, deep down, she knew she wouldn't want him to.

"Can I get you anything else, Sadie?" Randy asked.

She glanced at the table; everything looked wonderful. "No. thank you."

Carson unfolded his linen napkin and then draped it across his lap. He offered her a flute of Champagne and picked up his own. "To us, Kitty Kat."

She raised her glass and Carson tapped it with his. "No matter how many times I ask you to quit calling me that silly name, you refuse to stop."

"I'm a creature of habit."

"I'll have to agree with the creature part," she teased.

Carson gave her his best simper and traded his flute for a fork, picking up one of the oysters from the half shell. "Open wide, Sadie."

"You're not really going to feed me…" Before she could finish, the fork slipped between her lips. The aroma of butter and the taste of smoky cheese gave her no choice but to suck the oyster off the fork. She closed her eyes and groaned in ecstasy, remembering that taste too well. "You don't play fair, Carson."

Rewarded with a panty-melting smirk, he then sampled the delectable oysters, too.

Sadie took a sip of Champagne as she watched, then picked up her own seafood fork and helped herself to three more oysters. "What made you accept the contract with the Warriors over the Cowboys?" Though she'd moved out of state after their breakup, she'd still followed his career closely. And Barbi and Erika filled her in on all the hometown gossip.

"Two million in signing bonuses."

Impressive, to say the least, but she knew money alone wouldn't have swayed him. She shook her head. "It was never just about the money for you." Even in high school everybody knew Carson was destined for the NFL.

"You're right," he confirmed, "though it helps. I weighed the pros and cons—considered what Mom wanted me to do. And then I thought about living in Texas…"

"Weren't ready for cowboy hats and tacos for breakfast?" Carson snorted. "I love tacos."

"Plus you'd look hot in a cowboy hat, maybe a black Stetson."

"You think I'm hot?" Carson asked.

"Jesus," she sighed. "You don't need my admiration to figure it out, Carson. You know every woman who knows football or sees you on the cover of a magazine fantasizes about you, right?"

He waggled his eyebrows and laughed. "Now how would you know that?"

"My recent research about you and the team. Can't miss the marriage proposals or comments about your tight ass and sexy smile on social media."

He dismissed the praise with a wave of his hand. "Next year someone else will dominate the news."

"Unlikely," she said. This was the perfect opportunity to steer their conversation into a more professional area. "You're not just a trending topic on Twitter or Facebook, Carson. Social media is growing at an explosive rate. And when it comes to you, your brand holds up over time while the popularity of other players on your team has waned."

He refilled their flutes. "I don't give a shit about any of that right now, Kitty Kat."

"You should."

"Yeah—I know."

"Tell me why you think your fans are so passionate about you."

He circled the rim of his flute with his finger. "Maybe I don't lie about who or what I am."

His posting history confirmed it. Despite his wealth, talent, and growing popularity, Carson often shared personal insight, asked his fans for advice on how to improve his game, and never commented about controversial topics like religion or politics. Sure, he supported the military and demonstrated his patriotism, but it stopped there.

"Social media posts compete with others to survive…nine times out of ten, yours wins."

"Compared to who?"

"Take your pick. Athletes in general. NFL players. We can even narrow it down to quarterbacks."

"Is that what they taught you in that little private school in New England, how to measure trends?"

Sadie pursed her lips. "Dartmouth is an Ivy League school, Carson."

"I know, Kitty Kat. You did good." He reached out and caressed her cheek. Instead of pulling away, she leaned into his big, warm hand. "Better than me. Always did."

The compliment warmed her heart…or was that her second glass of Champagne? She'd always been a bit of a lightweight when it came to alcohol. "What do you mean?"

"I was born with the proverbial silver spoon up my ass." Carson's father owned a chain of successful Chevy dealerships in Alabama and northwestern Florida. When the economy tanked, so did his father's bank account. While Carson was in college, his father rejoined the military. "You started with nothing, Kitty Kat—earned that scholarship by merit alone."

Unfortunately, Carson's father died while on deployment in Afghanistan, once again throwing Carson's life into a tailspin. He started to drink again, the way he did after she broke up with him. "Thank you for the praise, Carson, but

I'm pretty sure money didn't give you that throwing arm."

"It helped," he admitted.

In desperate need of changing the subject, she asked, "How's your mother? Sisters?"

"You know how my mom is stubborn and prideful. I paid off her mortgage and offered her a generous allowance so she could stay home and take care of the girls. Flatly refused to do it."

"Is she still working at the insurance office?"

Carson nodded. "Yep."

"What about Genevieve? She's what, sixteen now?"

"Going on twenty-five."

Sadie remembered how Genny would follow them around, gaga over her big brother. "And Heather?"

"Heather, Stacey, and Suzanne are all blossoming into equal pains in the ass. If I have to hear about another Justin Bieber song or the latest gossip about a Kardashian, I'm going to hurl."

Sadie expelled a deep sigh. Barbi was right: relaxing and enjoying some great conversation with Carson is just what she needed. What harm was there in catching up? In admitting she'd missed his companionship? As long as they kept their clothes on, was he really dangerous? After a long look at him, she knew the obvious answer. *Yes.*

"How's your mom and dad?"

Sadie didn't want to talk about herself or her family. "I settled them in a nice condo in Huntsville a few years ago."

He scratched his stubbled jaw. "Why Huntsville?"

Casting her eyes downward to avoid his direct gaze, she tried to come up with a legitimate excuse beyond it was the farthest they'd go to get away from Fairhope and Carson. Her parents wouldn't leave the state. "Why not?" she tossed at him.

"What's wrong?" Carson claimed her hand again. "You can tell me."

Why hide the truth? Carson already knew most of it. Her father had suffered a debilitating injury on an oil rig and never recovered. Forced into early retirement, her dad turned to alcohol to manage his pain. "He's still drinking heavily."

"Sorry to hear it, Sadie."

"As for Mom, she can't really work. Dad requires around-the-clock care."

"You support them financially?"

"I help. Social Security doesn't pay all the bills."

"You've had a hell of a time, sweetheart."

Carson was an easy man to be around—so much so, she wanted to open up and tell him everything. But…Randy returned to the private dining room at the perfect time, rescuing Sadie from herself.

She eyed the overflowing plates on his tray. "It looks amazing," she told Randy. The decadent stuffed fish and rice made her mouth water like she hadn't eaten in a year.

"Do you prefer red or white wine, Sadie?" Randy asked.

"Surprise me." After all, Carson had been full of surprises so far, why ruin the streak?

CHAPTER NINE

Carson stretched his arms above his head and watched as Sadie finished her last bite of cheesecake. The girl had kept pace with him throughout the meal, devouring everything on her plate. The only difference was she was half his weight. So where did it all go? He knew better than to ask.

"Oh, my goodness," she said. "If I can't get out of bed in the morning, I know who to blame."

"I could help you with that, Kitty Kat."

She gave a nervous laugh. "One of your other areas of expertise, right?"

"You?"

"No, women in general."

"I'm not a saint, Sadie."

"Never thought you were."

He took a sip of water, then wiped his mouth on the corner of his linen napkin, his gaze never leaving her face. "I'm definitely an expert on you, Sadie. I know what you like—what makes you feel good."

A little panic registered on her face. The casual manner in which he talked about her and the fact that she knew he was right made her uncomfortable. The first time they'd made love was unforgettable. Not just because she'd lost her virginity, but because he'd done everything right, making her orgasm twice—a testament to their chemistry and his sexual prowess at a young age.

She fanned herself with her hand. "Is it hot in here?"

He grinned. "I'm perfectly comfortable."

"Well…" She rearranged the silverware a couple of times. "Thank you for a wonderful meal, Carson. However, I don't feel like we accomplished much on the professional front."

Carson checked the time on his watch. "Do you have a curfew, pretty lady?"

"No, but I bet you do."

"About that…"

"I thought the rules were pretty stringent during training camp."

"All depends on who you know and what pay grade you're at."

She propped her elbows on the table and rested her chin on her folded hands. "Why did you get sent to my class, Carson? You're hardly the type to get into trouble. In fact, your record is clean—no fines and no suspensions. Just the butt shot, which wasn't your fault."

"There's several reasons."

"I'm listening…"

"Jack Menzies has a lot riding on me—he considers me a franchise quarterback. Know what that means?"

"Tom Brady?"

Carson covered his heart like he'd been deeply wounded. "Of all the players you could have named."

"The title suits him."

"Yeah, it does," Carson agreed. The man was a legend he'd admired all his life. "Most experts say a franchise quarterback needs consistency, leadership, and football intelligence."

"Do you possess all of those qualities?"

Carson's jaw tightened. "My stats say I do."

"Do you think you do?"

He chuckled at her persistence. "As of last season, I have a 68.2 percent completion rate, threw for 3,623 yards, threw thirty-one touchdowns, was only intercepted twice, and my overall quarterback rating is 116." If that didn't impress her, nothing would, because Sadie was a statistical genius. In high school, she'd make complicated spreadsheets and advise him on where he could best improve his overall numbers. That's what the college scouts studied the most.

"Wow," she said. "I didn't realize…"

"What?"

"I haven't checked your stats recently."

"And?"

"Those are incredible numbers, Carson."

"Those numbers earned me more freedom than the average Warrior."

"Deservedly so."

"Ty, too," Carson said.

"You two are close."

"He's the only one I trust completely."

"I'm glad you found someone like that."

He'd like to add her to that short list again.

"What about the other reasons you mentioned?" she continued.

"Of why I'm in your class?"

She nodded.

"Coach believes in that whole no soldier left behind mentality. And since I'm one of the captains…"

"Do you agree with his philosophy?"

"Yep."

"Is there something else?"

Carson didn't want to tell her about the women. "Didn't you read the fine print in my franchise personnel file?"

"Briefly."

He bowed his head, finding it increasingly difficult to continue. Christ, Sadie had given up her virginity to him. "Two years ago…" He didn't want to relive the most embarrassing moment in his life, not with Sadie.

"The woman in the bar?"

His eyes grew wide. "You know about it?"

She touched his hand reassuringly. "I'm not judging."

"Another home game victory and a trip to Sullivan's with the team. The place was packed with fans. Everyone was buying rounds for us. Beers. Tequila. Probably the biggest celebration I've ever attended at the bar. I went to the bathroom, and *she* followed me inside."

"Who?"

"Diane."

Sadie's expression didn't change; she was listening intently.

"It surprised me to see her in the men's room. I even told her she needed to go. But Diane was so damned persistent."

"What did she do?"

"Told me she was my biggest fan—waited for me outside the stall—followed me to the sink, and when I turned around after I washed my hands..."

"You don't have to tell me, Carson. I can fill in the blanks."

He shrugged and looked away. "Isn't that what you're here for? To learn everything there is to know about the team?"

"The media gave enough details."

He gazed at her again, scooped her hand off the table and gave it a squeeze. "Don't know what the fuck I was thinking about that night...maybe nothing. But I didn't fight her off. And when the door opened and three guys walked in and found us, I didn't stop. You know the rest."

"The pictures were posted that night."

"Yeah."

"And the response on social media was mixed. It didn't hurt your overall likability, but a lot of women blamed you. Thought you seduced Diane."

"That's not how it happened, Sadie," he defended himself.

"I know. The interview she gave pretty much proved that. She wore it like a badge of honor."

Carson let go of Sadie's hand. "That's not who I am."

"Really?" She rolled her eyes. "If anyone knows that, I do."

"I've moved on. And I never get that shitfaced anymore."

"You don't owe me anything, Carson—not when it comes to your personal life. We broke up a long time ago."

"It's not that easy for me, Sadie. Separating the past and present."

She looked down. "It's been hard for me, too, Carson."

He wanted to believe it. Up until this moment, she seemed so cool and accepting of where they'd each ended up—like nothing from the past affected her.

"If it helps, Carson, I'm not angry about what happened with Diane. Surprised that you didn't handle it differently, but mostly disappointed that you'd open yourself up to that kind of abuse."

"Abuse?"

She shifted in her seat. "If the roles were switched, if you had followed Diane into the ladies' room…"

"Yeah." He didn't want to think about it. "You're a bigger person than I am. Not sure I'd like it if those headlines were about you." It would drive him crazy if he saw her in another man's arms.

She tilted her head. "Should I take that as a compliment?"

"Absolutely."

"You don't need to worry about your public image, Carson. If you want me to talk to the owner and your coach about excusing you from the class, I'd be more than happy to."

"No—wouldn't be right. Might suggest some kind of favoritism."

"All right. I'll treat you like everyone else. In fact, please show up early tomorrow. I'd like you to be my first appointment concerning the questionnaire."

"Whatever you want, Kitty Kat."

Their gazes locked then, and Carson was lost in a sea of deep green with gold flecks. Thick lashes framed her almond-shaped eyes. His attention dropped to the swell of her breasts and then dipped even lower to her tiny waist. "Let's get out of here."

What had started out as a business dinner had turned into an intimate occasion filled with laughter and deep insight into the kind of man Carson had matured into. Underneath all the football hero bravado was a vulnerable and compassionate man. It definitely caught Sadie off guard. She hadn't expected to feel so comfortable, to smile so much, to actually like him again. He'd always been and remained a force in her life. She honestly missed him. And after sitting through his agonizing explanation about Diane, that's when she knew he'd really changed for the better. The old Carson wouldn't have been so open about everything.

Driving in companionable silence, Carson crossed the Mobile River to Blakeley Island, headed north to the Spanish River overlook. Another location that held sentimental value for the two of them.

"Carson?" she said as he killed the engine.

"Yeah, Kitty Kat?"

"Did you plan a reunion tour for us?"

Carson was silent a minute before answering. "If I did, it was unintentional."

Sadie found herself taking in the surroundings, remembering hot steamy nights here spent in Carson's Corvette making love, drinking wine coolers or beer that Carson's college friends bought for him, sitting around a bonfire with their friends, or just listening to a thunderstorm rolling in from the Gulf of Mexico.

She opened her mouth to say something, to tell him she

didn't believe coming here was unplanned, but thought better of it.

"Something on your mind?" He pivoted in his leather seat, facing her.

Every fear she had about coming to Mobile was justified tonight. Carson was more dangerous than he'd ever been before. And since it had been two years since she'd made love…well, this closeness was screwing with her body and brain. Her flight instinct told her to jump out of his car and call a cab. But cell phones didn't work out here seven years ago, and she doubted it would be any different now. As for her fight instinct—that had all but disappeared.

What was left? An inner voice trying to convince her she had every right to touch him. His face, chest, arms, legs…

Carson reached for her, but she shrank away, wedged up against the door.

"Sadie? What happened between the restaurant and here?"

"I don't know."

"Look at me, sweetheart."

Without another word, she opened the car door and climbed out. Spending another minute alone with Carson wasn't an option. Too many feelings, old ones and new, were overwhelming her. She needed a breath of fresh air and a moment to think.

It seemed like forever before she heard the crunch of boots on the gravel somewhere behind her. And when she felt his fingers on the back of her arm, raising gooseflesh and giving her passion chills, she automatically stopped, waiting for what she knew came next.

"What's wrong, Kitty Kat?"

She turned to him. "Where should I start?"

"I thought we had a great time."

"We did. That's the problem."

He rubbed her arms reassuringly. "You're afraid of me?"

"Of course not. I'm afraid of myself."

He curled his fingers under her chin and tipped her head up. "Trust your gut, Sadie. If this doesn't feel right…"

Oh, it felt right, like it was their second chance. All the memories from this place washed over her—the hot kisses and sex—the endless talks—the joy of just having someone to be with. She gazed at the city lights in the distance and breathed in the salt air. Why couldn't Carson be a complete asshole? It would make it so much easier to walk away.

Barbi's words popped into her head, *Have fun for once. Treat Carson like he's an old friend. Share a good meal, have a few drinks, and don't be afraid to reminisce about the old days. It's normal and healthy.*

Denial wasn't healthy, but it was Sadie's normal. And in this familiar setting, with the man of her dreams in front of her, and a little alcohol to take the edge off, she was suddenly tired of lying to herself. Sick of depriving herself. She caressed his cheek with her fingertips, her hand shaking. "I missed you."

"Sadie," he whispered in that hypnotic tone. "I want to touch you. Need to feel you again. It's been too fucking long."

CHAPTER TEN

Too long was a ridiculous understatement. Carson closed his eyes, remembering a hot summer night when they were kids—when they'd spent the night on the same beach with a group of friends after a game victory. Funny how the whole world around them could celebrate, raising hell and drinking to the wee hours of the morning, but Carson and Sadie always managed to carve out their own existence, blocking out the noise—focusing on each other.

Shaking the thought, Carson wrapped his arms around Sadie. "I've missed you too, Kitty Kat."

She didn't try to squirm free. Instead, she took a deep breath. "So what does that mean for us? Because I can't handle another heartbreak, Carson."

Sadie avoided confrontation. How many times had she left to escape an uncomfortable situation? But she had to ask the question.

"Nothing's changed for me," he said. "I know we've moved

on, dated other people, but here we are, back where it all started. I don't believe in coincidence, Sadie."

"We're not teenagers anymore, Carson. This…" She gestured between them. "Is the product of seven years of silence."

Exactly what was she referring to? The sizzling, mutual attraction between them? The painful erection he'd been sporting all night? Did it matter? "That silence was one-sided, Sadie. You refused to take my calls or answer my texts. When that didn't work, I wrote a dozen letters only to have them returned, unopened."

She tilted her head. "What letters?"

Carson rolled his eyes. "Probably better you didn't read them."

"No. What letters, Carson?"

"The ones spilling my guts. I wrote half of them while I was drunk."

"I-I never received them."

He tried to wave it off. "Pretty sure it wouldn't have made a difference. They were returned unopened and I threw them away. Then you left. End of story."

"Maybe my parents sent them back, Carson. I'm sorry."

In his mind, things had never really ended; she simply broke up with him and then disappeared. "We had big plans, remember?" Plans she obviously didn't want to be a part of. He shook his head—knowing Sadie Reynolds still had the power to hurt him. The only problem? There wasn't any offensive line to protect Carson against whatever weapons Sadie had. Only him and her, one-on-one. And she was definitely his weakness—with her irresistible pouty mouth and wide green eyes.

"*You* had big plans."

"You're right, Kitty Kat."

Had she misheard him? He was admitting to putting his own dreams above hers?

"I never wanted to go to Florida. I wanted to experience something different—New York or New England. You had ten scholarship offers, three of them from schools I would have considered attending with you. But instead, you did whatever Coach told you to do."

"That's not fair," Carson said. "The man made it possible for me to go pro. I owed him…"

She shook her head. "You only hear what you want to hear. That's why I left, Carson. That's why I put myself first for once."

Carson had relived those heart-wrenching moments again and again, remembering every word and every look on Sadie's face the night she broke up with him. He'd suffered through the aftermath, overhearing all the ugly things people in their hometown had whispered behind his back about her, how she had used him in high school to get what she wanted and then dumped him the minute she received her scholarship. Those memories had scarred him—triggered his self-destructive mode, sending him on the longest drinking binge he'd ever had.

"Losing you nearly ended my football career before it even started."

"I know," she whispered.

"You knew?"

"You made the national news a few times that summer. And Barbi and Erika…"

"And that never made you want to reach out?"

"I-I..."

"Did it, Sadie?" She owed him that much. Because if there was any hope of him having a future, possibly a family, he needed to know. No woman could live up to Sadie. He'd always hoped they'd cross paths again, get a second chance. But after seven long years, that hope was about to finally faded to a fantasy unless she showed him that she still cared.

"Yes. Do you think I enjoyed watching your life unravel? Just because we broke up doesn't mean I stopped caring."

"If you'd just reached out once..."

"I did," she finally admitted.

Even in the dim moonlight he could see tears in her eyes—the regret. Yeah, he'd felt that way too many times to count. "When?"

"I-I called several times, but when you answered the phone, I lost my nerve and hung up."

He wracked his brain trying to remember those phone calls but couldn't. Everything about those first few weeks without her was fuzzy.

"Why? I was still the same, Sadie. Still loved you, and sure as hell wanted you back."

"I was an emotional wreck—fragile and so unsure of myself. I felt so naked without you, Carson. I don't expect you to understand this next part. I needed to find my own way, to prove to myself that I could stand on my own two feet."

"Why wouldn't I understand?"

"Because you've always had direction and confidence to spare. Your football career started in high school. The first time you threw a pass, everyone knew where you were headed."

"You're the most intelligent woman I've ever met, Sadie. Everyone knew you'd get a scholarship. It screwed me up."

"Why?"

"If you keep a butterfly in a bottle too long, it'll suffocate. I knew Fairhope was your bottle, sweetheart. You were never happy there. Eventually we had to face that fact. I wanted to return to Alabama after college, and you wanted to leave forever. I just wasn't able to see that so clearly back then. I thought being married to me would be enough to keep you there."

Sadie twined her fingers with his and raised his hand to her lips, placing a feather-light kiss on his knuckles. "I did love you, Carson."

His heart stilled at the familiar tone. The emphasis on those three words he'd have killed to hear from her just one time over the last seven years. Catching her face between his hands, his thumb moved nervously over her bottom lip. She didn't reject his touch; if anything, she stepped into him, pressing her cheek against his hand, indicating she wanted more.

He shoved his free hand through his hair. Should he take advantage of the moment? Push her boundaries, see how far she'd go with him? He held her chin between his thumb and forefinger, lifting her face so she was forced to look him in the eyes. "You're all over the place, Sadie. Condemning me one minute, giving me hope the next. Tell me what you want."

Carson knew what he wanted—to touch her—to make love all night long. Those comfortable leather seats in his Viper reclined…

She seemed to struggle for a breath, her eyes still locked on his. "I'm not sure anymore."

"Let me help you make up your mind." Tugging her close, his tongue tangled with hers, the kiss all-consuming. The time for restraint was over. Immersed in her sweet fragrance and equally delicious taste, his hands roamed boldly up her back. Sadie dug her fingernails into his arms, standing on her toes for better access to his lips.

Christ, he'd wanted this forever. His fantasy had suddenly and unexpectedly turned real. Lust boiled in his veins and the air crackled with desperation—the kind of desperation only years apart could make. Unanswered questions didn't matter anymore. Everything Carson needed to know could be found in Sadie's hungry kisses. In the way she looped her arms around his neck and plastered her tiny body against his.

On a growl, he greedily scooped her up, and Sadie locked her ankles behind his back. Cupping the nape of her neck, he deepened that kiss, not wanting it to end. Somehow, he made it to the front of his car and lowered her onto the hood. Spread out before him like a feast, he stared admiringly—her hooded eyes, kiss-swollen lips, slim legs opened wide enough to grant him a peek of the red panties she was wearing underneath her ass-hugging dress, all too much to take. It transformed him from the respectable man he'd intended to be tonight to the sex-starved animal he'd always been when it came to the girl he once loved.

His cock throbbed. "Sadie…"

She gazed up at him. "I know what I want."

They'd both had a bit to drink, but not enough to get drunk. Definitely not enough to make Sadie offer her body to him without knowing what she was doing. He'd hate himself, otherwise. As much as it pained him to question her choice, he said, "Tell me you're sure, baby. I need to know."

She nodded silently, then slowly lifted her skirt, revealing those lacy red panties. Carson moaned in utter lust as he leaned over his car, gently pushing her back down, using one hand to lower her underwear to her ankles, then completely from her body. His thin thread of restraint snapped. He couldn't tear his eyes away at the perfectly trimmed strip of red curls that crowned her pussy.

She lifted her hips in invitation, eyeing him. "Is something wrong, Carson?"

"Wrong?" he repeated, thinking her crazy for even asking. "No, sweetheart, everything is perfect." *Too* perfect.

Maybe that's why he feared what would happen after he caressed her the first time—what consequences would follow. Lust and a mixture of anger and desperation jabbed at his heart and cock at the same time. Did he still love her? Or was all of this just a way to prove to himself that she had suffered as much as he had? That she wanted him as much as he wanted her?

Gripping her legs, he pulled her toward him, close enough to bend at the hips to reach her delectable mouth. Breathing her in, he captured her lips in another possessive kiss, his right hand finding the wet warmth of her core.

At first, he gently stroked her, his fingers dancing over her soft flesh. When that wasn't enough to satisfy his growing need, he slid a finger inside her. She cried out, wiggling underneath him. Carson closed his eyes for a long second, the velvet smoothness of her tight pussy something he never wanted to forget.

"Carson…" She traced the seam of his lips with her fingertips. And when his mouth opened, she offered him two of her fingers. Sucking them into his mouth, he watched her respond to his touch, her sighs almost as gratifying as feeling her quiver. He rotated his wrist, increasing the pressure on her clitoris, teasing her.

His girl had always been wet and ready, never needing too much foreplay. Was she the same, or had her tastes changed? Whatever she wanted, he'd give it to her. The ripple of anticipation that started at his toes and worked its way up his body nearly had him shaking. Another example of the power she had over him. He growled and withdrew his hand from between her legs and stepped back.

She watched as he licked his fingers, her scent and taste triggering a new wave of memories. Carson unzipped his jeans and his erection sprang free from the restraint of his snug jeans.

Raising herself onto her elbows, Sadie didn't hold back. Her fascination with his body had never been a secret. And that hadn't changed after all these years, either. She reached for his cock, running her fingers down its hard length, meeting his hungry gaze as she lightly squeezed him over and over again.

"You're killing me, Kitty Kat," he groaned.

"Then what are you waiting for?"

Urging her back with a little more force this time, she bent her knees and pressed them into his chest as he positioned himself between her thighs. Condoms—hell—he didn't have any. "Sadie—we can't—I didn't bring any protection…"

"I'm on the pill, Carson."

"What about…"

"I have access to your medical records…as for me, it's been so long…"

"How long?" His ego demanded her to say it, that she hadn't felt right with another man.

"Two years," she whispered. "And I'm desperate to make up for lost time."

Hell. Carson drove into her with wild abandon, burying himself balls deep. Every muscle in his body tensed as he pumped his hips, holding her legs against his chest, dipping down to take those sexy lips again. Her tongue darted between his lips, wrestling for dominance with his, exploring the depths of his mouth.

She bucked underneath him, meeting him stroke for stroke, forcing him into a frenzied pace. Too much all at once. Her legs started to quiver uncontrollably and she closed her eyes, crying out his name. At the same moment he groaned violently, the friction and force of their movements causing him to explode inside her, the power of their shared orgasms stole their breath.

It wasn't enough for Carson. And not nearly good enough for the girl he'd always loved. Cradling her face between his palms, he eyed her. "I want more, Kitty Kat."

She cupped his cheek. "More," she repeated hoarsely, looking good enough to eat.

All the confirmation he needed, he pulled out and flipped her over, careful not to hurt her, not giving a shit about his car.

Not needing any prompting, Sadie positioned herself on her knees, her back arched, that heart-shaped ass high in the air. Carson gripped his cock, stroking it as he took in the perfect view.

Sadie straightened her skirt, smoothing what wrinkles she could. Carson had seen through her defenses—offering her exactly what she needed—him.

"You okay, sweetheart?" he asked, hugging her from behind.

She sighed as he kissed the top of her head. "Better than okay," she said, meaning it. She turned in his arms and gazed up at him. He looked happy. "Thank you."

"For what?" The effect of his sexy, boyish grin went straight to her core.

"For making me feel alive again, Carson. I'm so career-focused, I've neglected my personal needs."

His smile widened. "You don't need to worry about that anymore. I'm here now." He rubbed his hands down her arms.

Here now, but where would he be the moment something bigger and better than her came along? Although she'd given herself to him tonight, that didn't translate into renewing their relationship. Like she'd always known, his football career and the desire to stay in Alabama made it impossible for them to resurrect anything long term.

"I guess we should talk about that, Carson."

"Shoot, sweetheart." He leaned against the side of his car, crossing his long legs and arms, looking too cool and relaxed for comfort.

"We shouldn't kid ourselves about what happened tonight. It was amazing, and I'm sure it provided some relief for whatever residual feelings you have left from our time together."

"Jesus Christ, Sadie." He shook his head. "How can you disconnect so quickly? People don't just do what we did because there's unresolved issues from their high school relationship. Stop hiding behind our past and start accepting what's in front of you. I'm not a boy anymore, and you sure as hell aren't the same girl."

"What's that supposed to mean?" she asked, offended by what he might be implying.

"You're all grown up, sophisticated and independent, as polished as any New England white collar I know."

"Does that make you uncomfortable, Carson?"

He laughed. "Why should it?"

"Because you chose to stay close to home for college, and then moved back to play for the Warriors. That means you never really had to change."

"You already admitted I changed for the better, Kitty Kat."

"Yes," she confirmed. "You've managed to carve out this amazing career and stay true to the values I know your parents worked so hard to instill in you. Considering all the pressure you live with—playing like a superstar, pleasing the fans, earning all that money…It's admirable, believe me."

"But not good enough for you."

"You belong here, Carson. I don't."

"You were born in Alabama, raised here." He pushed off the car and came at her, resting his hands on her shoulders. "What are you afraid of?"

Why did all of her closest friends and family members ask her the same questions? What are you afraid of, Sadie? Why did you run away from the perfect life, the perfect man? Why can't you stay in one relationship long enough to build something meaningful? "I live in South Carolina, Carson. I have a great career. My parents live in Huntsville. The only connection I have to Fairhope is Barbi and Erika."

"You're avoiding the question, Sadie."

"Part of it is about my father—how everyone judged him, calling him the town drunk, the loser on disability. I didn't like the way people looked down on him and Mom, or me."

"I thought that stopped... We dealt with that."

"Just because I was your girlfriend didn't mean everyone supported our relationship. Fairhope is full of old money, Carson. People who expect things to stay a certain way."

"I'm sorry, Sadie."

"It wasn't your fault. Maybe I should have told you. But I can't move back here and be that girl again, Carson." He had helped her so many times, and his closest friends had been so accepting of her. She missed that part the most. The companionship, belonging to a group of people that would do anything for their friends.

When she went silent he returned to the car and opened the passenger side door. "Let's go, sweetheart."

Feeling relieved and sad at the same time, Sadie slipped into the seat. Carson had made her feel like a woman again, so why couldn't she accept that precious gift and just let fate lead the way?

As Carson joined her inside the car, she knew the other half of her answer—because he'd always had a set expectation of what a wife should be: a helpmate and mother, living her life around him and their children, definitely not focused on her own career. That, and his past selfishness, scared her more than anything.

She didn't blame him. They'd both grown up in a traditional Southern town that seemed to be stuck in a time warp from the 1950s. But she'd escaped. He hadn't.

No, Carson Savage was a sweet memory, one she'd cherish forever. And whatever time they spent together over the next few weeks would only add to those memories. But once she returned to South Carolina, that had to be the end of them, right? What else could she do? What was she willing to do? Sadie stared out the passenger side window, feeling more confused than she ever had.

CHAPTER ELEVEN

Nothing made sense. Not Sadie's emotional flip-flopping, or the way he was feeling after making love to her. What should have been a special moment had turned into Sadie explaining why she couldn't get involved in a relationship with him. Had she used him for sex? Not that he'd normally complain, but Sadie meant something—everything, really.

Carson let the hot water cascade down his shoulders, breathing in the steam from the shower. He'd walked Sadie into the hotel lobby, kissed her cheek, then walked out, not giving her the satisfaction of a backward glance. He drove home with classic metal blasting from his speakers, frustrated and confused by her denial, tortured by the lingering scent of their sex on his body.

Even Tamera eyed him speculatively when he walked inside, letting the screen door slam behind him. He'd stomped upstairs to his master suite and locked the door.

Once he rinsed the soap off his body, he leaned his forehead against the marble wall, unable to get the naked image of Sadie out of his mind. How many nights had he stayed awake fantasizing about her, dreaming of a second chance? That summer after high school, he'd tortured himself, trying to understand why she'd run away. All through college, no matter how hard he pushed himself to play ball, how many nameless girls he took home, or how much he partied, nothing could erase the three years he'd spent with Sadie.

When the Warriors and Cowboys competed for him right up until the draft, Jack Menzies making a backroom deal at the last minute to get him as the first-round draft pick, all Carson could think about was staying close to home just in case Sadie returned. Everything about his past with her had influenced the decisions he made about his future.

He didn't hide his feelings from his family—his mother was completely aware of why he hadn't settled down yet. She never judged him, never discouraged him from dreaming big when it came to Sadie. She simply told him if it was meant to be, Sadie would find her way back, no explanation needed.

Well, it'd finally happened.

Smacking his hand against the wall, Carson raked his fingers through his wet hair. He hit the wall again, finding it did nothing to ease his frustration. *What's going on in that beautiful head of hers?*

Turning the multiple sprayers off, he reached for a towel from the heated rack, wrapping it around his hips. As he stepped out of the glass enclosure, he caught his reflection in the floor-to-ceiling mirror across from the shower. He frowned. It didn't matter what he looked like, how successful he was, how many women he seduced, or how many properties he owned. Money couldn't buy happiness. Oh, it could make being miserable bearable, but it couldn't change anything—it wouldn't bring back Sadie for good.

Tamera rapped on the door, and Carson walked through his bedroom and opened it.

She considered him before she spoke. "Your mama is on the phone."

"Everything okay?"

"Just a friendly call, I think."

"Thanks, Tamera, I'll take it in here."

"Okay. What about dinner?"

"Already ate."

"Need anything else, sweetie?"

"A lobotomy," he said before he closed the door again.

Carson padded to the nightstand on the left side of his oversized bed. He picked up the phone, wondering why his mother hadn't called his cell instead. "Mama."

"Carson," she greeted him with much needed warmth in her voice. "The girls are spending the night at Auntie Beth's house tonight. Thought it would be a great time to catch up with you."

"Thanks, Mama," he said, trying to sound pleasant.

"Rough day at camp?"

Carson laughed. Whenever she asked him that question, it made it sound like he was a kid at summer camp. "Nothing I can't handle."

"Carson," she said, "I carried you in my body for nine months. Spent a lifetime making sure you were a happy little boy."

"I know."

"Your short answers indicate something is wrong. You know you can tell me anything, right?"

Blessed to grow up with parents that encouraged their children to communicate openly, Carson knew he should share the fact that Sadie Reynolds was back in town. Not to mention, if Tamera and his mama had a chance to chat, Tamera would definitely share the news.

"The commissioner and Jack Menzies are cracking down on anyone who violates moral clauses in our contracts, especially players who misuse social media."

"Sounds reasonable."

"We're not teenage boys, Mama. We're grown men, capable of making our own decisions—even if they're bad ones."

"Really?" she asked. "I might live in a small town, Carson. But the minute anything makes the news about the team or you specifically, my phone rings."

Carson regretted that part of his very public life—the effect it had on his mother and sisters. That was another reason he walked a straight path, staying out of trouble as much as he could. "I'm very careful…"

"Except for the occasional slip, right? Like the ass shot Genevieve's girlfriends were giggling over the other night on the internet?"

Carson's heart dropped into his stomach. "Jesus Christ."

"Don't take the Lord's name in vain, Carson."

"Sorry, Mama."

"Were you taking selfies in a mirror?"

"No."

"Then who's responsible for that indiscreet picture?"

"One of the rookies."

"Shame on that man. Maybe I should give the coach a friendly call and get the rookie's phone number. And once I contact that player, I'll remind him how fortunate he is to have such God-given talent. Maybe he needs to think about all the disadvantaged kids out there and how his time would be better spent..."

"I don't think that's a good idea. Coach and everyone else in the front office already knows."

"Oh."

"We've been put on notice."

She took a deep breath. "What do you mean?"

"If we don't clean up our public images, we might get fired."

"Not you, though."

"Mama..."

"Jack knows you're a good kid, Carson."

"I'm also responsible for the actions of my teammates and helping steer them in the right direction."

"All right," she said in her dissatisfied tone. "What's management doing about it?"

"Hired a social media expert to rehabilitate our profiles, to help change the public's perception of the team."

"Isn't that your agent's job?"

"Not everything is black and white, Mama."

"Is this expert reliable?"

"She's incredible," Carson slipped.

"What did you say?"

"She's credible."

"Carson," his mother started. "I distinctly heard you say *incredible*."

"Did I?"

"Are you fraternizing with a professional woman hired to work with your team?"

In every way. Now would be the perfect time to slip in Sadie's name. "Mama, it's Sadie Reynolds."

The gasp that followed indicated his mother's surprise. "*The* Sadie Reynolds?"

"In the flesh."

"Jesus."

Carson wanted to remind his mother not to take the Lord's name in vain, but he bit his tongue.

"How is she?"

"Fine, Mama. Successful, beautiful, and just as confused as she's always been."

"Poor girl."

"I know she didn't grow up the way I did. Her father is still struggling with addiction, and her mother is forced to stay home and take care of him. Though she's making a great living, she's so emotionally isolated."

"That's terrible, baby. The best thing you can do is offer support and be there if she needs you."

Carson rubbed the back of his neck and started pacing. In his mother's ideal world, that's what a man like him would do. But Carson flatly refused to let the opportunity to reconnect with Sadie slip through his fingers. A man of decisive action, he'd come up with a game plan, just like he did on the field.

"I need to go, Mama. I have an early morning. Say hello to the girls. I'll drive down on my next day off."

"Or I could come spend a few days with you? Auntie Beth

can take care of the girls, and I have a few personal days saved up at work."

Though he appreciated the offer, Carson knew his mother too well. She'd get too involved with him and Sadie. "Let me think about it, okay? My schedule is all screwed up right now. There's limited time before preseason." His mother knew the routine as well as he did.

"I love you, Carson. And I'm so proud of you."

"I love you, too, Mama."

"Give Tamera a hug for me. And please, tell Sadie I'd love to see her."

Carson hung up, unsure of what he was going to do about Sadie.

CHAPTER TWELVE

A couple of days after her date with Carson, Sadie finally finished up her one-on-one meetings with the team. The session with Carson had been intense and sexually charged. They couldn't keep their eyes off each other, and she had been tempted more than once to touch him. But he kept his distance. Plus, he'd been more than helpful and even offered to review her notes after she met with the other players. His insight would be invaluable once she finished building her spreadsheet for what the goals were for the team.

In the meantime, she had spoken with Leonard, and they'd brainstormed ideas for a new publicity campaign. It would be launched online, on television, and on the radio simultaneously. Surprisingly, she'd woken up with the perfect slogan and was excited to share it with Leonard.

His happy face popped up on Skype, and she smiled as she took a sip of coffee.

"Good morning, sunshine," he said.

"Morning."

"What do you have for me? The Warriors' public relations department generously sent over enough material to keep our production team busy for the rest of the year," he said.

"Hopefully great video clips and quality photographs."

"Yes," he replied.

"One less thing for me to worry about."

"Getting stressed out?" Leonard asked.

"Just anxious to start getting my hands dirty. You know how I am. The preliminary fact-gathering exercises are boring."

Lenny chuckled. "Only you would get bored surrounded by all that muscle."

"I sneak a peek once in a while."

"At what, exactly?"

"Let's stick to business, shall we?" She could spend all day talking to him about frivolous things; that's why they worked together so well.

"What do you think about 'Rediscover the Alabama in the Alabama Warriors'?"

He thought about it. "Catchy. Clean. Memorable."

"Isn't that the most common complaint, that the fans feel like they've lost touch with their team?"

"After the political shitstorm everyone's been embroiled in this year, I'd have to say yes."

"I think we need to focus on the locals—bring this team home."

Leonard picked up a pen and started taking notes. "Where do you want the videos to be taken? On the field? Locker room?"

"Small town clips. Fourth of July, Thanksgiving, parades, and maybe the individual players doing community service?"

"You think traditional will catch the fans' attention?"

"I think it will make them take a second look. The fame and glamour have a place, but let's think about this on a different level, Leonard. How much is an average game ticket?"

"Hold on." Lenny typed something on his computer. "Have it right here. Ninety-three dollars. That's an eighteen percent increase in cost over last year."

"So nearly four hundred dollars just for the tickets for a family of four? That's crazy!"

"That's football. And the Warriors rank pretty close to average for ticket costs."

"Let me guess…"

"Yep. The Patriots have the highest cost."

"Add in parking, programs, popcorn, hot dogs, drinks, and maybe a jersey or two for the kids," Sadie said. "We're talking, what, six or seven hundred dollars. That's a vacation for some families, Leonard."

He rubbed his chin. "Where are you going with this?"

"The median household income for Alabama is forty-one thousand dollars. I want to concentrate on that—highlight how much the players appreciate their fans. Recognize how special it is to come to a game."

"Hmm," he said. "You might have something here. Take the spotlight off the field and shine it on the average fan."

"Yes! Maybe we can get some fan quotes—clips of kids saying why they love the Warriors and have individual players respond on a personal level."

"I like it a lot, Sadie."

"How far am I supposed to go with this, Leonard?"

"Jack Menzies has deep pockets and high expectations. You're in control of this. If you think one of those guys needs a new wardrobe, hire a fashion consultant."

She laughed at that. "Somehow I can't picture Solomon Webster taking fashion tips from me."

"Is he still hostile?"

"Apprehensive, not hostile. I think the first day pissed everyone off, even Carson."

"How's that going?"

"I'll let you know later."

"That bad?"

"No," she said. "I'm just not prepared to discuss it right now."

"We had another team reach out and ask for a proposal."

"Really?"

"Guess word got out what the Warriors were doing. This could turn into something big."

"What does Charles think?"

Lenny huffed. "He's in Greece."

"Seriously?"

"Would I lie?" he asked.

"I'm shocked that he's traipsing all over the world while we're busting our asses to land this contract."

"The man is having a midlife crisis, I think. Ever since Shelly broke it off with him, he's been on a world tour to get laid."

Sadie cringed at the thought of any woman sleeping with her boss. "Maybe it's a good thing. Leaves you in charge, and he's not micromanaging me."

"Whether you know it or not, Charles admires you."

"Right," she replied sarcastically.

"He does, Sadie. You wouldn't be in Alabama if he didn't. Which leads to the next topic of interest."

"What?"

"I'm flying in next Friday."

Sadie leaned forward. "To Mobile? That's wonderful news!"

"I thought about what you said, and I did remember what is was like in the field. I've lost touch sitting in this office. So, if you'll have me…"

Sadie blew him a kiss. "I can't wait."

"You have the lead, sweetheart. I'm just along for the ride."

"You'll want access to the locker room."

He waggled his eyebrows. "What's on the agenda today?"

"I'm going to visit the practice field, see how these guys interact in their natural environment."

"Wildlife viewing, sounds fun."

"You're crazy, Leonard."

"So I've been told."

"Have a great day," she said.

"You, too."

Armed with a camera, she left her hotel room and headed for the field to watch afternoon practice. She'd been around the game long enough to follow the plays. She passed by the media area and overheard one of the reporters on camera.

"Thanks to the Warriors' front office, Carson Savage will be surrounded by talent this season. After drafting a new wide receiver, Donovan Quick, it should take some of the pressure off Carson. But the main concern today is whether the Warriors can clean up their act and join other teams like the Mustangs, who have taken the commissioner seriously when he demanded all teams clean up their acts. Jack Menzies, the owner of the Warriors, has gotten creative this year, holding a preseason minicamp. Word has it most of the players aren't happy with the idea, but judging by how many of them are here, I'd say they took the front office seriously..."

Sadie knew the pressure was always on Carson, whether it pertained to the game or serving as a leader. He was an out-of-pocket quarterback who took risks—he could barrel down field and take out a couple defenders before getting tackled. But her attention was on Tyrone Baxley today, the big and physical all-star tight end who never seemed to slow down, on or off the field.

"Seven-on-seven," the offensive coordinator called, clapping his hands.

Seven players, including Carson, completed a series of passing drills. Sadie understood the importance of timing and route combos—and Ty's explosive speed was breathtaking. She snapped several photos, then switched to video.

Tyrone had a bad habit of posting controversial content on Twitter, Instagram, and Facebook, expressing his political views and disappointment in dwindling NFL popularity, and he always shared intimate photos of the women he was dating. His favorite hashtag was #livingaplayerslife. But he didn't mean football player.

Sadie spent the next hour getting the pics and videos she needed, then sat in the bleachers with the lucky fans allowed to attend the practice.

After a few minutes, a guy sitting behind her tapped her on the shoulder. "With the media?" he asked.

Sadie turned around and smiled. "No. Just a fan."

He shook his head. "I saw you on the field. Regular fans don't have access to the field. We're only allowed to sit here and use the bathroom over there." He pointed. "You on a secret mission of some sort?"

Sadie considered the middle-aged man. He was dressed in jeans and a button-down shirt, had a Warriors ball cap on, and expensive tennis shoes—the average Warriors fan? Maybe she could turn this into a learning moment, find out what he loved about the team. "My name is Sadie." She extended her hand.

"Gerald Davenport." He gave her hand a firm shake.

"Are the Warriors your favorite team?"

"My *only* team."

"Would you mind telling me what players you follow on social media? What you like the best about them?"

He tilted his head. "I knew it."

"What?"

"Secret mission."

Sadie grinned, unable to disclose what her purpose on the field was. "Maybe," she teased.

"Nice to see a lady working with the team," he said. "I'll help you. I like Savage and Baxley, Hicks and Gonzalez. The running game was hot last season. And the Warriors and New Orleans were knocking on the championship doors last year. With the new talent, pretty sure we have a real shot at the playoffs again."

"What about social media?"

He pursed his lips. "Hate it, but consider it a necessary evil.

I'm a stockbroker, expected to stay up-to-date on things. I use Twitter and Facebook mostly. I follow a dozen players, post the occasional comment, nothing too serious."

"What's your overall impression of the team?"

"Depends on the time of year." He winked at her. "Savage and Hicks are local heroes, born in Alabama. Good ol' boys raised right."

"Does that make a difference to you? If a player is local or from another state?"

"Sometimes." He gestured at the field. "Ty Baxley is from New York—raised in the foster care system, no real roots. It shows."

"In what way?"

"Doesn't have a mama to keep him on the straight and narrow."

Sure, Gerald was referring to all the women Ty slept with, she didn't ask for clarification. "But you like him?"

"Who doesn't? He runs a 4.24-second forty-yard dash."

Talent overshadowed whatever moral shortcomings a player possessed? Sadie could work with that. In fact, that's why she'd been taking pics of Ty. Showcasing his talent on the field instead of his prowess in bed was the first step to reinventing him.

"Thank you, Gerald." Sadie stood.

"Leaving me already?"

Sadie leaned in and whispered. "Secret mission, remember?"

He chuckled. "Well, whoever the hell you are, Sadie, it was nice to meet you."

Carson headed off the field to grab a towel and some Gatorade. The June humidity was brutal. As he wiped the sweat from his forehead, he watched Sadie leaving the bleachers. God, she looked good in jeans and that off-the-shoulder shirt. While he'd been completing passes on the field, she'd been on the sidelines taking pictures. But not of him.

Ty joined him. "You seem preoccupied."

"Nothing I can't handle," Carson said.

Ty followed his gaze to Sadie and smirked. "You're full of shit. No one could handle her. She's out for blood."

Carson frowned. "She's here to help."

"Need to clear your head of that pussy fog. She's working for the front office, and in case you haven't noticed, there's a war going on here. Them against us."

"Don't take everything personally, Ty," Carson said. "Think we're the only team under pressure to clean up our public image? The league is losing money, big time."

"Not my problem."

"What's going on with you?"

His best friend poked him in the chest. "This shit drains the brain. I'm tired of coaching points and meetings. Tired of bleeding for this team and getting lumped in with the players who don't know their asses from a hole in the ground. Now Jack is trying to silence me, dictating who I can sleep with, what I can and can't post. It's like he wants to stop me from having an opinion."

Carson dropped his helmet on the ground, then crossed his arms. "You really think he's trying to silence you?"

"Well he's definitely limiting what we can share on social media."

"How many dick pics do you need to post?"

Ty shook his head. "None. That shit is sacred. The ladies post them, not me."

Carson rolled his eyes. "I've seen them. It's not like you remove the tags when women tag you."

His best friend laughed. "Like dick, do you?"

"I follow you on Twitter, asshole. That's why I'm worried about you. Tone it down some, okay?"

"Social media has nothing to do with how I play."

"Guess you should have read the fine print in your contract."

"Whose side are you on, Carson?"

"The team's. Yours. Mine." Carson retreated a step and sucked down his orange-flavored drink, throwing the paper cup in the nearby trash can. "Don't you ever get tired of the spotlight? The media up in your shit? The people using you for whatever scraps you're willing to toss their way? The late nights? The hangovers?"

Ty blinked. "Yeah. Sometimes."

"So, you do understand the problem, then? We don't get to live normal lives. This uniform"—Carson tugged on his number 8 jersey—"comes with responsibilities and privileges. Finding the right balance is the challenge."

"Maybe for you."

"No." Carson cupped Ty's shoulder. "All of us. Coach wasn't joking. Our asses are on the line. Especially yours and mine. Do you want to suit up in Dallas? New Orleans? Los Angeles?"

"Jesus Christ." Ty was silent for a moment. "You're always trying to be the squeaky clean white boy. Hell no, I want to stay here with you, baby."

Carson laughed and puckered his lips. "Come here, add a little color to my life."

Ty shoved him away. "Think there's been enough ass-kissing going on around here."

Glad the mood had shifted, Carson snagged his helmet off the grass.

"What about red? Where's that going, Carson?"

Ty knew his history with Sadie. Carson blew out a breath and shrugged. "Hell if I know. And I hope you aren't shooting your mouth off about us. The less anyone knows, the better. I'm not even sure if Sadie wants to keep seeing me."

The one thing he was certain of was that everything felt different. She hadn't answered his texts since the night they'd made love. But that was about to change.

CHAPTER THIRTEEN

Sadie closed the door to her small office down the hallway from the media room where she held her class. Scrolling through the shots of Ty on the field, she smiled, satisfied with the crisp images. She scrolled to her messages. A missed call from Leonard, one from Barbi, and three from Carson. Chewing on her bottom lip, she weighed her options of what to do about him.

Her body was still recovering from the multiple orgasms. Aroused by the memory of Carson pumping inside her, she reached for the bottled water on her desk. She unscrewed the cap and took a long drink. Isolating him would only give him more of a reason to pursue her. She traced circles around the mouth of the plastic bottle.

With a two-day break from training camp starting tomorrow, maybe she'd take the time to meet Barbi somewhere—rent a room on the beach and enjoy the sunshine.

The door to her office opened, startling her.

Carson filled the doorway. "Kitty Kat."

"People usually knock."

"I'm not people," he said, stepping inside and closing the door behind him.

Unnerved by his intrusion, she pretended to scan through some of the papers on her desk.

"Stop," he said.

She met his gaze. "Stop what?"

"Avoiding me."

She folded her hands. "All right, Carson. You want the truth?"

"Always."

"I made a mistake. *We* made a mistake."

"Is that what you call it? Stretched out on the hood of my car, screaming my name? What about the encore? Quite the performance for a mistake."

She groaned, picturing herself doggie style. "Hormones. Desperation. An overwhelming need to get laid."

He rubbed his stubbled chin, a spark of mischievousness in his fathomless eyes. "I like the last excuse best."

"You would."

He shrugged. "Can you blame me, Sadie? What am I supposed to think after seven years? You show up in Mobile, looking like you do—throwing me those fuck-you looks—challenging me at every turn..."

"I could say the same about you!"

"Maybe..."

Honestly, she'd dressed to impress him every day. That little extra shake of her ass, the lingering stares from across the class-room, the ridiculous formality she insisted on between them,

Mr. Savage this, Mr. Savage that. She couldn't hide the smile.

Carson moved closer to her desk. "I know that look."

"What look?"

"That smile."

"A private thought, that's all."

"Nope. You have the shittiest poker face, Kitty Kat."

Sadie's mind was reeling. After all this time, she still couldn't fool him. "Look, it's been a long day, Carson. I'm hungry and exhausted."

Inviting himself to take a seat in the guest chair, he leaned his elbows on the desk. "We connected, Sadie, on every level. I still make you laugh. Still make you hot. And definitely still drive you crazy. Are you going to keep denying it?"

He'd asked a similar question before. The only word to come to mind was *no*. Her heart twisted as she drank in his perfect features. He was threatening enough as a memory, but with the flesh and bone Carson sitting within arm's reach, she couldn't trust herself to do the right thing. Never could when it came to the two of them. They'd screwed their way across Alabama and back again as kids, on the beach, in his car, in his parents' bedroom, at the school—anywhere with a flat surface.

She unintentionally eyeballed the desk, feeling her cheeks flush.

Carson shot up from his chair. "Sadie?"

Very slowly, her gaze met his hungry eyes.

With a sweep of his giant hand, he cleared the desk off and then reached for her. An avalanche of emotions and raw desire crushed her as she tore her blouse off, crawling on top of the desk.

"Fuck…" Carson shed his shirt. "Looks like we're doomed to keep making mistakes together."

She really didn't care. All she wanted was his hot hands all over her body. On her breasts, ass, his fingers tangled in her hair. He took immediate control, tugging her over to his side of the desk, pushing her onto her back, and unbuttoning her jeans. She lifted her butt so he could ease the tight material down her hips. Growling with impatience, he paused to unzip her heeled boots, pulled them off her feet, and then tossed them across the room.

Sadie admired his physique, the ridiculous six pack and chiseled pectorals. His arms were thick with muscles and covered with tattoos. But one patch of ink caught her attention the most—on the left side of his chest, just above the heart. Scrolled in elegant lettering was *Sadie*. Her eyes went wide as she read her name out loud. She'd forgotten about that tat.

In a low voice he said, "Kept you close to my heart, Sadie."

Carson slipped his tennis shoes and shorts off, and his boxers followed.

Under the bright overhead lights, she could see every bruise and scar on his warrior body. The brutality he suffered through every day just to stay on top of his game. The need to touch and kiss every mark made her heart burst. Then her gaze dropped to his stomach, following the blond happy trail to his erection. His cock was thick and long—as perfect as the rest of him.

"Like what you see?" he asked.

She more than liked it.

Carson leaned over and whispered in her ear, "Every time you look at me like that, I want to fuck you."

As if on command, she spread her legs, inching closer to the edge of the desk—more than ready.

Carson grinned, then tugged her jeans off. "How long has it been since I've seen your beautiful body?"

Seven years and five days. She'd kept careful count. They'd been partially dressed the other night when they made love on his car, and it was too dark to see him. "Too long," she managed to whisper.

"Too long," he repeated, slipping his hand behind her back and unhooking her black bra.

As the last article of clothing from her body fell away, Carson sucked in a breath. "Stop denying us, okay?"

His hands covered her breasts, massaging gently at first, then squeezing them together as he lowered himself and circled her nipples with his tongue and fingers. They were made for each other. She knew it and needed to stop thinking about the past. Carson was right, he made her laugh, she loved talking to him about everything, and the awkwardness she'd expected to experience with him, well, it hadn't happened at all. It felt so natural being with him.

On a deep groan, Carson's hand drifted down her stomach, his fingertips feathering over her core. Tingling sensations shot up to her nipples. Sadie draped her arms over his shoulders, pulling him in for a kiss.

He tasted so good, felt incredible against her hot skin.

"One of these days," he started, "we're going to do this in a bed."

She nodded.

"Come home with me tonight."

She nodded again.

"Good girl. Now lift your arms above your head, Kitty Kat."

She followed his directions, just like she used to.

Carson stretched her out underneath him, gripping her tiny wrists with one hand while he slid two fingers inside her, caressing her clit with the heel of his hand. She closed her eyes, breathing in his scent, riding his palm—letting the pleasure take hold. No one else could make her relax and let go, only Carson.

"Baby…"

She opened her eyes.

"You ready for me?"

She blinked several times, smiling up at him. "Yes."

Carson captured her lips as his cock plunged inside her, filling and stretching her. Almost instantly, her orgasm started, the soft, slow pulse of pleasure that promised to bloom into a mind-melting explosion if he kept thrusting so deep and fast. Wrapping her legs around his waist, Sadie closed her eyes and remembered what making love with him felt like seven years ago when she still loved him—when their futures were hopelessly intertwined.

They'd been inseparable as teenagers. She opened her eyes and sighed, gazing up at him, finding that confident, boyish grin.

No doubt their bodies were making up for lost time—hearts desperate to recapture the past. And though that voice in the back of her head kept asking, *if it didn't work out before, why would it now?* She realized she should trust herself, and Carson. He'd told her to trust her gut the other day. And as she looked up at him, recognizing the powerful emotions in his eyes, she wondered if either one of them had ever really stopped loving each other. Maybe love was the wrong word at the moment, but the feelings were overwhelming and real.

"Carson...I-I'm going to..."

He silenced her with a demanding kiss, his tongue tangling with hers, his grip growing tighter around her wrists. Carson muttered a curse as he rotated his hips, his last thrust setting them both off.

A few minutes later, Carson rested his head against her chest, still breathing hard. "You're mine again, Sadie."

"Yes," she whispered. *As long as you don't hurt me again.*

CHAPTER FOURTEEN

As Carson's truck turned into the magnolia-lined driveway, Sadie rested the soles of her bare feet on his dashboard, breathing in the fresh air from the passenger-side window she'd just opened. For some reason, she felt completely relaxed, had even traded her heels for sandals, her jeans for shorts, and her typical business jacket for a girly T-shirt when Carson stopped by her hotel room for her to pick up some clothes for the weekend.

He'd mentioned his home in the College Park area several times. She smiled when the driveway curved to the left, the trees opening up and revealing a two-story house with a wrap-around porch on the bottom and a smaller one on the second floor. The main entryway consisted of two sets of intricately patterned beveled-glass French doors with black-shuttered picture windows on either side. Antique copper tubs filled with blooming roses lined the walkway to the stairs leading up to the porch.

Carson parked in front of a detached four-car garage,

climbed out of his truck, then walked around to the passenger's side and opened her door.

"The property is amazing," she said, getting out of the truck.

"Thanks, Kitty Kat. Wait until you see the gardens and the kitchen."

Her stomach protested as she started to follow him around the side of the house. Carson stopped and grinned.

"Are you hungry?"

"Starving," she admitted, cupping her stomach. "Orange juice and a granola bar doesn't qualify as a meal."

Carson looked at his watch. "It's four o'clock. That's all you've eaten today?"

She nodded.

"You know better than that." Carson slipped his arm around her waist, urging her to turn around.

They walked back to the front entrance and climbed the three steps to the porch.

Sadie admired the wicker furniture, a half dozen rocking chairs and three loveseats with matching footstools. On the far end was a two-man hammock. A dozen ceiling fans were on, providing some relief from the afternoon heat.

The front doors opened. "Sweet Jesus," a woman said.

"Tamera?" Sadie couldn't believe it.

Tamera smiled and opened her arms wide. "Give an old woman a hug!"

Sadie did just that, genuinely happy to see her. "It's been so long."

Tamera pulled back so she could look Sadie in the eyes. "Time has been kind to you."

Sadie's cheeks heated. "Thank you, Tamera. You haven't changed a bit."

Tamera shook her head. "Twenty pounds in seven years says different." She gazed at Carson. "His fault, of course. Ever cook for a football team?"

Carson laughed and threw his hands up. "Cook doesn't mean eat."

Tamera chuckled. "Have you ever met a Southern woman who doesn't like to sample what she cooks?"

"Never," Carson answered.

"That's right," Tamera confirmed. "Now move out of the way so I can get this pretty lady out of the heat."

Sadie followed Tamera inside. The spacious foyer featured a stairway and what Sadie guessed was the original tin-tiled ceiling. The tiles matched the intricate diamond design on the beveled French doors. Smiling, she stepped closer to the nearest wall to get a better look of a series of framed photographs—surprised to see several that included her.

Memories flooded her mind as she gazed at faces she hadn't seen in so long. A shot outside the school in front of the buses before the team left for an away game. Another group picture at the lake. But the one that really made her heart skip a beat was from their Disney-themed junior prom. Carson and Sadie had reenacted the spaghetti scene from *Lady and the Tramp*.

She swallowed back the raw emotions from the shock of knowing the same photograph was hanging in her home—a prized moment she never wanted to forget.

The heat of Carson's body behind her made her shiver. "What's wrong, Kitty Kat?" he whispered close to her ear, his hot breath on her neck making her body sizzle with desire.

"Nothing," she lied.

"Did you think I'd ever really let you go?"

Turning around, she gazed up at him, gauging his sincerity. The headlines surely showed he'd more than let her go. How many women had she seen him with over the last seven years? Twenty? Thirty? All supermodel types who likely wanted to benefit from his fame or were after his fortune. "I don't know, Carson. Didn't you?" She arched a brow, interested in hearing what he'd say. Would he make excuses? Feed her the usual line most men used—none of them meant anything? After all, she'd only had two lovers since they'd broken up.

Before Carson could answer, Tamera coughed politely, obviously reminding them that they weren't alone. "Dinner will be ready soon," she announced before trotting away.

"She's amazing," Sadie said. "I can't believe she's here."

"Try telling Tamera no. She's already earned a full retirement and should be passing the time on a beach in Hawaii or jet setting around Europe. Instead, she wants to be here with me. I offered to hire a maid and she told me she wouldn't let a stranger work in our house."

"You're lucky to have her."

"I know," Carson said. "And I'm lucky to have you, too."

Their gazes locked, and Sadie struggled to take a steady breath.

"You mean the world to me." Carson slanted his mouth over hers, stealing a kiss.

As he pulled back, Sadie closed her eyes. Years of emotional and physical deprivation had made her hungry for more than

Tamera's cooking. "Carson," she whispered, staring at him.

"You okay?"

"I've missed you so much." In all honesty, she couldn't accurately describe what she was feeling.

"It will all be okay, Kitty Kat," he assured her. "There's no pressure here. I want you happy and comfortable. Let me give you a tour before dinner. We can grab your bag after."

"Did you decorate this place?"

"Most of it," he said. "Mom and Tamera helped with the antiques, and some were included with the house."

Carson escorted her through another set of French doors that opened into a sunny room with a cove ceiling. A padded seat ran the length of six windows—the perfect place to spend an afternoon reading a book. Candles decorated the fireplace mantel, and the mahogany dining room set must have been from the eighteenth century.

"Elegant," she commented, impressed with Carson's taste. "The windows are my favorite thing about this house."

"That's what caught my eye," he said. "The natural light."

She'd always wanted a home with lots of windows and wood floors.

He showed her the living room next, then his office, den, and kitchen, before she followed him upstairs. The landing overlooked the first floor and had a sitting area with more windows. The master suite was on one side of the landing, the remaining bedrooms on the other.

Carson's suite was done in bold gold with white trim, the theme carried over to his study and bathroom.

"If I lived here…" she started.

"You'd never leave?" he finished for her, that cocky grin deserving a kiss.

Choosing to ignore his innuendo, she continued to explore. The balcony gave her a perfect view of the gardens. "Beautiful," she said.

Carson joined her outside. "Thanks, Kitty Kat."

"Your walk-in closet is bigger than my condo," she teased.

"Maybe you need more square footage. If I remember correctly, you had enough clothes to fill two bedrooms."

"My second bedroom *is* a closet."

He laughed.

"I like my neighborhood and the community swimming pool."

"Don't you miss home?"

She looked in his direction. "Sometimes."

"South Carolina? What's it got over Alabama?"

You don't live there would be the candid answer. But he wasn't the only reason she'd left. Growing up poor in a small town made a lasting impression on her. Some people accused her of dating Carson because he had money. Worse yet, they accused her father of faking his disability so he didn't have to work anymore.

"My job," she said, giving the safest reply.

He nodded. "You enjoy what you do?"

"I like helping people turn their lives and businesses around."

"Why not do it here?"

She shrugged, knowing he was testing her. "Why'd *you* stay?"

Carson clenched his jaw. "Let's save that story for another day," he suggested. "I bet dinner is ready."

She licked her lips thinking about Tamera's cooking. Today had been full of surprises—like making love on her desk and agreeing to spend a few days at Carson's place. Eating a home-cooked meal prepared by one of the best cooks she'd ever met was the cherry on top. "Does she still make that sweet corn-bread?"

"And that black-eyed peas recipe with bacon."

Sadie rushed for the door. "Try to stop me," she challenged him, hitting the stairs with a smile plastered on her face.

CHAPTER FIFTEEN

Carson hung back on purpose so he could stare at Sadie's luscious ass as she descended the stairs in front of him. The heavenly aroma of fresh-baked cornbread permeated the lower floor of the house. They walked into the kitchen, catching Tamera as she was transferring the food from the pans into dishes.

"Pot roast with potatoes, carrots, celery, and okra," she said.

"Cornbread?" Sadie asked.

"Over there, sweetie." Tamera pointed to a bowl on the counter that was covered with a towel.

Without hesitation, Sadie helped herself, forgoing butter. Kernels of corn were baked in the bread, adding to the flavor. Sadie's mother wasn't a bad cook; she just never had the time to make things from scratch. And though Sadie could cook fairly well, her culinary abilities paled in comparison to Tamera's talent in the kitchen. "This is *so* good, Tamera."

"Eat to your heart's content," she said. "There's three more loaves in the oven. I'll be sure to send you home with a loaf."

Sadie looked at Carson.

"Sadie is spending the weekend with us."

Once they were seated in the dining room and Tamera served their meal, she started for the kitchen.

"Aren't you going to eat with us?" Carson asked, standing up and pulling out Tamera's usual chair.

Tamera gazed at Sadie and Carson. "I can handle eating by myself tonight. You two have a lot to talk about."

"But you'll have dessert with us, right?" Sadie asked.

Tamera winked at her and left the room.

Carson watched Sadie take a few bites of pot roast, enjoying the utter look of pleasure on her face. It was something he'd missed about her. She was never able to mask her emotions, and he'd always appreciated the way she reacted to different situations so openly—good or bad. In this case, food—which, for Sadie, might equal the intensity of multiple orgasms. After another moan, he couldn't hold back his laughter.

"If I'd known how much you missed her cooking…"

"I ate dinner with your family every Sunday for three years, Carson. How couldn't I miss it?"

He just stared at her, looking thoughtful.

"What?" she asked with her mouth still full of food. "You'd dangle that temptation in my face to get me here sooner?" She laid her fork aside and took a sip of red wine.

"Something like that."

"Well, I'd have probably come."

Carson smirked and rubbed his chin. "Already took care of that little detail, Kitty Kat. Several times."

She rolled her eyes. "Don't you ever think of anything else?"

"Football."

"So that's the extent of your thoughts? Sex and football?"

"Not necessarily in that order."

"Okay...football and sex. Or sex and football depending on the day of the week."

Carson smiled. "Put that on my profile."

"I think the front office is looking for something a little more wholesome."

Carson swallowed a generous portion of beer before he answered. "You read my personnel file. I make regular visits to the children's burn unit at Saint Francis Hospital, sponsor a football camp every summer, and appear regularly at Big Brothers Big Sisters."

"Who do you mentor?"

"Charlie Silva—since fifth grade."

Impressed by his dedication, she asked, "How old is he now?"

"Thirteen, just started middle school."

"Wait..." Sadie did the math. That meant... "When did you start mentoring Charlie?"

"Before I went pro."

"Why don't you go public with it? Share the special moments with your fans?"

"No," he immediately refused. "Promised Charlie's mom I'd keep a low profile with her son."

"But if you managed it the right way, we could turn this into a fundraising opportunity for Big Brothers Big Sisters."

And a photo op to benefit the team. *Nope.* Carson shoveled a generous portion of roast into his mouth. "Just cut a one hundred-thousand-dollar check for them last quarter."

"What if the public matched you dollar-for-dollar?"

That caught his attention. Might be worth it if Sadie could find a way to do it without involving Charlie. "How?"

"There's so many ways—silent auctions, a community fair, or perhaps a mini training camp."

"I like the fair idea best. Dunk the quarterback."

"You'd sit in a little glass box filled with water and let everyone throw balls at a target to see you get wet?"

"For the kids?" He lifted his eyebrows. "Yeah."

Carson could see her formulating, thinking about how to pull it off in such a short span of time.

"We should plan several events. Drop off some groceries at a shelter. Cleanup day at a park." She rested her cheek on her palm. "As long as you let me take some pictures and video footage."

"I still don't understand why Jack went to all this trouble." The front office had never mentioned the depth or severity of the team's publicity issues. "You'd think they'd try asking us to turn things around on our own first."

Sadie folded her linen napkin and dabbed at her lips. "Easier said than done."

"How so?"

"It's not just one or two players, Carson. Remember what I said the first day? Congress has a better approval rating than the Warriors?"

"Off the field, maybe."

"Yes—there's no loss of confidence in your playing ability."

"This is our year, Kitty Kat, I can feel it." He scanned her beautiful face, looking for a sign of faith in him.

Her gentle smile was all he needed. "I never doubted your talent, Carson. Every year the team gets better."

"I knew you were watching me." He reached for her hand, caressing her knuckles with his thumb. "I was always showing off a little in case you were."

"You don't have to prove anything to me."

"Sure, I do." Having her here, in his house, meant everything. And if she took the time to think about it, she'd see her lasting influence over him everywhere she looked. He might have been a selfish ass, but he never forgot anything she confided in him—her dreams, especially. "How about we take a ride after dessert?"

"Okay," she agreed. "Where?"

"It's a surprise."

A few minutes later, Tamera cleared the plates and returned with a pecan pie. Sadie accepted a small piece, attacking it with the same enthusiasm she showed for the cornbread.

Tamera chuckled as she took a forkful of pie. "There's more if you'd like another piece."

Sadie laid her fork aside and covered her mouth as she chewed and swallowed the last bite. "I'm so sorry. I have horrible table manners, Tamera."

"Don't apologize for enjoying food. It's one of the pleasures in life."

Once they were finished, Sadie helped Tamera clear the table, then Carson took her to the garage behind his house, the one where he stored his collection of exotic cars. "Pick one."

"What?"

"Surely there's something you've always wanted to drive?"

She walked between the two rows of vehicles, sixteen in total, stopping in front of the Viper.

His lips lifted in humor. "Kind of special, isn't it?" He'd never think of that car in the same way again.

"Mm-hm."

Joining her by the car, he opened the driver's side door and grabbed the key from the ignition, then dangled it in front of her face. "Want to drive, sweetheart?"

"More temptation?"

"You can have anything you want." Including a Super Bowl ring if she stuck around long enough.

"You drive," she said.

"All right."

"I can't believe you leave the key in the ignition. Aren't you afraid someone will steal your car?"

"State-of-the-art security system and the fact that this is *my* house? Nope, never gave it a second thought." If someone had the balls to break in and try to steal his cars, they'd have to get through him first.

Once he got her situated in the car, he climbed in, started the engine, and drove out of the garage, closing the door with his remote.

Twenty minutes later when he turned onto Highway 98 south, Sadie's demeanor changed. She looked uncomfortable. Carson squeezed her hand. "I'm not taking you to Fairhope."

"No?" She frowned. "Isn't that where the highway goes?"

"We're going to Point Clear."

"Point Clear?" she repeated, looking confused.

"Yup."

Seemingly satisfied with his explanation, she settled back down, searching for a radio station she liked. She stopped when she heard Disturbed, turning up the volume. Carson watched her get into the music, bobbing her head up and down to the unforgiving beat, singing the words to "Stupify" like she meant it. Several songs finished before he turned off the highway and onto a dirt road.

Outside of his teammates, Sadie was the only other person Carson wanted to show the farm to. The place had belonged to his great-grandparents in the 1930s, and he couldn't pass up the opportunity to restore the farmhouse and barn to their original glory.

Carson planned on surprising his mother and sisters with it soon. No one deserved a life of relaxation like his mother did. After his father died during his second deployment with the Marines in Afghanistan, Carson's mom had to go back to work. The farm was one of many luxuries he could afford to give his mama now.

The land was flat but lush and green, acres of viable farmland stretched out as far as the eye could see.

"Where are we, Carson?"

"Stanhope Farm," he said.

"Are you taking me berry picking?" she asked.

Alabama was full of farms where you could go and pick whatever fruits and vegetables that were in season for ten dollars. "Better than that," he said, taking the final turn. The gravel driveway ended at the barn and farmhouse. "This property used to belong to my great-grandparents."

"Really?" She got out of the car. "I think I remember you talking about it."

"Jonathan and Rose Stanhope, my mother's grandparents. Moved here from New York in the early 1930s to start a farm. I had an opportunity to buy it awhile back." There was nothing remarkable about the property except that it belonged to his family again. The old white house looked better with the fresh coat of paint the caretaker had recently finished. The double-crib barn was a work in progress. Carson had insisted on reclaiming the original materials to rebuild the structure.

A dark-haired man exited the barn, smiling as he walked over to where they were standing. "Carson," he said, shaking his hand.

"Good to see you, Rex. This is Sadie Reynolds."

"Ma'am." The retired Marine bent his head respectfully. "Anything I can do?"

"Just here for berry picking," Carson said, slipping his arm around Sadie's waist.

"There's baskets on the porch. Nice to meet you, ma'am," he said, walking back to the barn.

"Who is he, Carson?"

"Captain Rex Dubois, served with my dad in Afghanistan."

"How'd he end up here?"

"After Dad died, we stayed in touch. Made me feel better having someone to write to who knew my father. Rex retired a few years ago, suffers from PTSD. The place needs a lot of repairs and upkeep, so I offered him the job."

Sadie was silent a moment. "Wait a second…He didn't *need* a job, did he? He's an officer, probably draws a comfortable retirement."

"He does," Carson admitted. "But sometimes the best therapy for a man involves using his hands."

"And you pay him?"

"Of course I pay him. And he lives here rent-free."

She looked around again, in the direction of the house, then at the barn. "What kind of berries do you grow here?"

"Mostly blackberries."

"What else?"

"Beets, potatoes, tomatoes, and there's an apple orchard west of the house that my great-grandfather planted."

"Perfect," she said, typing something on her cell phone.

"Sadie, what are you doing?"

"Taking notes."

Hell, did the girl ever stop thinking about work? "No."

"No, what?" she asked, trying to sound innocent.

"The world doesn't need to know about this place."

"Of course they do."

Carson crossed his arms over his chest. "You're relentless. I like my privacy, Sadie. So does Rex."

"What are you worried about?"

"I don't need the press camping out on my land—harassing Rex—disturbing the peace around here."

"We don't even need to say where the farm is. Just the idea of the farm, and what you're doing for Rex is enough to garner that positive image we need to focus on."

"Sadie..." He scrubbed his face. "I plan on gifting this farm to my mother and sisters in a few weeks. Mom needs to retire, and the girls should learn something about their family history, maybe how to work the land some."

"Listen to me, Carson. I've been struggling to find a way to repackage you without duplicating what the others are doing. Everyone expects the players to visit sick kids or donate money to whatever charitable organization you prefer. But this...A Marine captain who served with your father recovering from PTSD while he rebuilds a historical property? And you? Keeping this a secret so you can reward your mother for years of hard work? Think about it. It's genuine and fresh. Not a photo op or staged. The locals will connect with you on a deeper level."

"Rex wouldn't like it."

"Actually," Rex said, interrupting them.

Sadie turned to her right, finding the captain holding a couple of baskets.

"Thought you'd want these."

"Thank you," she said, taking them. "I'm sorry if you overheard our discussion."

"No." He smiled. "I like your idea." He gazed at Carson. "You should listen to the pretty lady."

Carson waited for Rex to get out of earshot before he spoke again. "Damn it, Sadie. Still charming the shit out of any man."

"I've been accused of worse things." She licked her lips.

"Keep doing that and the only thing you're going to be picking is grass off your backside after I get done fucking you in that field over there."

She followed the direction of his gaze, then deliberately licked her lips more suggestively.

Carson growled, tugging her into his arms and kissing her. "You shouldn't have done that, Kitty Kat."

CHAPTER SIXTEEN

After Carson rolled off of Sadie, she sat up, tall enough to see over the long grass. He'd delivered on his threat, half dragging, half carrying her to the field. Of course, she didn't fight too hard to get away. There was something sexy about the spontaneity between them. "We still didn't make it to a bed," she commented as she straightened her bra and T-shirt.

Carson stood up, zipping his jeans. "We'll finish this in my bed tonight." He offered his hand, and Sadie took it, getting pulled to her feet. "Let me help you clean off that perfect ass."

She chuckled and turned around, plucking grass from her hair. "I know you haven't had much time to think about it, but please let me feature the farm. It's the best option for you."

He slapped her ass and chuckled. "You win, sweetheart. But we need to establish a few ground rules, okay? And I don't want to forget our Big Brothers Big Sisters discussion."

Facing him, she chewed on her bottom lip as she admired his blue eyes in the sunlight. "Absolutely, anything for the kids. In fact, my manager is flying in next Friday. He's the perfect addition to the team, and he's organized some world-class charity events, Carson."

"Why didn't you tell me sooner?"

"I've been kinda busy with something else."

He smiled. "I made you forget?"

"Almost."

"Only almost? I'm losing my touch!"

"Never," she said, hugging him. "Now about the farm…"

"I don't want the name of the farm revealed or the exact location. I know it could be found eventually, but we need to be careful, okay?"

"I understand."

"Just tag it as somewhere in Alabama."

"You do know a simple title search on the property…"

"I don't really want to think about it, Sadie. I like my privacy—more than you know."

"I'm accustomed to dealing with high-profile people. I promise to utilize the protection mechanisms I've regularly used for past clients."

"OK, but Rex doesn't spend much time around people. He makes a trip to town every couple of weeks for supplies, maybe stops at a bar for a beer. I don't want him to feel cornered. It can trigger an episode."

"Is he on medication, seeing a psychologist?"

"Negative."

"Why not?"

"Drugs can't fix everything, Sadie. He doesn't like the side effects—the numbness."

"I can't imagine what he's been through."

Carson kicked at something in the dirt, sighing. "He watched my dad die."

The sad news wrenched her heart. "I'm sorry, Carson. Maybe we should forget about it." Christ, she was an insensitive idiot. Sadie blinked several times, unsure what to say. She'd grown up around Carson's family, loving his father—everyone did. His sense of humor and ability to make anyone feel important made him an unforgettable character.

"No," Carson said. "Rex expressed interest in something outside of the farm. That's real progress for his recovery. Interacting with the public is a big challenge for him. I'm good with it, really."

Sadie wanted to believe it. "I'm going to watch out for you, Carson. I've already told the front office you don't belong in my class. But for some reason Jack and your coach insist on you being a part of the process."

Carson shoved a hand through his hair. "Apollo never catches a break, believe me."

Sadie crinkled her nose. "I never liked that nickname."

For the first time since they'd started spending time together, Carson seemed unsettled. "Do what you need to do, okay?"

She touched his arm. "Does the offer still stand for picking blackberries?"

His eyes lit up. "If we can find the baskets in this grass."

Sadie bent over and started searching through the high grass. A few minutes later she squeaked with disappointment. "Oh no!"

"What?"

"Look." She held up the crushed basket so Carson could see it.

He waggled his eyebrows. "Collateral damage."

"The other one should be here."

Carson joined the effort and finally found the second basket, in perfect condition. "We have dozens of these in the barn," he said. "We get a steady stream of customers visiting this time of year."

"How long have you owned the farm?"

"A little over a year."

"It's a wonderful thing you're doing here. Offering Rex a second chance, giving your mom the perfect home."

"If she'll accept it. Silly woman doesn't like taking my money."

"Independence is a great quality."

Carson clicked his tongue. "She's just stubborn."

"A little of that, too," Sadie agreed. "Guess that's where you get it from."

For the next hour they picked berries, enjoying the sunshine. Just as they arrived back to the house walking hand-in-hand, a car pulled up. A couple with two children climbed out of the sedan. Sadie froze, eyeing the man.

"Sadie?" Carson whispered. "Something wrong, sweetheart? You're crushing my fingers."

"I…I'm sorry." She released his hand, unable to look away from the visitors.

"Stay here," Carson said, handing her the basket and then stepping forward to greet the family. "Can I help you folks?"

"Mommy," the little boy said. "Is he Carson Savage?"

The young mother looked at Carson, then back at her son. "The quarterback?"

"Yeah."

"Maybe you should ask the man yourself."

The little boy couldn't be more than six years old. But Sadie lost interest in him as soon as the boy's father stared her way, studying her closely. *Jason Millar. It had to be.* An asshole who'd always taunted her in school after she refused to date him. Sadie's hackles went up, that fight-or-flight instinct kicking in.

Jason took a few steps in her direction, and Sadie wished she could just disappear. This is why she didn't like Alabama. Everyone knew each other. And though they weren't in Fairhope, Point Clear was only a few miles away. The chance of running into someone she grew up with were ridiculously high. The proof was standing in front of her, all six-foot-plus, with dark hair and black eyes.

"Sadie Reynolds?" he asked.

Run! That's what the little voice inside her head suggested—demanded. But she couldn't. "Hello, Jason," she said, fighting to keep her composure.

"I can't believe it," he said. "How many years has it been? Six or seven?"

"Seven," she confirmed, grateful her sunglasses were dark enough to hide her eyes. "Is that your family?" She gestured at the kids.

Jason looked over his shoulder. "My niece and nephew. They live in Denver. Janice brought them down for a visit. You remember my sister, don't you?"

How could Sadie forget Janice Millar—the leader of the bitch clique that often targeted Sadie because she didn't wear the right clothes or hang out with the right people, even after she started dating Carson. "I remember her."

"I can't believe you and Carson are back together."

Sadie started to say something, but it was too late—Carson was on his way over, smiling. He stood beside her, draping his arm over her shoulders, holding her close. "Been a long time, Jason. Thought you moved to Reno."

"I did," Jason said. "Moved back home four years ago."

"Small world," Carson continued. "We were just leaving. And the farm is closing soon. There's other places to go."

"So no berries?" Jason pressed.

Carson gazed at Sadie, and she forced a smile. He nodded at her as if he understood, then took the basket from her hands, thrusting it into Jason's arms. "Take these."

Jason didn't get a chance to respond. Carson steered Sadie to his car. Once she was inside, he told her to wait for him. He closed the door and jogged toward the barn. Sadie sank down in the comfortable leather seat, her gaze focused on Jason, who was busy talking to his sister.

Lord, talk about bad timing. Or was this fate trying to tell her something? Giving her every reason to stick to her plan of leaving Alabama as soon as her job was done? She didn't care if it had been seven years since Jason and Janice had made her life a living hell. But if she was going to be with Carson, she'd have to get used to all the drama again. She wasn't sure how their relationship would work but if they continued to see each other she'd have to spend at least some time in Alabama. And life in a small town came with a hefty price. But she appreciated the way Carson had dismissed the asshole and his sister. It gave her hope for the future.

Turning the key in the ignition so the radio would turn on, Sadie forced herself to focus on the music. Jimi Hendrix blared through the expensive sound system, drowning out her thoughts.

Maybe Barbi was right to reschedule that trust-building workshop. Sadie needed to let go of a lot of deep-rooted negativity. If she wanted to stay with Carson and build a successful relationship, she'd have to learn how to deal with her emotions and get rid of the fears that often kept her on edge, even when she was in South Carolina.

She deserved better, and so did Carson. It just wasn't going to be easy.

CHAPTER SEVENTEEN

P lease don't mention anything about me to the family out there," Carson told Rex in the privacy of the barn.

"Is this about you and Sadie?"

Carson nodded. "The price you pay growing up in a small town only a half hour away. People still talk about us."

"That's why I left California," Rex said. "Nowhere seems far enough away."

"And that bastard"—Carson grimaced—"doesn't think I know how much he hurt my girl."

"You two getting reacquainted, then?"

"Better than that."

Rex's grin stretched ear to ear as he slapped his arm. "Happy to hear it. Remember the letters you wrote to me after you graduated? You told me everything about her. They're in the house somewhere if you'd like to show her."

"No." The last thing Sadie needed to read were those letters. She already had missed out on the ones he'd written to her. The ones to Rex were even more volatile. It would give her a taste of the desperate, angry man he'd turned into after she left him. What he'd really like to do is grab Jason by the throat and beat the shit out of him for mistreating Sadie. But Sadie didn't know that Carson knew everything Jason had done. "Be courteous, but get them the fuck out of here as soon as you can."

"Got it, boss."

Carson shook his head. "I'm not your boss—we're friends."

"You sign my paychecks."

"Couldn't have done any of this without you, Rex." He gave Rex a hug, then headed outside, more than ready to get home and make love to Sadie again.

Halfway to Mobile, Sadie cursed as she was scrolling through her messages on her cell phone.

"What's up?" Carson asked.

"Pull over," she demanded.

"We're on the highway, Sadie. Can it wait?"

"No. Please pull over."

He took the next exit, ending up in the parking lot of a gas station. He turned in his seat so he could see Sadie.

"Can you believe it? We've only been gone thirty minutes and that asshole has already posted our picture all over Facebook." She shoved her cell into his hand. "Look."

Carson read the post on Jason's page:

Out for a casual drive with the family today. Never expected to run into Carson Savage with his favorite piece of ass from high school. Guess who's back in Alabama? Sadie Reynolds. Did red ever look so good?

He eyed a picture of Sadie from high school and then the

new photo Jason had obviously snapped while they weren't looking. Yeah, red never looked so good…unless it was a bloodstain on Jason's goddamned shirt after Carson punched him in the face.

Frustrated, Carson slapped the steering wheel with both of his hands. "Sonofa—"

"Don't," Sadie said. "It's my fault, not yours."

"How, sweetheart?"

Her lips formed a thin, tight smile. "I never should have come here, Carson."

Did she mean Point Clear or Alabama in general? "Can you be more specific?"

"We should have stayed in Mobile."

Breathing out a sigh of relief, Carson grabbed her hand and kissed her fingers one at a time. "I know you've been away for a long time. And I know you never liked the politics of Fairhope, how everyone was always in involved in other people's business…"

"That's an understatement."

"The dynamics of living in a small town. But there's an upside, Sadie."

She arched a brow.

"Whenever there's an emergency—you can count on your neighbors to be there."

Sadie looked at him like he was crazy. "Maybe for you."

Carson shook his head. "Do you know what happened after you left?"

"I don't want to know, Carson."

"I don't understand why you're so anti-Fairhope. So many people missed you. They still talk about us."

"My point exactly! We're old news. If they haven't moved on yet…what does it say about them? About their lives?"

Carson shrugged. Alabama wasn't the same as other states. And Fairhope definitely was unlike any other town he'd visited. Generations of families stayed there for any number of reasons. Whether he liked it or not, it was home, and not just for him. Sadie couldn't deny her roots. "I'll take care of Jason," Carson assured her. "But he doesn't represent the majority of people in Fairhope, Sadie. If you'd just take a ride with me…"

"No." She withdrew her hand, not looking happy.

"Sadie? I feel like I'm missing something big here."

Averting her gaze, Sadie stared out the window. "Tell me, Sadie. Please."

She laughed nervously. "Why? What good would it do now?" She faced him again. "We were bigger than life back then, weren't we? The perfect couple destined for a great future together. You'd play ball and I'd have kids. We'd move back home after college and put Fairhope on the map."

A sad smile crept across Carson's face. "Yeah, we were. And what's wrong with being the perfect couple?"

"It was too much pressure for teenagers to deal with. When I broke up with you, Carson, a lot of people blamed me for your downward spiral that summer."

"I'm not the only player from Fairhope that had aspirations for the NFL."

"No, but you're the first to really make it. And everyone knew it. I jeopardized that future, and people didn't want me to forget about it." Suddenly tears threatened to fall from her beautiful eyes. Carson reached for her cheek, but she avoided his touch.

"No," she chastised. "You can't make me feel better with a hug."

"Jesus Christ, Sadie. Did someone hurt you?" Rage started to uncoil in his gut. If she didn't hurry up and explain, he was close to driving to Fairhope to find out on his own.

"Yes and no," she said.

He raked his hand through his hair, his blood pressure spiking. "You're killing me, Kitty Kat."

"I never wanted you to know…really, I didn't." She sniffled. "I received death threats, Carson. So many people shunned me—wouldn't even greet me on the street. It could have been anyone."

"Death threats?" His control was unraveling.

"Relax. Please. I'm okay."

"Shit."

"Emails, anonymous phone calls…"

"Did you report it to the police?" He wished she would have told him back then. It would have given him great pleasure to destroy whoever it was. He cracked his knuckles, trying to recover from the shock and rage.

"Yes."

"What happened?"

"Chief Isaac dismissed it as crazy fans caught up in the moment. I believe his exact words were 'It's not an immediate threat.'"

"Asshole."

Sadie shrugged. "Another realty of small-town life. The chief was one of your biggest fans, I think."

A moment of silence passed between them, and Carson couldn't take his eyes off her. "I'm sorry, Kitty Kat."

"Not your fault, Carson. Can we go back to Mobile now?"

"Yeah," he said. "I think we could both use a good night's sleep." But rest was the last thing on Carson's mind.

Sadie hurried up the stairs, not wanting to see Tamera. In fact, she wanted to be back in her hotel room alone or, better yet, in her condo in South Carolina. But that wouldn't be fair, not to Carson or to her. He'd done nothing wrong, and only wanted to share his life with her. Normal people did that. But Sadie felt completely out of sorts.

Standing in the middle of Carson's luxurious bedroom, she eyed the king-sized bed with its ornate wood headboard and high-end comforter. Dozens of plush pillows tempted her to just curl up under the covers and shut out the world for a night. A gas fireplace was situated on the left side of the room, next to the doors opening to the balcony. It would be too easy to make herself at home here. A glass of red wine, maybe a favorite book, definitely a cozy fire, dim lights, and the soft lingering scent of roses in the air from the gardens below.

Carson had indeed done well.

"Sadie?" He came in with her overnight bag. "Can I get you anything? Maybe a hot bath? Glass of wine?"

"No, thank you," she said. "Would you mind if I slept in one of the guest rooms?"

His expression changed from one of concern to deep disappointment. "Of course."

"It's nothing you did..."

He held his hand up. "I understand, Sadie. Come on." He turned and walked out.

The guest bedroom was smaller than the master suite, but no less comfortable. Carson set her bag on the end of the bed.

"There's an intercom system if you need anything. Just give me a call, or better yet, come and find me." He pointed to a white box on the wall by the bed. "Don't feel guilty if you wake me up. And just so you know, I understand that you need some adjustment time. Jason and Janice are assholes. But not everyone in Fairhope is like them. I promise."

Sadie wrung her hands, trying to find the words that would let Carson know how much it meant to her that he understood. If Barbi were there, she'd tell Carson how far Sadie had come in just a few days, facing her fears and ignoring that little voice that always told her to avoid uncomfortable situations. That little voice that told her to run away. She may be sleeping in a different bedroom, but at least she wasn't running back to South Carolina. It was progress.

"Carson."

"Sadie." They'd both uttered each other's names at the same time.

"Breakfast, eight o'clock. Okay, beautiful?"

"Okay. Thank you for not pushing anything. Good night."

"Night."

Her heart tightened as he walked out and closed the door.

"Stupid," she muttered as she unzipped her bag, searching for her toiletries case and nightie—a sexy, white lace ensemble. She'd intended to wear it for Carson.

After soaking in the jetted tub for half an hour, Sadie dried off and slipped into her lingerie. She combed out her hair in front of the mirror, deciding to leave it down to dry naturally. Knowing Carson was just down the hallway made her feel strange inside. Had she reacted too harshly to everything? After all, who was she punishing? Carson or herself? He had an endless stream of women available, that much she knew. The zing of jealously surprised her. But what about her? She'd banished her last boyfriend, cutting him off without an explanation.

Her bedroom was like a desert, barren—until now.

Staring at her reflection in the mirror over the sink, she frowned before she squeezed a generous amount of toothpaste onto her electric toothbrush. "You're an emotional coward."

After she finished brushing her teeth, she turned out the lights and reluctantly climbed into bed, tucking the covers under her chin. She felt like a little girl in the oversized bed. As a child, she'd always feared leaving any part of her body exposed—afraid the monsters would get her. Well, not much had changed, because everyone seemed like a predator at the moment, out to get her for something.

Just as she relaxed her head on the pillows, her cell dinged.

Mumbling, she crawled out from underneath the sheets and walked to the bathroom where she'd left her phone. Unlocking the screen, a simple message waited for her...

You never should have come back.

CHAPTER EIGHTEEN

The long, cold shower did nothing to alleviate Carson's conflicted emotions. Standing on his bedroom balcony with a cold beer, he stared across the open expanse of his property. A full moon had risen, casting silvery light everywhere, reflecting beautifully off the fountain pool. Just when he thought he'd made progress with Sadie, winning her trust again—something gave her reason to retreat behind those defensive walls he'd tried to tear down.

Goddamned past wouldn't move out of the way to make room for a future they could easily share if she'd let them.

Taking another swig of beer, he sighed when someone knocked on the door. Assuming it was Tamera, he set the bottle on the nearby table and hurried to his door.

He opened slowly, but it wasn't his housekeeper.

Sadie held up her cell, fresh tears in her eyes.

"What happened?" He rushed to her side, tugging her into his arms and taking the phone from her.

"Read the text message," she said.

The words *You never should have come back* filled his line of vision, sparking a new fire inside him. The number was blocked, but Carson knew it was Jason trying to fuck with Sadie and him. He turned with Sadie in his arms and tossed the cell on the bed. Then, as gently as possible, set her away from him so he could cradle her face, forcing her to look up at him. "You're safe with me, Sadie. That text is just immature bullshit. Jason couldn't live with the fact that you wanted me and not him. If I ever see him again, I'll make him regret it. Trust me."

"You'd punch him for me?" She sniffled but also giggled as she snuggled against his chest.

"I'd break his neck."

"That's a little extreme. But I like the idea of you protecting me."

"How did he get your number?"

"That's my work cell phone. Anyone can find me on social media."

He fisted his hands, feeling possessive and desperate to show her he cared. "I don't like it."

"What do you want me to do? Tell my boss I can't deal with my past and don't want my contact information on a public profile?"

He tipped her chin upward. "Being very public can be a bad thing."

"Not when your livelihood depends on public perceptions. An image expert who can't handle a little cyberbullying doesn't sound like the kind of professional I'd want to hire."

"You're the victim."

"It would raise too many flags, Carson."

"I understand." He guided her to the bed. That's when he noticed what she was wearing—the sexiest fucking lingerie he'd ever seen. The lacy material stopped just below her navel, granting him a peek at the matching, see-through panties. A hint of red hair between her toned thighs gave him an instant erection.

Though he preferred to take the lead, Carson wanted to empower her, to give her complete control. He positioned himself on the edge of the mattress and patted his leg. "Come here, beautiful."

Sadie didn't hesitate, she came to him and straddled his lap, wrapping her arms around his neck, pulling him into a demanding kiss. Her tongue teased his lips open, and he could taste fresh mint in her mouth. She'd always had that clean smell, like freshly washed clothes hung out in the sunshine to dry. Pure—something he had little of these days. It made him want her more, made him remember the younger Sadie he'd instantly fallen in love with the day he rescued her and that damn kitten from the tree.

Enveloping her in his arms, he kissed her, their tongues tangling together, her tiny sighs as satisfying as the wet heat he could feel through her panties. Holding on to her still, he scooted to the top of the bed, undid the knot in his towel, and reclined against the mountain of pillows.

She threw her head back, rotating her hips, her beautiful red hair damp from a shower. The top of her nightie left little to his imagination, revealing more than a hint of her full breasts. He reached, tracing the outline of her hard nipples through the thin material first, then gently pulled it down, revealing her soft, white flesh.

Dipping low enough for him to capture one of her nipples in his mouth, he sucked it hard while he caressed her other breast. Carson growled, shoving her panties aside, filling her with three fingers.

Sadie cried out his name, riding his hand. He closed his eyes, lost in everything about her.

"Carson..."

He didn't need her to say anything, he could feel how wet she'd gotten as he pumped his fingers in and out of her. Once she came...

As she started to pulse around his hand, he tangled his fingers in her hair, pulling her down for another ragged kiss that expressed everything he wished he could say to her. But how could he speak the words? *I love you* might scare her off. But he did. The realization hit him hard. She belonged there, with him, not in South Carolina, living a separate life. In fact, the root of all of her inhibitions probably came from denying herself the life she was probably meant to live. He wanted her to have her job, to have her dreams, but he wanted to help her achieve them. To build a life with her.

She broke the long kiss, her hair draped all around his face. Their eyes locked and she smiled, caressing his cheek.

"Do you feel good, sweetheart?"

She nodded.

"Ready for more?"

Instead of speaking, she reached down, gripped his erection, and circled her thumb over the tip of his cock. The pressure made his balls tighten and ache for release. A look of satisfaction lightened her features as she let go of him and slowly maneuvered herself down his body. Straddling his lower legs, she licked his length at first, massaging his balls at the same time.

"You're so hard," she said.

"I'm something," he whispered, fisting his hands in the comforter, waiting for the right moment to strike—to flip her over and fuck her from behind.

He moaned as she wrapped her hot lips around his cock, her tongue flicking down his shaft. Her fingernails followed behind her tongue, tickling and teasing, bringing him closer to exploding inside her mouth. But that's not what he craved tonight. Carson needed to possess her, to claim every perfect inch of that tiny body—to remind her what it felt like to be loved by him. Wanted. Needed. To know she was safe. Worshipped. And thoroughly fucked.

"Sadie." He lifted his head off the pillows, loving how she looked with his dick in her mouth.

She stared up at him.

"I don't want to hold back, baby. Tell me it's okay." He'd never hurt her, but sometimes he needed it a certain way—hard and relentless.

Her tongue stroked up and down his shaft a few more times before she released him. "Yes," she whispered.

Carson launched himself at her, capturing her mouth with his, tearing her panties off at the same time. "Fuck, Sadie." He smoothed her hair away from her face, gazing deep into her eyes. "This is real, baby."

She nodded, eager for him to do what she knew was coming. He lifted her hair off her right shoulder, nibbling her soft skin, then bit down.

She squeaked, but dug her fingernails into his shoulders, signaling she liked it. He did it again, sliding his hand down her back and then underneath, grabbing a handful of her tight ass. *His ass.*

"Take me," she whispered against his lips, dark need swirling in her eyes.

Carson helped her get into position, nudging her legs farther apart, urging her to arch her back more. Nothing pleased him more than to see her on her hands and knees in front of him, waiting for him to pound inside of her. He trailed a finger down the crack of her ass, kneeling behind her.

"I love you, Sadie." The words escaped as he slid into her, wild with frustration and tired of holding everything in. His feelings were alive, as uncontainable as his talent on the field. Nothing could steal this moment or convince him to take back his confession.

"Did you hear me?" he asked, hammering deeper.

She turned her head, catching sight of him over her shoulder. "Yes," she whimpered as he reached around her hip and caressed her clit.

"Good, baby, that's all I need to know." And it was. He would never pressure her to say it back, but as he fingered her core, not missing one sigh or cry of his name, he realized it didn't matter if she repeated his words. He could tell by the way she surrendered to him, let him do whatever he wanted to her body, that she had never stopped loving him. And in Carson's mind, that was the sweetest victory he'd ever tasted.

CHAPTER NINETEEN

Two days later, from the privacy of her hotel suite, Sadie held a video conference with Leonard. "Did you have a chance to review the notes from the questionnaires the players completed?" she asked.

Leonard was at his desk in the office even though it was after hours for him, his tie loosened, his shirt unbuttoned, and a glass of red wine in his hand. "That's it, Sadie? No hello, how are you? Just strictly business?"

"I'm sorry," she said. "It's been a long week."

"How so?" He leaned back in his chair, studying her. "You look different, Sadie."

Was it that obvious? "What do you mean?"

"I don't know…More color in your cheeks. Did you gain some happy weight? Sleeping better?"

All of the above. Happiness had a way of making someone feel and look better. There was no denying the joy she felt when she was alone with Carson, especially in bed. As for the slight weight gain, she needed the extra pounds. Life on the road usually meant skipping meals or not eating enough nutritious food. "You can determine all of that on video chat?"

His smile widened and he laughed. "You're wearing a Carson Savage jersey, Sadie."

"Oh no!" She looked down at her chest, having completely spaced out her attire. "Would you feel better if I slipped on a business jacket?"

He shook his head. "Not at all, sweetie. I just assumed…"

"What?"

"Are you getting cozy with the quarterback?"

Should she just get it over with and confess? Apparently, Lenny and her other office mates hadn't checked Facebook lately. Though she'd taken every step available to protect her personal profile from the constant stream of comments coming in from the damned post Jason had made, there was still some residual activity. "We're friends," she offered.

"Friends," he repeated, not sounding very convinced.

"Friendly?"

"You're talking nonsense. There's no one here, Sadie, if that's what you're worried about."

Since leaving Barbi and Erika behind in Fairhope, Lenny had been the closest thing to a BFF she'd found. He never let her get away without hearing the sordid details about his weekend affairs—with men *and* women. He lived for it, rather enjoyed shocking her with naughty tidbits of his sexual exploits. Sadie, on the other hand, never had anything to share—until now. "God, Lenny." She reached for her own glass of wine on the nearby table and took a long drink. "He's so…he's so irresistible."

"I knew it!" Lenny jumped up from his chair, gesturing like his favorite team just scored a touchdown, pumping his fist in the air. "Sadie Girl got laid."

She rolled her eyes, her face heating with embarrassment. "Are you done yet?"

He gazed at her, finding his chair again. "Hell no. I'm just getting started, sweetheart. Ready to shout it from the rooftops if you'll let me."

Swallowing another mouthful of wine, she waited for Leonard to settle down again. "Why would you want to tell anyone?"

He leaned forward, his enormous head filling her screen. "Come here, Sadie."

She got closer to her laptop. "Yes?"

"Whenever a beautiful woman rejoins the human race, it's time to celebrate."

She waved him off, sighing as she scooted away from her computer. "I'm highly selective."

"No," he countered. "You're unattainable."

"I'm on the clock, Leonard." Maybe they should focus on work-related items instead of personal issues.

He shrugged. "So am I. What Charles Longley doesn't know…"

The mention of her boss made her stomach churn. "Somehow I think he wanted me to come here and get involved with Carson to benefit the company."

Lenny coughed. "Just figured that out?"

"So, we're no longer just a PR firm, we're a matchmaking service, too?"

"Why not?"

"And what's supposed to happen when I'm done here, Lenny? Did you ever think about that?" Lately, that's all she could think about. Carson Savage was embedded in her brain.

"I love you, Sadie Girl, but someone needed to clear the cobwebs from your hoo-hah."

She couldn't swallow the laughter—his pet name for female genitalia was outdated and ridiculous. "I prefer cobwebs."

"You don't do dead from the waist down very well."

Sadie cleared her throat. "Tomorrow I'm conducting a focus group at a neutral location. Thirty fans from the Mobile metroplex volunteered. Ten of the players will join me, observing from behind a two-way mirror."

"You're so freakin' creative," he praised her. "What's the catch?"

"We're going to play a little game."

"Such as?"

"Name recognition. I name a professional football player, and the fans tell me the first word to come to mind."

"Try me," he begs.

"Tiger Woods."

"He's not a football player!"

"Nope," she says. "But what name recognition."

"Affair."

"Tom Brady."

"Hah!"

"I say Tom Brady and your first thought is *hah*?" she asked.

"Deflate Gate."

"That's two words."

He rolled his eyes.

"Michael Vick."

"Next."

"Okay." She drummed her fingers against her cheek, thinking of another high-profile athlete. "Michael Phelps."

"God."

"What?" she asked.

"He's a fucking demigod, I think."

"When I hear his name, I think fish," she replied.

"Fish? That's almost insulting. What about penis—he definitely inspires mine."

"Gross."

"What's gross about my penis?" Leonard looked devastated.

"Nothing! I've never seen it, and I certainly don't want to talk about it." How had they gone from discussing the planned exercise for tomorrow to athletes who turned Lenny on?

"Thanks a lot, Sadie."

"I didn't mean it like that!" She laughed so hard she nearly choked on her own saliva. "Let's stay focused. Serena Williams."

"Hot," he replied.

"You get the point of the exercise yet?"

"Yeah—it's great. But what about the players?"

"I'm hoping the hard truth will make them more cooperative," she said.

"Are you having serious issues, then?"

"Nothing I can't handle."

"Egos get in the way, I'm sure."

"There's some of that, mixed with the holier-than-thou

routine. No one seems to understand the permanency of what they share on social media. It's like walking into a classroom full of teenage boys. The testosterone levels are scary."

"I'll be there at the end of the week. Lenny knows how to handle the big boys."

"Why are you talking about yourself in third person?"

"Makes me sound more important." He steepled his fingers under his chin. "I'm proud of you."

"Thanks."

"Sure. Can you manage the Carson thing?"

"Which part?" she asked sarcastically.

He raised a brow. "Is there an area of concern? Because if you need pointers in the bedroom…"

"Not at all."

"Hugs and kisses, then. I'm headed to the club."

Chats with Lenny often took longer than necessary, but Sadie always felt better afterward. She closed her laptop and moved it to the desk. Thank God she didn't have to see anyone tonight. Carson had a prescheduled event he couldn't get out of, and what she needed more than anything was a full night's sleep.

The next morning, she arrived at the off-site facility where the volunteers for the focus group were set to show up at nine. An unmarked van carrying the players pulled into the nearly empty parking lot a half hour before the volunteers. Sadie checked the roster on her clipboard as the players disembarked, making sure everyone was there.

"Mornin', red," Ty said as he stepped down. "Anything I can help with?"

"Good morning," she said, smiling. "Thank you for agreeing to attend the focus group."

He checked the time on his gold Rolex. "I could be back at camp having eggs and bacon."

"Our hosts have generously provided breakfast. It's waiting inside."

"How are things going with Carson?"

Sadie didn't know how to answer that. She preferred to keep their relationship secret until she finished her job. But Ty was Carson's best friend, eventually she'd have to get used to him knowing. "Good," she said.

"He's happy, Sadie."

"We both are."

"Keep it that way, okay?"

"Hey, red," another player called.

Sadie looked past Ty, putting a check mark by Jag Patera's name. "Hello, Mr. Patera."

Jag gave her a lopsided grin and gazed at Ty. "I think it's kind of sexy when she calls me Mister."

Ty chuckled. "Don't let Carson hear you say that."

Patera's forehead creased. "Why not?"

Sadie shot a pleading glance at Ty, silently asking him not to say anything more.

Ty nodded at her. "He's here to make sure we all behave."

Just as Sadie sighed in relief, Carson appeared from inside the van and waved at her.

He was dressed in gray warmups and a matching team

T-shirt, a ball cap on his head and his eyes hidden by sunglasses, and his smile suggested he was in a good mood. Sadie waited for him to join them by her rental car.

"Hello, Ms. Reynolds," he teased.

"Hello, Mr. Savage."

"Jesus Christ," Ty said.

"What?" Carson removed his sunglasses.

"Nothing. Can we get on with it already?" Ty begged.

Sadie took a last look at her attendance sheet, then glanced at the players standing around her. For a moment, she wished she could take a picture and send it to Barbi and Erika. She was surrounded by so much hotness. Barbi would definitely appreciate the visual proof. So would Lenny.

"All right, gentlemen. Thank you for showing up on time. This should only take an hour or two, depending on how receptive our volunteers are. The plan is pretty simple. I wanted you to witness firsthand feedback from local fans. This is all about perceptions, how people feel about the most prominent players on the Warriors."

"I'm a prominent player?" Nick Acevedo asked, puffing out his chest.

"Yes, Mr. Acevedo, you're a fan favorite."

The tight end grinned. "Thanks."

"I doubt you required confirmation from me."

"Maybe not," he said. "Still nice to hear it from a pretty lady."

Sadie had learned quickly how to tune out the compliments.

"If you'll follow me…" Sadie had rented space from a full-service company that provided turn-key facilities for business needs. In this case, a suite for focus groups.

They walked through the reception area, the administrative staff stopping to gawk as the guys walked by. After they turned down a long hallway, Sadie stopped midway and opened the door to the comfortable lounge where the players would be observing through the two-way mirror. A long table containing coffee, tea, bagels and spreads, fresh fruit, and yogurt waited.

After the team settled down, Sadie pointed to the two-way mirror on the far wall. "You'll be able to see and hear everything I do, but the volunteers won't know you're watching."

"Isn't that unethical?" Solomon Webster asked.

Though Solomon had become more cooperative, he still questioned Sadie since their initial confrontation.

"Not in this case," she explained. "We're not conducting clinical trials. This is a simple exercise meant to discover how your fans feel about you as individuals."

Solomon sat down on one of the sofas with a cup of coffee. "I like the idea. Sometimes it's easy to forget who we really play for."

"I understand," Sadie said. "You have one of the biggest followings. And I'm impressed with how well you manage your social media and public appearances overall. However, we need to focus on less controversial posts. Nothing about being able to do a better job than the NFL commissioner, and you probably shouldn't call any of the Cowboys pussies. And there's the video clips where you work out in a thong."

"What's wrong with my thong?"

"Um…it's not very kid-friendly. Maybe you could wear shorts or warm ups?"

Solomon scratched his head. "What about chaps?"

"No," Sadie said. "Remember—think families."

Solomon laughed. "You're gullible, red. Yeah, I'll switch to shorts. I'm all about the kids."

She couldn't believe he'd gotten the best of her so easily. "I'd like to join you next week when you visit the hospital."

Solomon took a sip of coffee. "Sure. As long as you don't mind handing out stuffed animals."

"I'd love to donate some. How many kids are we visiting?"

"About thirty. I can have my assistant send you the information."

"Please do," she said. "Any other questions?" she addressed the rest of the players.

No one said anything, so Sadie distributed a worksheet that explained everything she would do today. Twenty-three players were listed.

"Meryl isn't even part of the class," Ty said, scanning the paper.

"That's intentional," Sadie said. "With the exception of the ten of you, the name selection was random to keep it fair."

"Fair?" Acevedo questioned.

"We needed a true representation of the team. Less controversial players mixed in with your names."

After spending a few more minutes with the players, Sadie excused herself and went to the room where the volunteers would be arriving shortly. She checked the tables to make sure all the supplies they'd need were ready. Fifteen minutes later, the participants arrived. She greeted them warmly, directing them to the refreshments table.

Twenty-eight of the thirty showed, which satisfied Sadie. She closed the door and started the session. The general mood of the volunteers was pleasant, so she had high hopes for the group.

Taking careful notes, she opened the exercise with Solomon Webster's name.

"Thunderbolt," a man in the front row said.

Several participants laughed.

"Tenacious."

"Powerhouse."

"Political."

"Rude."

"Risky."

Solomon drew a mixed impression.

Sadie moved down the name list, finally stopping on Ty. "Tyrone Baxley," she said.

A woman cleared her throat. "Man-whore."

"Dangerous."

"Ultimate talent," a gentleman said.

"Try to limit it to one-word descriptions, Mr. Wright," Sadie reminded him.

"If we were talking about anyone else," he said, "I could."

"All right," Sadie said. "Let's run with this." She walked up to the white board and wrote Ty's name. "Give me everything you have, Mr. Wright."

After shooting off three paragraphs worth of positive adjectives, Sadie smiled at Mr. Wright. "Now that you can visually assess how you feel about Tyrone Baxley, what's your favorite word on your list?"

Mr. Wright scrubbed his face. "Does it have to pertain to football only?"

Sadie shook her head. "Not at all."

"Prowess," he said.

Sadie circled his choice on the board. "Prowess is a wonderful descriptor. Can you explain how this applies to Tyrone Baxley?"

"On the field and off."

"Can you be more precise?" Sadie urged.

"Women."

Yes! That's what Sadie was looking for, the truth. "Are you a friend of Mr. Baxley's?" she asked.

"No."

"Then how can you quantify your description of him?"

"Don't you follow him on social media? Watch the news? Read the papers?"

"My affiliation with Tyrone Baxley is unimportant, Mr. Wright. I'd like to know more about your opinion."

"The man has everything, talent, speed, money, looks, and women."

"You admire him, then?"

"I love him."

Sadie scribbled down a few notes, then moved on to another player's name, recorded the results, then called Carson's name.

"Apollo," a woman said.

"Accuracy."

"Honest."

"Secretive."

"World-class."

As the compliments flew, Sadie couldn't help but smile to herself, thinking about a few choice words she'd use to describe Carson, too.

"You get Apollo, and I get man-whore," Ty complained.

"What did you expect?" Carson asked.

"Don't my stats mean anything?"

"When the number of women you've slept with in a season equals your rushing yards, what do you think your fans are going to pay attention to?"

Ty scratched his head and laughed. "Never thought of it that way."

"Maybe Sadie deserves a little more consideration."

"The same kind you're giving her?"

Carson gave him a push. "Don't go there."

"I didn't, but some of the players are talking."

"About what?"

"Come on, man. They're not blind."

"My personal life has nothing to do with this."

"Technically, no. But there are a couple guys who are envious of what you have with our teacher." He gestured at the mirror. "She's exceptional."

"I didn't want everyone to find out yet, but I guess it's hard to hide when we're all working together in close quarters. Just let them know she's taken."

"Hey." Ty raised his hands. "According to Sadie, I already have my hands full with too many women."

Carson laughed. "Do I need to worry about Sadie getting hit on?"

Carson didn't want any added drama. With the preseason on its way, the front office and his coach up his ass, and his relationship with Sadie, there wasn't any room for problems. Carson had limits. And the next person who tried to get in his way might suffer the consequences of the temper he'd spent a long time learning to control.

"You know I have your back."

Carson trusted Ty implicitly. Yet the question remained as he gazed at his other teammates. Could he trust them? The competitive nature of football in general made it impossible to always keep the peace. Add a beautiful woman into the mix—especially one who had access to the team—it could start trouble. "But?" he pressed his best friend. "Do I have to worry?"

Ty gritted his teeth and gestured at the rookie, Jag Patera, known as the Greek Freak. "I've heard him make some lewd comments about her. Locker room trash talk. Might be time to make your relationship more public."

Maybe Ty was right. He'd have to talk to Sadie first. If she agreed, Carson knew it would take care of the problem. And if it didn't, he'd handle it some other way.

CHAPTER TWENTY

Sadie waited in the main terminal of the Mobile Regional Airport with a sign that read SEXY ALMOST BALD GUY. As soon as Lenny appeared, she waved, thrilled to see him. He smiled and rushed to her side, pulling her into a hug.

"Look at you!" he said, spinning her around.

"I'm so happy to see you, Lenny."

After grabbing Lenny's luggage, they were in her rental car and driving to the stadium.

"You made it in time for Family Night," she said. "We're unveiling the first video online tonight."

The video clips had been taped around Mobile, at the hospital where Ty and Carson volunteered, at the local parks on Big Brothers Big Sisters play days, at a couple elementary schools, and even at the stadium. Sadie couldn't believe how nurturing Carson was with the kids…like he had a dozen children of his own. As for Ty—there was more to that man than he let on. Sadie smiled—the big softie would make a great father one day.

"The production team did an incredible job, didn't they?"

"That's an understatement. They captured everything I envisioned for the campaign. Starting with Ty Baxley and ending with Carson was brilliant. And the kids…"

"I loved the little boy at the end," he said.

"He's adorable. I love that he asked Carson why he chose the Warriors."

"Did you like Carson's answer?" Leonard asked, rubbing his eyes.

"Hey, are you too tired to attend the event? I could drop you at the hotel instead."

Sadie worried about Leonard because he never took time to rest. He was either at work or partying. Now that he was there, she'd encourage him to stay in a few nights and catch up on sleep.

"No, I'm fine. What about Carson's answer?" Lenny asked.

"When he said it was all about Alabama? I loved it—really meshed with the slogan—'Rediscover the Alabama in the Alabama Warriors.'"

"Charles suggested a series of videos."

Sadie stared at Lenny, then back at the road. "I didn't know he was keeping up with the project."

Lenny nodded. "When he can."

"Here we are." She pulled into the vast parking lot of the stadium, driving up to a security shed and flashing a badge that gave her access to all the team areas.

The guard waved her through.

"Now that's power," Lenny teased.

"There's a pass waiting in my office for you, too."

"Really?" He laughed maniacally and rubbed his hands together. "Does it grant access to the locker room?"

"Should I be worried about Carson?"

"Afraid of a little competition?"

She parked the car and pulled the key from the ignition before raising her hands in mock surrender. "You'd win."

Lenny grinned. "Glad you recognize my superiority where men are concerned."

She rolled her eyes. "Is it difficult carrying that big head of yours on your shoulders?"

Lenny snorted as he climbed out of the car.

Sadie enabled the alarm and slung her backpack over her shoulder. "I'll give you a quick tour of the administrative building, then we can get outside and start taking some pictures and video footage."

They walked to a side door where another security guard was stationed. "Hello, Ms. Reynolds." The guard smiled.

"Hello, Richard. This is Leonard, my coworker. I have a pass for him in my office."

"No problem. I trust you." He opened the door, and Sadie and Leonard stepped inside.

Sadie led the way down the hallway, then turned left. "There's several offices on this wing," she said. "Two media rooms, a conference room, and classrooms." She opened the door to her office and flipped on the light switch. "Small but functional."

Leonard set his briefcase on the desk and loosened his purple tie. "You're comfortable here."

"What do you mean?"

"The way you carry yourself, more relaxed than I've seen you in a while."

She shrugged. "Blame Carson."

"Blame me for what, Kitty Kat?"

The sound of Carson's deep voice aroused her, and she could read the excitement on his face. He was wearing full pads and leaned against her office door.

She gazed at the wall clock, surprised he'd cut it so close to the practice game time to see her. "Aren't you supposed to be on the field warming up?"

"Sure," he said. "But I wanted to check in and make sure Leonard got here okay." Carson turned to Lenny. "Heard a lot about you. I'm Carson."

Sadie held her breath, hoping Leonard wouldn't drool all over Carson's extended hand.

"I'm a big fan," Leonard said, shaking his hand. "Looking forward to the exhibition tonight."

"Thanks." Carson stepped around the desk and kissed Sadie's cheek. "Ready for tonight?"

Sadie nodded and scooped up the schedule for the featured activities. "I memorized everything. On-field football drills, six to seven; Care and Share Family Night Picnic in the west parking lot, seven to eight thirty; and the ever-important Fan Walk of Dreams, an interactive, confidence-building training area with a football toss, photo ops, obstacle course, and other fun for the whole family..." she read out loud.

"Someone's been doing their homework," Carson praised her.

"Well, it's a great opportunity to make you guys look good.

Plus, someone needs to set an example for the bad boy quarterback and his rowdy offensive line."

Carson gave her a crooked smile. "Did you think about what I suggested last night? Attending the after-party together? It's important to make a good impression on our new sponsor for the stadium. And I'm pretty sure you'll charm him into a generous donation." It was the best solution Carson could think of to show the world he and Sadie weren't just a hookup.

She dropped the program on her desk. "Yes, I have."

"You hesitated."

"I did," she admitted. "Though there's no policy in my contract discouraging me from fraternizing with a player..."

"You should go," Leonard injected.

Carson nodded in his direction. "You're invited, too."

"I appreciate the offer, but I have some paperwork to catch up on and should probably get some sleep. You two have fun. I'll grab a cab to the hotel after the game."

"Are you sure, Leonard?" Sadie asked, not wanting him to feel left out.

"Stop worrying about me and go show the world how happy you are."

Why did Leonard have to be so direct in front of Carson? She didn't have any doubts about being with Carson, just about how everyone would react to them getting back together. There were so many things to think about—especially whether or not they could deal with a long-distance relationship.

Carson took Sadie's hand and squeezed it. "No wonder you like him so much."

Sadie couldn't hide her smile. "He grows on you."

"I just want what's best for my girl," Leonard said. "And I've always told her, run with the big dogs or stay on the porch."

"Advice to live by," Carson said. "I have to go, sweetheart. See you on the field."

Sadie gave Carson a quick hug. "Good luck."

The walk through the tunnel that led to the stadium field felt eerily lonely, the usual twang of excitement in his gut absent. Count that as a first. The reason he kept playing was because of the butterflies he always felt right before a game. Didn't matter if his team was on a winning or losing streak or how many fans were in the stands. Carson loved the game. Plain and simple. When Sadie had been at his side during his high school career, it'd been that much sweeter.

He paused halfway down the tunnel, spotting his team lining up ahead. Looking in the opposite direction, toward the locker room, he wondered what it would feel like to march back inside, hang his jersey and helmet up, and then simply walk away—quit. The desolate feelings that thought provoked were similar to how his heart felt without Sadie. Carson was tired from teeter-tottering on the unknown. He wanted Sadie and wasn't sure he could keep her if he stayed in Alabama.

"Carson!" Coach called.

Carson snapped out of his thoughts, shoved his mouthguard in, and then secured his helmet on his head. As he jogged the rest of the way to his team, catching the sound of the fans above stomping their feet to the rhythm of "We Will Rock You" by Queen, he couldn't resist smiling. A man with half his heart full trumped a man with an empty one. That's what he'd focus on tonight as he ran out of the tunnel and into the spotlight— thirty thousand fans jumping up from their seats, clapping and screaming his name.

Though tonight was only meant to showcase the talents of the offense and defense for the fans, Carson never threw a ball half-assed.

He stepped up to the line of scrimmage, placed his hands under his center, and yelled, "Red sixty, red sixty, alpha-omega, hut-hut."

Jag Patera snapped the ball, and Carson dropped back, looking for an open receiver. He spotted Ty, throwing a perfect spiral that ended up in his best friend's hands. With a grin plastered on his face, Carson raised his fist in the air, celebrating the forty-yard pass and equally impressive catch and run Ty had made.

Then he searched the sideline for Sadie. She was there, camera in hand, not missing an opportunity to take positive pictures for the Warriors.

Dressed in a navy blue mini dress and black heels, hair in a messy bun, Sadie decided to attend the party with Carson. She credited Leonard's adage—*run with the big dogs or stay on the porch*—for giving her the final nudge she needed to just go and not worry about what anyone else thought. This was her life. And Carson deserved a confident girlfriend, not one who would run away every time she felt uncomfortable. She'd already let Jason get the best of her once, and that wouldn't happen again.

She'd misjudged Carson and her own feelings. How long

had she lived under the disillusionment that she didn't need intimacy, that she could keep living by herself without opening her heart? Not that she was ready to surrender her heart quite yet, but the early signs of deeper feelings for Carson were emerging. It frightened her.

Leaning against his truck, she waited patiently as players started to file out of the team facilities. Family Night had been a success, and Sadie hadn't missed a chance to take intimate photos and video footage of her players interacting with the public.

Ty had a way with children, and she'd already posted several pictures on his social media pages of him working one-on-one with boys and girls at the youth obstacle course. The response was overwhelmingly positive, hundreds of mom fans liking and sharing the pics. She checked his Facebook page again, smiling at the early results. It had been a week since the star tight end had posted any controversial content. Though he complained incessantly about keeping his bad boy image, she knew he wasn't serious.

There were so many positives to concentrate on. However, that didn't negate the darker elements of being a football player. The alcohol and drugs, wild parties, and the biggest risk—the gorgeous women who seemed to line up for any of the players.

"Hey, beautiful," someone called out.

Sadie looked around, wondering who the compliment was for.

Jag Patera stopped in front of her, running his hand up her arm. "Did you enjoy the drills?"

Sadie took a step to the side and smiled. "I enjoyed the kids the most."

"What are you doing in the parking lot all alone?"

"Waiting for Carson," she said, hoping he'd show up soon. Jag didn't exactly creep her out, but he had a predatory air about him that made her nervous. "Have you seen him?"

"Yeah. Still in the shower playing with his…" He gazed at her. "Never mind. Let me give you a ride to the party. That's where you're going, right?"

She nodded. "*With* Carson."

"You two a thing?" Jag crossed his arms over his chest.

"We're something," she said.

Jag cocked his head. "When you're done playing around with the quarterback, come see me." Sadie shook her head as he walked away, wondering what in the hell that was all about.

"Looked for you inside," she heard Carson say a couple minutes later.

She turned around, happy to see him.

Carson lifted her hand to his lips and planted a feather-light kiss on her palm, then twirled her about, whistling at her. "You clean up nice, Kitty Kat. I'm guessing by the way you're dressed, you decided to step out with me?"

"Yes. I'm okay with the world knowing we're together."

He was silent for a long moment. "You sure?"

"I'm sorry for making you wait. I'm trying to overcome some of those old bad habits of mine, Carson. This is a big deal for me."

"You don't know how happy it makes me." He tugged her into his arms and kissed her. "You're beautiful."

So was he. He looked edible in his charcoal-colored suit, the light blue shirt underneath unbuttoned low enough to show off his blond chest hair. His curls were damp and slicked back with a touch of polishing gel, the subtle citrusy scent of his cologne teasing her senses.

Maybe they could skip the party and go to her hotel or his house and make up for some lost time.

"You're quiet," he said.

Hooking her arms around his neck, she pulled him in for another kiss, nipping his bottom lip.

Carson growled, lifted her off her feet, and wedged her between his body and the door of his truck. "I've missed you," he said near her ear.

"Can we skip the party?" Lust bloomed inside her.

Carson planted a hand on one side of her head, then raked his fingers through his hair with the other. "I wish we could, sweetheart. This is a private party—potential sponsor for the team. I promised Jack I'd make an appearance. Now, how long we stay…" He ran a finger between her breasts, stopping when he noticed the pendant she was wearing. "Sadie? Is this…?"

The first gift Carson had ever given her, the gold and jade carved dragon held special meaning to her. She always traveled with a jewelry box, and before she left South Carolina, she slipped the piece in with her collection of otherwise business-appropriate pieces.

"You kept it?"

"I have everything you've ever given me, Carson."

He rested his forehead against hers, gazing into her eyes. "You never stop surprising me."

Feeling vulnerable, Sadie averted her eyes. Carson cupped

the base of her neck, massaging the anxiety away. "Ready?"

"Absolutely. It's been a long time, going out like this with a man."

He placed a finger over her lips. "Shh. I don't want to know about your other men."

She understood—Carson had been her first lover. "There's not much to tell."

Breathing in, Carson's expression softened. "Sorry, Kitty Kat. I shouldn't let my petty jealousy get in the way of letting you explain. God knows you've seen enough of my conquests in the news."

She nodded in appreciation. "I dated David Hemmer my freshman year in college. Didn't work out very well—he couldn't live up to the Carson standard."

"The Carson standard?"

"A term Barbi coined a long time ago."

He rolled his eyes. "I miss that girl."

"She's one of your biggest fans."

"Tell me more about this standard?"

She swatted his arm. "You're such an attention hound. I'm trying to tell you something important. I felt so alone without you," she confessed. "So, I tried to replace you. Blond hair and blue eyes were the primary prerequisites."

His lips hitched up, the warmth of his smile as potent as his touch. "You've only dated one man in seven years, Sadie?" Why did he look so hopeful?

"No, I've dated a dozen men since we broke up—but only slept with two."

"God, I love you." He crushed her against his chest, stroking her head. "I'm afraid I haven't been a saint, Kitty Kat. I regret what I've done on most days."

The beat of Carson's heart against her cheek made her feel safe. "You don't need to explain. I may not like what I know, but I understand why, I think."

"You do?"

"You were trying to do the same thing, replace us—searching for the same feeling but never finding it."

His embrace grew tighter, his rhythmic breaths a sign that he was in deep contemplation over what they'd just shared with each other. "I used sex to cover up my true feelings."

"Did you ever actually like any of them?" She pulled back so she could see his face.

"Maybe one or two, but it never went anywhere. My heart was desperate to get you back. Then I'd get shitfaced to cover up the pain."

"I'm sorry, Carson."

"You'll never know how sorry I am, too, Sadie."

Their gazes locked again, and Sadie knew there was a lifetime of things she wanted to share with him.

"We should go," he said, walking her to the other side of the truck.

As she climbed into the seat, he paused. "Don't run away again, Sadie. Promise me."

Carson had remained a constant in her life, influencing the decisions she made, the people she dated, even the self-imposed misery her heart lived in. Could she trust herself to take this leap of faith and have a normal relationship? She took in his features, not missing the hope in his eyes. "I promise," she said.

CHAPTER TWENTY-ONE

Carson pulled into a curving driveway in a gated community, finding a long line of vehicles waiting for the valet. "Might take a bit," he said, reaching for Sadie's hand.

She gazed out the windshield. "Whose house is this?"

"Martin Solese, owner of Alabama Solar."

"He's the new sponsor?" She looked surprised.

"A big maybe," he said, pulling up another couple of feet.

"His estate is beautiful."

"Three thousand acres of pristine pastureland, orchards, and vineyards."

"He owns a winery?"

"Several."

"I can't imagine having that kind of money."

"Neither can I." He pointed at the main house. "What's the point of building a new home that's a replica of a plantation? Do you know how many dilapidated properties are available around here? Ones the Historical Society is hoping someone will come along and restore?"

"New money," Sadie offered. "Wants the charm and prestige, but none of the headaches that accompany a hundred-year-old-plus property. Whoever designed the place should win an architectural award. The symmetrical façade, stacked porches, and Greek columns look authentic. Extravagant."

"Wait until you see the interior."

"You've been here before?"

"Twice."

After fifteen minutes, a valet finally opened Sadie's door, and she climbed out. Carson joined her, placed his hand at the small of her back, and smiled. "Ready, sweetheart?"

The grand foyer was crowded, but that didn't keep Sadie from admiring the double staircase and elegantly designed iron railings, the intricate design of the white and gold marble floor, or the black glass chandelier overhead. Every time she discovered something new to praise, she looked up at Carson, which made him chuckle. He'd like to spoil Sadie one day, give her the freedom to decorate his home—the house he wanted to share with her.

"Carson!" Martin, their host, called from across the space and headed toward them. He extended his hand, appearing genuinely happy to see him. "Welcome. I enjoyed the exhibition today."

"Martin." The one thing Carson hated more than anything in a man was a weak handshake. Not that he expected Martin's grip to equal his, but… "This is Sadie Reynolds."

The host's indiscreet appreciation for Sadie's beauty showed on his face. "A pleasure to meet you." He took her hand and brushed a kiss over her knuckles.

Carson gritted his teeth. Maybe he should have opted out of the party after all. Martin threw extravagant parties all the time, invited the upper echelon—including dignitaries from around the world—and liked to push the legal limits for what qualified as acceptable entertainment.

A server with a tray full of Champagne stopped in front of them.

Martin instinctively grabbed three flutes, handing one to Sadie and one to Carson, then quickly downed his own. "The Champagne is made here in Alabama, Sadie. May I call you Sadie?"

"Of course." She took another taste and licked her lips. "Delicious," she praised.

Martin smiled and placed her hand in the crook of his arm, leading her through the foyer, down three stairs into an oversized den packed with people, past a media room with a theater-sized screen and at least twenty leather recliners, past a music room, then out a back door. Carson followed silently, ready to snatch the billionaire by the scruff of his neck and give him a good shake. But he didn't. Sadie seemed to be enjoying their conversation.

They ended up inside a party tent in the back garden. Several players, including Ty, fist-bumped Carson as he walked through, eyeing the decedent surroundings. There was a crystal Champagne fountain, oyster bar, sushi bar, fondue station, a buffet-style grill set up with a chef, six-piece orchestra, dance floor, and dozens of tables.

"What's your temptation?" Martin asked Sadie.

"My temptation?"

"Anything." He raised a brow.

"I enjoy a bold Cabernet."

"So do I," Martin offered. "But I meant more exotic—forbidden tastes, perhaps?"

To Carson's relief, Sadie reached for his hand. "Chocolate."

Martin rumbled with laughter. "She's very charming, Carson."

"And not accustomed to these kinds of parties."

"Of course, I understand. But such naïveté cannot last forever, can it?"

Sadie looked between them, searching for clarification.

Carson pulled her tight against him and whispered in her ear, "Martin hosts a food club."

"Really? How interesting. What sort of cuisine do you feature? I'm not afraid to try something exotic."

"Perhaps the best way to understand what I mean is to let you sample something very different." He excused himself.

"I believe Martin is a bit eccentric," she observed as the host walked away.

Carson was expected to spend time here to help his team. With talk of a new stadium, the franchise would need private donors like Martin to make it happen. This was his third such party at Martin's home. And just beyond the tent, Carson knew what he'd find: another tent where the *real* party was—banned food and alcohol, high-dollar call girls, cocaine, and probably a high-stakes poker game. Only VIPs were allowed inside, and an armed guard was posted at the entrance. Carson didn't want to expose Sadie to it. She wouldn't understand. Hell, *he* could barely stomach the idea.

Martin returned with a silver bowl. "Please," he said, offering her a forkful of delicate, black eggs. "Try this."

Sadie tasted the caviar. "It bursts with flavor."

"Yes," Martin approved. "It's Almas, otherwise known as black gold. The most sought-after caviar in the world."

Sadie's eyes went wide as she handed the fork back to Martin. "Thank you for letting me sample it."

He waved a server over and then placed the bowl on her tray. Turning back to Carson, he said, "I'll leave you to get settled. The invitation stands, Carson."

Once Martin was out of earshot, Carson blew out a breath. "Jesus Christ," he complained. "I can only handle small doses of that man."

"Why?" she asked. "I rather enjoyed his company."

"Sweetheart." Carson fingered a strand of her soft red hair. "Martin just fed you illegal caviar."

Sadie covered her mouth. "W-why didn't you tell me? That's horrible."

"Don't get upset. Wild beluga caviar is one of the tamer delicacies he offers."

"What are you saying? What else does he eat—elephants? Shark-fin soup? Puppies and kittens?" Her voice raised an octave. "Hasn't anyone informed the police of his illegal activities?"

Carson shook his head. "Martin and his cronies are untouchable. Too much money, and every politician within a thousand-mile radius of Mobile considers him an important friend and ally. He has better security than the president."

Sadie sighed. "What about Jack?"

"He doesn't get involved with these kind of events or fundraising. His sons do. Maybe after you're done rebranding the team, you can focus on what goes on behind the scenes. How about we forget about Martin and focus on dancing?"

"Did I hear you correctly? You're asking me to dance?"

"Yep."

"This is new," she said, pleasantly surprised.

"You always wished I was a more enthusiastic dancer."

"What changed your mind? Or should I say who?"

"Jealous?"

The orchestra started to play a waltz and Carson didn't wait for Sadie's reply, he guided her to the dance floor, holding her close—breathing in her scent. She rested her cheek against his chest, swaying to the soft music. She belonged to him. As his hand slipped up her back, he wondered if this could last forever. Was this really their second chance at happiness?

A half hour later, Carson found an empty table for them to sit at and then wandered off for drinks and food. He returned with two beers, sushi rolls, and chocolate-covered strawberries.

Sadie eyed the temaki. "Should I be nervous about what's inside the wrap?"

"Not at all," he assured her. "Anything served out here is safe."

"But..."

"Martin was just showing off before, sweetheart. He liked you."

Braving a taste of sushi, she made a satisfied noise as she swallowed her first bite. "The crab melts in your mouth. Taste it."

Carson took a sip of beer, then grabbed a piece of the cone-shaped sushi. He bit into it, crab, spicy tuna, and rice filling his mouth.

"Well?"

"I'd rather hand-feed you in my bed."

Sadie shifted on her seat. "That can be arranged."

"Can it?" he asked.

"Absolutely," she said, reaching for a chocolate-covered strawberry. She took a delicate bite, then offered the rest to Carson. "Like this?"

He licked her fingertips as he accepted the treat, undressing her with his eyes. He'd never be able to get enough of her. "I think I'm ready to go now."

"That was too easy."

"Nothing easy about it," he assured her. "I'm dying to get inside you, Sadie. And if we don't hurry up and go, I'll find an empty bedroom here—though a closet or bathroom will serve just as well."

She dabbed at the corners of her mouth with a linen napkin, then folded it neatly and set it on the table. Crooking a finger at him, Carson had no choice but to lean closer to Sadie. "How desperate are you to make love to me?" she asked.

"Incredibly desperate." Now everybody was going to know about them, but Carson didn't care. He wanted his relationship with Sadie to go public. It would show her how serious he was. "Do you need more convincing?" This time he offered her a strawberry, enjoying the way her full lips wrapped around the decadent dessert, her pink tongue licking the trace of chocolate from her bottom lip.

He closed his eyes for a brief moment, imagining what her tongue could do to his cock—what explosive passion her tiny, warm hands could inspire.

"Carson?"

He grinned. "Sorry, Kitty Kat."

"Kitty Kat?"

Carson frowned at the male voice, finding Jag standing next to Sadie. "Jag," he said, extending his hand, irritated by the intrusion.

Jag shook it. "Not joining us in the VIP tonight?"

"I have plans."

Jag's gaze slipped to Sadie. "I can see that."

"Tell the team I'll see them at practice tomorrow."

"Mind if I dance with the lady before you go?" Jag asked, focusing on Carson again.

Carson stood. "Yeah, I do mind." He offered his hand to Sadie, and she took it, rising from her chair.

"Does she?" Jag gestured at Sadie.

Carson's body went rigid. "What do you think, sweetheart?"

She gazed up at him, then glanced at Jag. "Thanks for the tempting offer, but I'm not done playing with the quarterback."

She squeezed Carson's fingers, signaling she was ready to go. It pleased him to witness her shutting Jag Patera down. But something kept niggling at his gut as they walked through the house and out the front door. What did Sadie mean by saying *I'm not done playing with the quarterback?* Jag had obviously approached Sadie before. It pissed him off, but he wouldn't push the issue right now. It just meant he'd have to keep a closer eye on his teammate—and on Sadie, because he didn't trust Jag to respect boundaries.

The valet delivered his truck, and once they drove away from the house, he turned on the radio and rested his hand on her knee, trying to concentrate on the road. A couple miles into the drive, he sighed, overcome with both desire and anger. "That's it," he declared as he pulled off the street, putting on his emergency lights, and killing the ignition. "I can't wait."

As if she felt the same, Sadie unbuckled her seat belt and then opened her door.

"Where are you going?" he asked.

"Out here." She closed the door and started for the woods a few feet away from the shoulder.

"Sonofabitch." Carson climbed out of the truck and followed her, more than ready to make love in the woods.

CHAPTER TWENTY-TWO

Three days later, Sadie and Carson met for lunch at a downtown café. She'd chosen a patio table, away from the crowd, overlooking the busy street. He arrived on time, wearing jeans and a Disturbed T-shirt, a baseball cap, sunglasses, and boots. As he wound his way through the maze of tables, Sadie couldn't help watching the way people reacted to his presence. Whether they recognized him or not, he was impossible to ignore.

He reached their table and leaned down to kiss her cheek. "Hope I'm not late, Kitty Kat."

"Not at all," she said.

"So why here? We could have met at your hotel or at the stadium."

Sadie opened a menu and scanned the list of lunch specials. "I thought neutral ground would serve best."

"Neutral ground?" The crease between his eyebrows deepened. "Is something wrong?"

"No." She looked up. "Sorry if it came off that way. We

just don't need any distractions, like a bed or desk."

That made him smile. "What about wrought iron tables?" He patted the table top. "Seems sturdy enough."

Sadie cleared her throat. "In the middle of the lunchtime rush?"

"Since when has that ever stopped us?"

She thought about it. Nothing ever deterred them from making love. "We're not teenagers anymore."

"Thank God," he said with a wink. "I prefer the grown-up version of Sadie Reynolds and everything she has to offer."

Folding her hands to keep from touching him, she cleared her throat. "That's enough innuendo from you, Mr. Savage."

"Is it now?" He lowered his sunglasses on his nose, peeking at her.

"I meant this to be a professional meeting."

"Yes, ma'am."

"I've been thinking about how we could move forward with sharing the farm experience with your fans—giving them a candid look into your life without being too intrusive."

"I already agreed to do whatever you wanted. I like the idea overall, as long as there's no backlash with my mom and sisters."

"That's just it…"

"What?"

"Good afternoon." A server approached the table. "What can I get you to drink?"

Sadie had been craving a cup of Turkish coffee but changed her mind the moment Carson had arrived. "Gin and tonic with extra lime," she ordered.

"What about you, sir?"

"Iced tea."

As soon as the server walked away, Carson resumed the conversation. "What's just it, Sadie?"

Resting her elbows on the table, she decided to speak freely. "I know there's more work to do on the farm, but I think it would be a great idea to present the property to your mother early. And to hold a charitable event at the same time for Big Brothers Big Sisters. Maybe a picnic—we can hire a band and have face painting and a magician for the kids. I'm sure local restaurants would be happy to sponsor the event."

Carson's expression remained unchanged as he leaned back in his chair. "That's impossible."

It wasn't the reaction she had expected. "Why?"

"Because it goes against everything I told you. Asking Charlie Silva to appear is challenging enough. Asking Mom and the girls to step into the spotlight is selfish."

"Not if we plan it carefully."

"No."

"You're being stubborn."

He shook his head. "I'm being protective."

"Stubborn."

The server arrived with their drinks. "Are you ready to order?"

"Give us a few minutes," Carson said.

"Carson..."

"Ask anything else of me."

"Won't you even take the time to review my proposal?"

"Proposal?"

"Yes." Sadie scooted her chair back and reached for the

leather briefcase sitting on the ground at her feet. She opened it and pulled out a file. "I've taken the time to draft a timeline complete with a synopsis of what I'd like to achieve." She handed the folder to Carson.

With a quirk of his lips, he opened the file.

The server returned, and Sadie ordered a chef salad for herself and a French dip and fries for Carson.

"Sadie…" He watched her intently for a long moment. "You've contracted a professional camera crew to follow us around the farm?"

"Proposed," she corrected.

"All right, *proposed*," he repeated. "That doesn't change anything. KTCA gets exclusive reporting rights in exchange for the use of one of their camera crews."

"Yes, simple economics for that part. KTCA is an award-winning station. They have an extensive audience—especially online. What better way to connect with your fans and make new ones? Plus, they'll handle the Big Brothers Big Sisters involvement—as well as Rex's relationship to you— with care."

He nodded and returned his attention to the paper. "So, you're suggesting multiple interviews and visits to the farm? And you want to involve my teammates?"

There'd be no regrets on this project. She'd spent the better part of two days coming up with the final plan. "Like a miniseries," she said.

"So now I'm expected to be a reality star?"

"The interviews will be featured on the evening news, but the extended episodes about your family, the kids, and farm will be on the internet. We'll schedule several live feeds so fans can ask you direct questions."

Carson scrubbed his chin, looking more and more irritated. "Sadie."

"I know it sounds intrusive. But it's not. You can't buy that kind of promotion, Carson. Think about the money we'll raise for Big Brothers Big Sisters. And if we're successful, maybe it can be an annual event. Getting kids out of the city for the day is a wonderful thing."

The server brought their meals. Carson took a bite of his sandwich and chewed aggressively.

"There's some time to think about it," she said.

She ate a few forkfuls of salad, nervous Carson might blow the whole thing off. Yes, she'd pushed the limits, but she just had a feeling if he agreed to the terms, he'd see the value in it once they started working together to organize the event.

"If I agree to this, I want to tell my mother and sisters about the farm in private first."

Sadie thought about it. Capturing their emotional reactions on film when Carson surprised them with the property was half the appeal of her idea. But she understood why Carson wanted to protect his family. "We can work around that."

"I love the idea of involving Big Brothers Big Sisters, Sadie. They're my favorite charitable organization."

"I know." She smiled. "I can't wait to meet Charlie."

"He's a great kid. Loves math and science."

"Wait!"

"What?"

"You just inspired another idea"

He leaned forward, resting his elbows on the table. "Does it involve taking our clothes off?"

"No." She smacked his hand. "Work first. Play later."

"All work, no play makes me a dull boy."

She snorted. "Seriously, Carson. Instead of the typical kind of entertainment for the kids, what if we sponsored an imaginarium?"

"Like a museum?"

"Yes. Interactive learning, math, science, the arts...We can do whatever we want, really."

"That's a great idea, Kitty Kat." He rubbed his stubbled chin. "My mom and sisters would love a chance to help."

"You're actually getting excited about it now?"

"Sadie..." He cradled her hand in his. "This reminds me of the way we used to be in high school. Working together on projects and..."

"I tutored you, Carson."

"I know. But we clicked, didn't we?"

"Yes," she admitted. "And we did a damn good job organizing fundraisers for the team."

"Yeah." He grinned. "That's why this feels right."

"I have one demand," she said.

"What?"

"The dunking booth. That stays."

"I'll do it."

"Really?" she practically squealed.

"On one condition."

She'd do anything for him. "Everything is negotiable."

"Glad to hear it, Kitty Kat. Because if I have to step out of my comfort zone, so do you."

She set her fork aside and folded her hands on the table. "What are you suggesting?"

"Spend the weekend with me in Fairhope."

Her flight instinct kicked in. She reached for a glass of ice water and took a long, nervous drink. "That's not possible."

"Why? Help me understand what's so intimidating about going home."

Sadie couldn't explain it, didn't want to. But if she expected Carson's cooperation, she'd have to give in. "I'm horrified by the prospect of seeing anyone we used to know. You saw what happened with Jason."

"Well what if we just see Barbi? Erika? What about my mom?"

She cocked her head. Her resentment of the place where she grew up was as strong now as it was back then. Never mind that she was educated and successful and had nothing to be ashamed of. But the very thought of walking down Main Street and having someone recognize her, especially one of her you-ruined-Carson's-life accusers, made her want to curl up in bed all day. "Where would we stay?"

"I keep an apartment."

"Where?"

"A studio off Fairhope Avenue."

She laughed. "Widow O'Brian's house?"

His face lit up. "You remembered?"

"How could I forget? She was one of your biggest fans. How is she?"

"Still as ornery as ever."

"With all your money, I can't believe you don't just buy a condo or house there."

Carson shrugged. "I like helping her out."

"Do you ever do anything for yourself, Carson?"

"Beyond football?"

"Yes."

"Only when I promised myself I'd win you back again after seeing you in that classroom."

Warmth radiated through her body. The man never failed to have the right words, to give the right look, to know when to touch her. "I-I…"

"You don't have to say a thing, Sadie. I know how you feel."

Did he? Or was he just guessing? Because underneath all the bravado was a brokenhearted boy who'd lost her. "Tell me." She stared at their joined hands, liking how perfectly her smaller one fit in his.

"You love me, Sadie. Plain and simple. And if I ventured a little further, I'd say you never stopped."

She blinked, giving no indication of whether he was right or wrong. Yes, Sadie loved Carson Savage. "You're so arrogant," she teased.

"Confidence is different."

"Says who?"

"The experts."

"What experts?" she asked.

"My mother."

That made Sadie smile so much it hurt. "You win, Carson.

I'll go to Fairhope with you. But promise we can keep the public appearances to a minimum."

"Dinner and drinks with a few friends on Saturday night?"

"Agreed."

They finished eating and Carson paid the bill. She watched him with even deeper interest now, the way he interacted with people and carried himself—like he wasn't an NFL quarterback with a multimillion-dollar contract.

He slipped his arm around her shoulders as they walked out of the restaurant and down the sidewalk toward the parking lot. "Going back to the stadium?" he asked.

She nodded. "I have some paperwork to finish up and a scheduled meeting with my boss."

"I'll follow you, then," he offered.

As she climbed into her car, Sadie knew she never wanted to leave Carson Savage again.

CHAPTER TWENTY-THREE

With the regular camp starting in four weeks, Carson's practice time had been cut in half to avoid injury. He reported to the strength and conditioning coaches more than anyone now, and he had some extra time to review film footage and finalize his playbook. Once he finished for the day, he decided to make a quick trip to Fairhope to prepare for the upcoming weekend. Sadie needed to feel safe and comfortable, to learn how to love her hometown again.

Carson parked in the Liberty Insurance parking lot and knocked on the back door of the office where most of the employees entered/exited the building. He'd known the secret knock since college: bang on it three times, pause, then knock twice again. A few seconds later, Gretchen Black, one of the agents, opened the door and smiled.

"Is your mother expecting you, Carson?"

"Nice to see you, Gretchen. She's not expecting me. Am I allowed to come in, even if it's a surprise visit?"

She swatted at his arm and waved him inside, then closed and locked the door. "Give an old woman a hug."

Carson gave her a toothy grin and dragged the older woman into his arms, giving her a good squeeze. "Where's Mom?"

"Grabbing a cup of coffee in the break room, I think."

"Mind if I wander around some?"

"Go ahead, I have a conference call in ten minutes. Good luck with the opening game." Gretchen walked down the hallway.

He turned right and found his mother in the break room sitting at a table with her back to the door, her face buried in a newspaper. Standing quietly for several minutes, he admired the woman who had taught him to believe in himself, to keep his word no matter how insignificant the promise he'd made might be, and to always tell the truth. Sometimes he faltered as a kid, not living up to her high standards, but she'd always forgive and say it was never too late to start over.

"Mama?" He stepped into the room.

Betty Savage turned around immediately, her bifocals perched low on her nose, her blond hair tied up in a tight bun, her bright, blue eyes focused on her only son. "Carson? Is everything okay?"

"Of course, Mama." He leaned over and kissed her cheek. "Had some business in Fairhope and thought I'd stop by."

"Business? With who?"

"I believe it's time to pay my rent."

Her eyebrows hitched up. "In the middle of the month? And don't you usually use auto pay through the bank?"

Carson claimed the seat across from his mother. No matter

how old he got, he always felt like a little boy whenever he sat at a table with his mom. "Can't hide anything from you, can I?"

Betty removed her reading glasses, tucking them in her blazer pocket. "How's Sadie? How are you?"

Carson couldn't stop the smile—whenever he thought about his girl, how far they'd come in such a short period of time, the happiness came gushing out of him. "We're good, Mama. Really good, actually."

She studied him for several seconds. "I want to believe you, Carson, really I do. But this is the first time you've popped in unannounced. And if you're anything, Carson, you're a creature of habit."

He couldn't deny it. "Sadie agreed to spend the weekend in Fairhope with me."

Betty folded her hands on the table. "Things are getting serious, then?"

"It's like we've never been apart."

"Then why do you look so concerned?"

"Did you know anything about the hellish harassment Sadie suffered after she broke up with me?" Carson had been obsessed with the issue ever since he saw Jason at the farm. It needed to be taken care of before the regular season got under way, before he was expected to travel, leaving Sadie alone and vulnerable.

His mother took a sip of coffee and sighed. "Why are you asking about it now?"

"It came up in a conversation we had last week."

"How rude of me," she said suddenly. "Can I get you something to drink? Coffee? Bottled water? A soda?"

"Mom?"

"Yes?"

"You're avoiding the question. Why?" He reached for her hand. "I'm okay—just want some answers."

She stared at the floor for a second before she looked at him again. "Yes, I knew about her problem. The chief came to see me a few days after Sadie left town."

Carson understood why. He'd raised hell about the breakup, made a fool of himself all over town. In fact, he probably should have gotten a couple DUIs, but the Fairhope PD protected him. "The chief blew her off, you know."

"An unfortunate thing."

"She's still devastated, afraid to come to Fairhope."

"Really?"

Carson sighed and nodded. Then he told her about running into Jason and Janice Millar, how they treated her, and the post the little asshole, Jason, had made on Facebook.

"Some people never change," Betty said. "He always resented you for dating Sadie. And hated Sadie even more for rejecting him."

"He better stay away from her."

"Don't get into trouble, Carson. Better to leave this alone."

"I'll try, Mama. What about dinner with Sadie?"

"She's always welcome, Carson. I just want you to make sure she's ready for all of this attention. Lord knows the excitement you're going to stir up getting seen together again after all these years. I don't want her to get overwhelmed and run away again."

"She promised she wouldn't."

"I'm sure she meant it when she said it, but…"

"She did."

Betty caressed his cheek. "I'd very much like to see the two of you build a life together."

"I'd marry her tomorrow if I thought she'd say yes."

Tears filled Betty's eyes and she sniffled. "Stop getting me all worked up."

"Sorry, Mama."

"Don't be," she said.

"One last favor," he said as he stood up.

"Hmmm?"

"Would you mind if someone wanted to interview you and the girls?"

"About what?"

"Me," he said mischievously.

Betty rolled her eyes. "Hasn't everyone had enough of Carson Savage yet?"

"Have you?"

"Of course not."

"That's all that matters, then."

She joined him near the doorway and gave Carson a big hug. "I'll do the interview if it helps. Stop by the house and say hello to the girls before you head back to Mobile, okay?"

"I will. Love you, Mama."

"I love you, Carson."

The next stop was Barbi's flower shop. He parked out front and walked in, the bell over the door ringing. Only a couple of customers were inside, so Carson explored the shelves, looking for something Sadie might like. He picked out a crystal vase, thinking a couple dozen white roses would look beautiful in it. If she'd let him, he'd send fresh flowers to her every day. She deserved it.

After the last customer left, Carson made his way to the counter, where Barbi was busy arranging some fresh-cut flowers. He placed the vase on the counter. "Be with you in a sec," she said, not looking up to see who he was.

"Is that any way to treat an old friend?"

She immediately set the flowers aside and glanced his direction. "Holy shit," she said, wiping her hands on the green apron covering her blouse and jeans. "Wait…" She paused, her smile fading. "Is your mother well? The girls? Sadie?"

Why did everyone assume his sudden appearance meant something bad? Maybe he should make more of an effort to spend time in Fairhope. "Everyone is just fine."

She held her hand to her chest in relief. "Thank God. It's great to see you!" She rushed around the counter and hugged him tight, then backed up so she could see him better. "So, you and Sadie…"

"Yup."

"That's all you can say?" She smiled.

"She's so damn beautiful."

"That's a start."

"Intelligent. Funny. Sweet."

"Scared shitless," Barbi added.

"That, too," Carson agreed.

"And you're here to get some advice?"

Carson smirked. "If I followed your advice on relationships, I'd have a dozen ex-wives."

Barbi chuckled. "Hey. Don't blame me. I haven't found Mr. Right yet."

"Pretty sure you don't want to."

"Variety is the spice of life."

"And here I thought you were just a cynic."

Barbi slapped his arm and chuckled. "Come on, I'll close the shop for a bit. We can chat."

She walked to the entrance, turned the hanging sign over to closed, then locked the door. "Want a drink?"

"Do you still keep some of that strawberry lemonade in the fridge?"

"Always. Have a seat at the table over there, be right back."

The shop was divided into two sides, the actual floral area and the space where Barbi held crafting classes. He sat down, looking at the numerous pictures hanging on the walls—some watercolors of southern Alabama landscapes, local farms, and the beach. The floor had obviously just been retiled, and the walls freshly painted a mint green. Matching curtains covered the two picture windows at the front of the classroom, and there was a leather sofa and matching chair along the far wall by the bathroom.

Carson had known Barbi since kindergarten and had grown up hanging out with her older brother, Cory. It had been a co-incidence that she happened to be Sadie's best friend. But now he was grateful for that fact, hopeful she'd be able to talk some sense into Jason.

She returned with two plastic tumblers brimming with ice and lemonade and set them both on the table, sitting next to him. "All right, superstar, tell me everything."

Carson ran a finger around the edge of his cup, contemplating how to approach the subject—gently or aggressively. Barbi was a no-nonsense kind of girl. "She means everything to me."

"I know."

"What happened after we graduated…"

"Stop, Carson. You don't owe me an explanation. You were young. She was confused."

"I fucked up."

Barbi nodded. "You're here now."

"I am," he agreed wholeheartedly. "It's just," he hesitated, overcome with emotions he couldn't harness. "No matter how close we seem to get, I can't completely trust the fact that she's going to stay in one place."

Barbi sipped her drink. "She's been trying to work through her fears."

"She has?"

"Yes. Before she came to Mobile, we were at a retreat where she was supposed to complete a workshop about trusting people and herself more."

"How'd it go?"

"Zip lining and Sadie Reynolds don't mix well."

"Zip lining? Christ, she's afraid to climb a tree."

"Right? But she tried it, even made it halfway across the river before she screamed and made the attendant shit his pants."

Carson couldn't suppress his deep-bellied laughter. Imagining his girl clipped to a wire over a river, racing for the other side, seemed impossible. "Did she finish the workshop?"

"God, no. Dropped her cell phone in the water while zip lining and then retreated to her hotel room to watch movies. I had to reschedule because she refused to finish the workshop and instead took the job and came here."

"She loves her job."

"That might be stretching it a bit. She relies on the job to keep her sane. Not saying she doesn't appreciate the money or opportunities it's afforded her. But ever since she moved to South Carolina, she's been lonely. Not depressed. Just quieter, more reserved."

"She's been away from everyone and everything she knows."

"Yeah."

"Until now."

Barbi leaned forward, resting her arms on the table. "What are you trying to say?"

"I want her to stay."

"So do I."

"She wouldn't have to work."

"Carson," Barbi chastised gently. "That's one of the reasons you lost her before. She doesn't want to be kept. Sadie is very independent and extremely talented at what she does."

"I know. You should see how quickly she's taken control of the team."

"I know all about it. She's more determined than ever to succeed."

He tasted the lemonade, chewing on a piece of fresh strawberry. "This is good."

"Wins best lemonade at the state fair every year."

"How's Cory?"

"Married with three kids—loves Oklahoma."

"Send my best wishes."

Barbi's lips curved into an understanding smile. "You're not here to catch up, Carson. Don't get me wrong, I'm happy to have you in my store. And if I had half a brain, I'd make a couple calls and get the ladies down here to make a fuss over you. But I know something is weighing heavy on your conscience. I'll help if I can."

Carson appreciated her candor and looked her directly in the eyes and told her about Jason. "And since Sadie agreed to spend the weekend in Fairhope, I don't want any distractions. And Jason is a big one right now."

"The bastard is still doing it? After all these years? Shit. He harassed her all the time, called her, and even left her some pretty threatening notes. I'm so happy she's coming home, even if it's just for a weekend. I don't want him to ruin it."

"He sent notes?" Why in the hell hadn't anyone clued him in back then?

Barbi jumped up from her chair. "Does it really matter anymore? There were fifty assholes like Jason who treated Sadie like crap because she broke up with you. We need to put all the bad memories behind us and focus on welcoming Sadie home. The only way she's ever going to be comfortable here is to see that we all love and miss her."

Carson took a deep, calming breath, trying to purge some of the rage over the way Sadie had been treated from his mind and body. "You're right, Barbi. I'll focus on Sadie if you can let Jason know the next time he tries to contact Sadie or posts something about her, I'll hunt him down myself."

"With pleasure," she said.

"Thanks, I need to go." He kissed her forehead. "Dinner Saturday night?" he asked as he approached the door.

"Where?"

"The old hangout. We're having a small get-together. Invite Erika, too. Okay?"

"Wouldn't miss it for the world," Barbi said. "As for you, take care of my girl or I'll hunt you down!"

Carson laughed and left the flower shop, excited at the chance to bring his girl back to Fairhope.

CHAPTER TWENTY-FOUR

I analyzed the shares of earned media interactions against each player," Sadie said, gazing at the paperwork in her hand, waiting for Leonard to reply as he sat across from her, reviewing her statistics report.

"Let's focus on the column where you report on the number of people our earned media efforts are reaching. Several of the players, Solomon Webster, Jag Patera, Carson Savage, and Nick Acevedo hit six digits—up ten to twenty percent in the last two weeks. However, Ty Baxley is down fifteen percent. Why?"

"The only logical explanation I have is we're in the process of flushing out the social media followers who stick with Ty for one reason."

"Being?"

"They're scandal whores."

Leonard stuck his finger in his ear and pretended to clear it. "Scandal whores?"

"Very funny. You know perfectly well what I mean. It's been two weeks since he's posted controversial content. Long enough for certain types to unfollow him and look for their entertainment somewhere else. We need to give him more time to recover from the drastic changes I've made, give new followers a chance to catch up with him."

"Would the occasional bikini-wearing supermodel perched on his knee at a nightclub be such a bad thing if it keeps his followers engaged?"

Sadie sighed. "Leonard, you directed me to clean up the Warriors' image—not to compromise. Ty Baxley is an outlier."

"He lost a hundred thousand followers in two weeks."

"And in three, he'll gain double that number."

Leonard scratched his head and tossed the papers aside. "Too much of a good thing can be a bad thing."

Disappointment flooded Sadie's body. She'd absolutely done her best to ensure that Ty's relaunch would be a success. Yes, the numbers were shocking if you looked at them the way Leonard was, but the data behind those numbers is what mattered the most. There was a damn good reason for the drastic changes in Ty's metrics.

"Did you see his social engagement metrics?"

"No. What column?"

"Sixteen."

"Up eight percent," Leonard observed.

"The best he's done in over a year."

"How is his brand being amplified?"

"Though he's lost a significant number of followers, the remaining fans, ones I consider long term, are engaged by the positive change in content. They're sharing more, perhaps inviting friends to take a peek at Ty's pages. This is a textbook case of quality over quantity."

Leonard swiveled in his chair and grunted. "You might be right."

"*Might* be?"

"I'll have the research team take a closer look."

"Thank you," she said with relief.

"What about the farm?" Leonard asked.

"Carson has agreed to all of my terms."

"Jesus Christ, Sadie. This is huge."

"I know." The most important proposal of her career—and if she delivered—it would catapult her career to the next level, perhaps a promotion and a significant raise. "Carson expects something in return, though."

That piqued Lenny's interest, and he transformed from her tight-mannered manager to his gossip-starved self. "Is it professional or personal?"

Sadie twirled a long strand of her hair around her fingers. "Personal."

"And? Don't leave me hanging, girlie."

"I agreed to spend the weekend in Fairhope."

"Ballsy," he said.

"Necessary," she corrected.

"So if it weren't for the project, you would have said no?"

"You know how I feel about Fairhope. There's nothing left there for me, not really."

Lenny coughed and muttered, "Bullshit."

"Hey!" she chastised. "Not everyone grew up with perfect

parents in a perfect house, in the best town, surrounded by the best people. You even had the perfect dog."

"So much for perfect," he said. "Look what my mother and father ended up with. A bisexual son who thinks the ideal marriage would be to a man *and* woman."

Sadie laughed at his self-doubt. Leonard was a Harvard grad with the best future prospects. It wouldn't surprise her if he started his own firm five or ten years from now. "At least you know what you want."

"Don't sell yourself short, kid. From where I'm sitting, you're closer to getting everything you were supposed to have. Just stop self-sabotaging. Don't be a ball buster, Sadie."

"Ball buster?"

"Give Carson Savage a chance to be the man you need."

"I've never needed a man before."

"Stop lying to yourself. Everyone needs someone, Sadie. In what capacity depends on the person. But for you…well, I'm sure he's the only one out there that gets you. Want me to pull out that long list of guys you've tried to connect with?"

"No."

"Now get out of my face and go work that quarterback, or I'll get it done myself."

Sadie laughed as she gathered her files and shoved them in her briefcase, more than ready to spend the weekend with Carson.

CHAPTER TWENTY-FIVE

Carson stuffed Sadie's overnight bag in the back of his Jeep and then joined her inside, pulling away from the roundabout in the front of the hotel. "Ready, sweetheart?" he asked, still worried whether she was truly prepared to return home after seven long years.

"I'm okay, Carson." She smiled, the warmth reaching her green eyes. "All roads lead home, right?"

"That's what they say."

"Thought they said run with the big dogs or stay on the porch?"

"They say that, too." She reached inside her purse and pulled out her sunglasses. "This is your last free weekend for a while, isn't it?"

"Yes. Training camp starts soon."

"After watching you on the field at Family Night, Carson, I believe you'll get that Super Bowl ring this season. I'd love to see it."

The high praise gave him hope that she'd be here well into the season, attending the away and home games—cheering for him from the stands where all the players' wives and girlfriends sat. A very exclusive VIP club that she'd never wanted to be a part of before. "Care to make a bet?" he asked.

"What kind of bet?"

"If I throw two touchdowns in the first ten minutes of the preseason opener, one for you, one for the team, you have to attend my first regular season game in Denver."

"Isn't betting against franchise rules?"

He shrugged. "Who cares?"

"Okay." She held up her pinkie. "Pinkie bet."

He reached over and wrapped his pinkie around hers.

"What if you lose?" she asked.

"I won't."

She smiled. "But if you do?"

"You can have whatever you want."

Carson said gazing at her, then focused on the busy road. She let go and relaxed in the bucket seat, kicking off her flip-flops and resting her feet on the dashboard—a move Carson appreciated because it meant she was comfortable.

"Any idea on the final roster?" she asked.

"Kaminski and Jones were cut yesterday. Chelsea was offered a spot on the practice squad. Sparrow might get traded. Otherwise, the lineup is solid, I think."

"I hate waiting to find out who made it."

"Too bad Patera didn't get cut."

She lowered her sunglasses and narrowed her eyes at him. "You're jealous of Jag?"

"Not in the way you think. He's a dog, Sadie. Always waiting for sloppy seconds. And I'm pretty sure he's the one who posted that ass shot."

"Thanks a lot for the compliment."

"Not you!"

"Mm-hm."

"Subject change?" he half begged.

"Does sloppy seconds have a choice?" She gave him her best pout, and he chuckled.

"Not really. Mom looks forward to seeing you tonight."

"It's been a long time, Carson."

"I know, sweetheart. We'll stop by the apartment first."

Sadie turned on the radio, switched it over to satellite, and turned on the Beatles station, singing the lyrics to "Love Me Do" in unison with Paul McCartney. It started to rain as they passed the WELCOME TO FAIRHOPE sign. He immediately drove downtown to the Fairhope pier, giving Sadie a chance to see how beautiful the water looked. The gardens were in full bloom, Mobile Bay slightly choppy from the breeze. He stopped in the main parking lot and turned in his seat.

"How do you feel now?"

She disconnected her seat belt and quietly exited the vehicle. Carson couldn't imagine what it would feel like coming home again after all this time. Respecting her privacy, he waited patiently as she walked toward the pier. He'd been damn lucky to grow up in a place like this. Loved and adored by everyone. At one time, they'd called him Fairhope's first son. And when Sadie came into his life, the town opened their hearts to her.

She'd been the perfect girlfriend—pretty and shy, smart and respectable, a good girl.

She'd brought stability to his life and given him a reason to do better. And he had, almost immediately. His grades improved and so did his attitude.

Everything deteriorated emotionally the moment she decided to break it off with him. Though he'd made it through college, won the Heisman trophy, and was a first-round draft pick, Carson had become mechanical—numb. His storybook career brought renewed interest to his hometown, attracting more tourists and bringing much-needed dollars to the local businesses. Hell, the Warriors had even invested in Fairhope, donating enough money to build a new athletic department for the high school and improve the public parks. But something had been missing, and he knew without a doubt who it was.

Just as he focused on Sadie again, her hair lifted in the breeze, showing off her slender neck and shoulders. Two of his favorite spots to lick and nip her delicate skin. God, he wanted her in every way. Wanted to marry her and move back to Fairhope and start a family. Somehow, he needed to figure out how to balance his career and hers without asking her to make any big sacrifices. Sadie's independence was very important to her. She wouldn't be satisfied living a small-town life. At least he didn't think so.

Sure he'd given her ample time to be alone, he joined her outside, slipping his arm around her waist and tugging her close. "Like it here?" he asked.

She gazed up at him and smiled. "It's strange to be standing here again. This park was an integral part of all of our lives—so beautiful."

"You made Fairhope a better place, sweetheart."

She clicked her tongue in disbelief. "That's a ridiculous statement."

"Is it?"

"Um, yeah."

"Did you know your scholarship was announced in the newspaper? That you're the only student from Fairhope to ever receive a full scholarship to an Ivy League school? Do you know how many people asked about you, wanted to celebrate your accomplishment? You didn't stick around long enough to experience it, but you were missed. I know you didn't always see that side of the town, but it's true."

"My mother sent me a copy of the announcement."

"I saved a copy, too."

She kissed Carson's cheek. "That's the sweetest thing you've ever told me."

"It is?"

She nodded. "The more time we spend together, the more I realize how alike we truly are. I have scrapbooks full of newspaper clippings, photographs, and social media posts I printed about you. When I say I followed your collegiate and professional careers, Carson, I wasn't exaggerating."

What could he say to that? He tugged her closer, wishing he could actually pull her inside him, where he'd shelter her from any fear and pain. They stood in companionable silence for a bit, enjoying the sights and sounds around them, the rolling waves and gulls screeching overhead.

Half an hour later, he checked the time on his Rolex. "We should go."

When they reached his apartment, Carson took their bags upstairs.

The studio consisted of a main room with a king-sized bed, dresser, plush area carpet, a leather loveseat and ottoman, and a flat screen TV mounted on the wall. An arched window provided generous light, and the kitchen and bathroom were on the far side of the space. Sadie immediately threw herself on the bed, testing the mattress.

"How long have you been renting this place?"

"Three years."

"And you furnished it?"

"I paid someone to pick up everything. Why?"

"The décor is so masculine. And this bed…" She laid back and spread her legs wide, stretching her arms above her head. "Luxurious."

Carson couldn't take his eyes off Sadie. All he wanted to do was climb on top of her, thrust inside her, and make love to her over and over again. His balls tightened, begging for release. He checked the time again—three o'clock. They were due at his mother's house at six. Plenty of time to remind his girl how much he cared about her.

Without another thought, he kicked off his tennis shoes, unbuttoned his jeans, and stripped off his shirt. He threw his clothes in a neat pile on the floor, arriving at the bedside in his boxer briefs.

Sadie hadn't said a word, only watched as he undressed, as fascinated with his body as he was with hers. He straddled her hips, running his fingers through the soft length of her hair. Dipping down, he captured her mouth with his, his tongue easing between her lips. As the kiss intensified, he cupped her breasts—circling her erect nipples with his thumbs. She cupped the nape of his neck, locking him in place, her other hand slid up his back.

He flinched at the slight sting of her fingernails digging into him, more than ready to get skin-to-skin. "Sadie…"

She dropped her hands to her sides, and Carson lifted himself off of her enough to help unzip her shorts and slide them down her legs. Next came her white lace panties.

"Touch yourself, sweetheart," he said, gripping his cock.

Sadie smiled and licked her fingers before she reached between her legs. Carson loved watching her caress herself, the way her fingers looked sliding in and out so slowly. His cock throbbed with excitement and Carson pumped himself again, never taking his eyes off Sadie.

As she cried out, Carson knew she was close to orgasm, and instinct took over. In an instant, he was on top of her, using his knee to open her legs. He positioned himself between her thighs, circling his hips, saturating his cock with her wetness.

Sadie locked her hands behind his neck, lifting her ass of the bed. "I want to feel your hot mouth all over my body, Carson. Please."

Carson groaned—shifting downward, his tongue swirling across her stomach, then kissing her silky skin. He nipped and kissed his way down her left leg, his free hand skimming over her sex, gently pinching her clit. Switching to her right leg, he worked his way from her ankle to her core, sinking two fingers inside her, kissing the tender spot right above her sex, before he buried his face between her legs—sucking her clit mercilessly.

She was naturally squirmy, and Carson gripped her calves, holding her in place while he drove her crazy with more licks and kisses—unwilling to stop until she came in his mouth.

Their chemistry sizzled, and Carson remembered the secret places that made her hot and wild. Like the ticklish spot behind her left knee, where if he kissed or licked, she'd practically come on demand. Or the tender places on the insides of her wrists…Carson snatched up one of her hands, turned it over, and nibbled the skin.

Sadie cried out, her legs quivering.

"Fuck," he whispered, doing it again. Just the sound of her pleasure-soaked voice brought him close to losing it. "Say my name, sweetheart."

"Carson."

"Tell me what you want, baby."

"Fuck me, Carson. Now."

Her dirty talk set him on fire, and he grunted as he shifted into a more comfortable position on top of her. He rested his forehead against hers, staring into her green eyes. She blinked up at him, massaging the small of his back.

"Carson…I-I…"

"I know, Kitty Kat. You love my ass."

She laughed so hard she had tears in her eyes.

He grinned at her reaction. The fear of losing her again, of all of this ending before it had a real chance to take root, scared him. Carson didn't like feeling helpless and out of control, though he knew Sadie would never intentionally hurt him.

Her natural defensive mechanism was to run away when she felt threatened. The only solution was to keep gently reminding her how much he cared. "You know I want you, Sadie, right?"

She nodded.

"I love you."

Reaching up, Sadie cradled his face between her hands, her eyes focused on his. "Carson—I never stopped loving you."

His heart stopped. The past collided with the present, her words conjuring a sacred memory. The first time they'd made love in high school. The first time she'd ever spoken the three words that had changed his life forever. *I love you.* Something primitive took over, and he sealed his lips over hers, thrusting hard and deep inside her, claiming her body and soul.

Whether she knew or not, in that moment, Sadie had finally come home.

CHAPTER TWENTY-SIX

Carson pulled up in front of his childhood home, and Sadie climbed out of the Jeep. Rushing to the trees, she quickly found the one where Carson had carved their names in the trunk when she was sixteen. Tracing the lines of the heart first, then his name and hers, she smiled.

Carson came up behind her, slipping his arms around her waist. "Did you ever think you'd be back here?"

She shook her head. "When I left Fairhope, I swore I'd never step foot in this town again. Seems I was wrong. *Very* wrong."

"Glad you were." He kissed the top of her head. "Ready to see Mama and the girls?"

She turned in his arms, gazing up at him, liking the way his smile touched his eyes. "Absolutely."

Taking her hand in his, Carson led her to the front door. He used a key from his pocket to let them in, and before the door closed, the heavenly scent of freshly baked bread hit Sadie's nose. She'd never get tired of that smell.

"Carson? Sadie?" Betty called from the kitchen.

"Hello, Mama," Carson said.

"You're early!" As soon as Betty appeared in the short hallway that connected the foyer with the kitchen, Sadie dropped her clutch on the floor and rushed into Betty's arms.

"Sadie." Betty gave her a squeeze and kissed her cheek, then held her away from herself so she could get a better look at her. "Carson didn't exaggerate, child. You are lovely."

Warmth filled Sadie's heart. "You haven't changed a bit, Mama." The name of endearment slipped out as if she'd been around the last seven years. "How are you? Where are the girls?"

"A little older and wiser, but the Lord has been good to us. And thank you for saying I haven't changed—but there's plenty of gray hairs on my head to remind me about the years slipping away. The girls walked to the market to get some ice cream for dessert."

Betty guided Sadie to the kitchen, leaving Carson by the front door.

"Mama?" he called.

"You know your way around, Carson."

Sadie laughed and sat down at the table situated in front of a picture window that overlooked a deck and the backyard. Hanging flower pots with an array of colorful blooms decorated the handrails on the deck. The backyard was spacious, with a swimming pool and swing set.

Betty joined Sadie at the table, setting a cup of coffee in front of her. "Congratulations on the job, Sadie. You must be thrilled having a chance to work with the Warriors."

"Sadie. Mama. I'm going to find the girls while the two of you catch up." Carson stuck his head in the room.

"They went to Maverick's," Betty said.

"OK. Be back soon."

Sadie liked the way Betty's gaze lingered where Carson had been standing. "He's a wonderful man."

"Yes," Betty agreed. "I'm proud of him. The whole town is proud of him. He deserves to be happy. So do you."

Sadie swallowed the small lump in her throat—feeling unusually sentimental. She'd expected some awkwardness with Betty after not seeing her all these years. But honestly, it didn't feel strange to be back. "Until Carson and I started talking again, I was focused on my career."

"And has it given you everything you hoped for?"

Sadie nodded. "Yes. The chance to do what I love and financial independence, and I enjoy living in South Carolina. How have you and the girls been?"

"We've been fortunate here, Sadie. Carson is a blessing, so much like his father…" Betty sniffled, and Sadie squeezed her hand.

"You miss him," Sadie observed gently.

"Every day."

Sadie understood that pain. "I'm so sorry."

"Don't make the same mistakes I did," Betty warned. "If you want to be with my son, and he makes you happy, find a way to make the relationship work, okay?"

"I-I…"

"It's okay, Sadie. I'm not going to stick my nose where it doesn't belong. I just wanted you to know I've always loved you like a daughter. And if you and Carson are meant to be together—the Lord will show you the path. I put off marrying Carson's father for four years. Four good years I could have spent with him."

"I never knew."

"Yes. It's not something I'm too proud of. Before I became Betty Savage, I wanted to be an actress."

"As in Hollywood?"

"Exactly."

"What happened?"

"My father reluctantly paid for acting school and set me up in an apartment in a nice area of Los Angeles. For the first couple of years, I showed some promise—did some modeling and starred in several commercials. I even did a couple walk-on roles on a soap opera."

Sadie smiled. "Why'd you come home?"

Betty stared out the window, shifting on her chair. She sighed, and then looked at Sadie again. "About the third year I lived in LA, Carson's father came for a visit."

"You fell in love?"

"I already loved him. And he knew it. He just needed to remind me where I truly belonged. We spent a week together. Three months later, I found out I was pregnant."

Sadie leaned forward, surprised Betty was opening up to her.

"I returned to Fairhope, too afraid to tell anyone the reason why. To make a long story short, I miscarried and spent the next year locked in my bedroom, suffering from depression. Carson's father did everything he could, but I didn't have the strength or heart to tell him the truth. Even my parents didn't know. Once Carson's father joined the military, I had to make a choice. Risk losing him once he deployed or marry him so we could be together."

Sadie shook her head and grabbed Betty's hand.

"I had Carson two years later."

Betty's story resonated with Sadie.

"Are you all right, Sadie?"

"Yes—just thinking about everything you shared. I'm grateful your life turned out so happy. You had a fairy tale romance. Five children. A beautiful home. Friends who adore you."

"You and Carson could have the same."

Sadie wouldn't confirm or deny it. She'd always been her own worst enemy. Leonard considered it self-sabotaging. Sadie called it self-preservation. Regardless, there was so much to consider. If she decided to fully embrace this newfound happiness with Carson, there were so many logistics to work out. Where to live. Where to work. How to just live without maintaining that tight control she seemed to have such a hard time letting go of.

Twenty minutes later, Carson arrived with his four sisters, who exploded into the kitchen and hugged and kissed Sadie, asking a hundred questions about where she'd been all these years and if she was staying in Fairhope.

The dinner with Carson's mom and sisters had gone better than he'd hoped it would. Sadie had always flourished with his family, like she belonged with them, which gave him even more hope, and every reason to convince her to stay with him as his girlfriend or wife. The latter being his first choice. "The girls were happy to see you."

"Genny and Stacy look like your father." She turned the volume on the radio down.

"I know."

"Heather is so beautiful," Sadie observed.

"And Suzanne is going to win a Nobel Prize."

Sadie chuckled.

"Do you think it's a strange goal for a twelve-year-old to have?" Carson asked.

"No. She dreams big."

"Did you bother asking her *how* she plans on winning it?"

"Yes, of course. She named a couple ways, including for literature."

"Suzanne doesn't write."

"Not yet," Sadie said. "But I encouraged her to follow her dreams."

"Did you enjoy your time with Mama? Did she say anything interesting while I was gone?"

"We reminisced about your father mostly. She told me how she ended up in California after high school."

"She did?" Carson couldn't believe it. He knew the story, but his mother guarded her secrets carefully, mostly ashamed about the choices she'd made when she was young, though Carson disagreed with her completely. His mother had just wanted to fulfill her dreams.

"She's lonely Carson. And she hoped her story would demonstrate why we should treat each other differently."

"And do you think we can?" Carson asked.

"I think we already are. We've learned the hard way, Carson. Being alone isn't what I ever wanted." She gazed at him. "But it's easier than risking your heart."

"There's no risk here, Kitty Kat. You've owned my heart from the beginning."

Carson decided to stop by the Fairhope pier so they could talk and enjoy the night air. He parked, then walked around to the passenger side of the Jeep and opened Sadie's door. "You're not feeling uncomfortable, are you?"

"No. Don't worry so much, Carson. If I have a problem, I'll speak up, promise."

Carson threaded his fingers with Sadie's as they circled the fountain located between the parking lot and pier. "I remember dancing with you here, Sadie."

She nodded. "Ray Dresher's seventeenth birthday party, right? The chief received several complaints about the loud music, but didn't do anything about it. Told anyone who called that the football team had delivered another state title and deserved to party as much as they wanted to."

"Yep." Carson rubbed his knuckles on his chest. "Fairhope royalty."

Sadie rolled her eyes. "Have you devolved all of a sudden?"

Carson let go of her hand and perched on one of the nearby benches. "Being here makes me feel nostalgic. And if that means resorting to the arrogant, badass high school quarterback I used to be, so be it, because it means I still have you, too."

"That's very true."

Carson reached inside his front jeans pocket and pulled out some change. "Make a wish, sweetheart."

Sadie chose a couple pennies and walked to the edge of the fountain. "Should I tell you first?"

"If you say it out loud, it won't come true."

Sadie threw him a cute smile before she tossed the pennies in the fountain. "There. I made two wishes, one for you, and one for me."

Carson was damn happy to be sitting in the same park he'd spent so much time at as a kid with the only girl he'd ever loved. She'd chosen him again, and he felt lucky. "Come here, Kitty Kat." He patted his knee as he reclined on the bench, making room for her to sit on his lap. Just after nine o'clock, the park was relatively empty, just a few fishermen out on the pier.

Sadie didn't hesitate, she sat on his lap sideways, slipping an arm around his shoulder. "Tell me about the dinner tomorrow."

"It's supposed to be a surprise."

"Really? I already know about it."

"Not the finer details." He massaged her back, then kissed her cheek.

She gazed up at him, blinking rapidly like a Southern belle. "Then do tell, Mr. Savage."

"We're going to Chasers for dinner with Barbi, Erika, Lori, and Maggie."

"What? You keep in touch with *all* of my friends?"

"Wait…that's just the beginning. Harp, Georgie, Miguel, and even Jonathan are coming tomorrow, too."

"The Front Five back together again? I didn't know they all lived in Alabama."

"Harp and Miguel stayed in Fairhope. Georgie lives in Mobile. Jonathan is catching a flight from Atlanta."

"I didn't realize how much this meant to you, Carson."

He didn't realize it, either, not until Sadie had agreed to spend the weekend in Fairhope. It did something to him inside, made him want to share his joy with the people he grew up with and loved. Sadie had touched all of their lives once she started dating Carson. When she left Fairhope, their tight-knit group fell apart. It had taken years to recover emotionally for him, even longer for the Front Five to reestablish their close friendships.

"You mean the world to me, Sadie. Don't blame me for wanting to let everyone know we're together again."

Sadie's cell phone vibrated, and she hopped off his lap, pulling it from her pocket. She answered it. "Sadie Reynolds," she said.

Carson focused on the waterfront, wanting to take a walk on the pier. Just as he was about to say something, Sadie cried out.

"Who is this?" she demanded.

Carson shot up from the bench. "Give me the phone, Sadie."

She did, and Carson put it on speaker. But whoever it was hung up.

"Jesus Christ." Carson said. "The number is blocked again. Do you think it's Jason?"

"I don't really care," she said. "Carson?"

"Hmm?"

"Can we go back to the apartment now?"

"Sure, sweetheart."

"I'd like to fall asleep in your arms."

He'd like to do a lot more than hold her. Carson felt an almost insatiable need to make love to her—to keep reminding her how much he cared. How much he loved her. But tonight was about Sadie, not him.

The ride home was short and quiet. Once they were inside, Sadie changed into her pajamas, a Warriors T-shirt and panties. Carson nearly exploded inside his pants, she looked so hot.

"You curl up under the covers. I'm going to take a quick shower." *A cold one.*

By the time he finished, Sadie's little half-snores filled his apartment. He laughed and crawled between the sheets, pulling her against his body, breathing in the clean scent of her hair, wanting to hold her forever.

CHAPTER TWENTY-SEVEN

Sadie did a final touchup on her makeup, dusting her cheeks with translucent powder and then freshening her red lipstick. She'd dressed fashionably casual in a pair of expensive skinny jeans, a white lace off-the-shoulder peasant top, and black heels. Her hair was swept up in a loose bun, with curly tendrils everywhere. A gold choker and oversized hoops completed the sexy look. She smiled at her reflection.

"Ready, baby?" Carson called from the other side of the door.

"Ready," she answered, opening the door.

Carson pretended to get weak-kneed as soon as he saw her, stumbling back a couple of feet. "Maybe we should stay in tonight. Not sure I'm ready to share you with the world after all." He crept close and nibbled on her collarbone, raising goose flesh all over her body.

"Carson…" She ran her long fingernails up his arms and he shivered.

"You're beautiful, Sadie."

She didn't know what to do, because Carson wasn't just saying it to be nice. Love shined in his blue eyes—the consuming kind of love women spent a lifetime searching for. And all of it was for her.

He looked handsome in stonewashed denim, a short-sleeved ribbed T-shirt, and Lucchese cowboy boots. "Thank you," she whispered.

Then Carson produced a delicate, black velvet box. She covered her mouth with both hands, her heart beating erratically.

"It's okay, baby. Listen to me. I'm not going to ask anything of you right now." He opened the box, revealing a perfectly cut, oval-shaped blue diamond set in yellow gold with five rubies. "I've never seen a more perfect stone, Sadie. I struggled with it, trust me. My feelings, what I needed to do to keep you. To love you."

Tears stung her eyes, but Sadie refused to cry. She loved Carson.

"If we never get any further than this, I want you to have this ring, to wear it, to remember this moment by. To know how much I love you. That I'm ready to drop to my knees and beg you to marry me. I won't yet—not until you're ready. But I can't keep my feelings a secret any longer. You complete me, Sadie. You drive me crazy. And I'll be damned if I'll ever let you go again."

He had the courage to tell her everything she was already thinking. That she'd fantasized about being Sadie Savage forever. That she wanted a big family—five or six kids—maybe their own football team. That she never really hated Fairhope the way people thought she did, it was just that it was unbearable to live there without him. Yes—the town had turned on her, and that had scared her away more than anything. But today, she had the courage to reclaim her life. To hold her head high, step out in public as Carson Savage's girlfriend—to love him openly and honestly.

"Will you wear the ring, Sadie?"

Blinking back more tears, Sadie held her left hand out for Carson.

"What finger?" his voice cracked.

"My ring finger," she whispered.

"Does that mean…"

"Ask me tomorrow," she said, captivated by the way his hand trembled when he slid the ring on her finger.

Carson stepped back and eyed the ring on her hand.

"Thank you," she said, admiring the stones. "I love you so much." She flung herself at him, and he caught her in his arms—capturing her mouth with his, kissing her so passionately she nearly fell down. But Carson held her up, giving her strength and hope that she'd finally found true happiness.

He broke the kiss, resting his forehead against hers. "This isn't over, Kitty Kat."

"I know." And she did. Carson never did anything half-assed. And he never relented, not until he got what he wanted. Another reason she wanted this man. He'd never given up on her. Ever.

"We're going to be late."

They arrived at Chasers ten minutes later. The two-story brick building was located in the downtown historic district. It had been converted into a sports bar in the 1980s—the most popular place in town. The inside was exclusively dedicated to Alabama sports teams, with framed jerseys, team photos, and even a high school wall of fame.

As soon as Sadie stepped inside, she couldn't miss a signed Carson Savage Warriors jersey hanging over the hostess station. The couldn't-be-older-than-sixteen employee squealed. "Oh. My. God."

Sadie struggled to hold back her laughter. The girl was obviously a huge fan and couldn't believe Carson had just walked in.

Composing herself enough to speak again, the teenager grabbed two menus from the table behind her. "Good evening, Mr. Savage. Are you here for dinner?"

Carson looked at the nametag on the girl's uniform. "We have a reservation in the bar, Elise. Thank you."

Obviously disappointed, she put the menus back on the table and turned back to Carson. "I'm not allowed in the bar. But if you walk through the double doors over there," she pointed, "one of the cocktail waitresses will seat you."

"Only if you let me take a selfie with you first," Carson said, holding up his cell.

"Really?" Elise asked excitedly.

"Do you follow me on Twitter? Facebook?"

"Of course."

"After I take the pic, give me five minutes and then check for a new post. Okay?"

She nearly ran around the podium and stood next to Carson, making the peace sign before Carson snapped a couple pics.

Once he finished, he placed his hand at the small of Sadie's back and gently guided her through the doors that opened into the busy bar. Big screens were everywhere, the NFL Network and ESPN blaring through the sound system. It didn't take long for someone to point their direction and say, "It's Carson Savage and Sadie Reynolds!"

The room grew eerily silent for a moment, and Sadie melted into Carson's protective body.

Carson must have sensed her discomfort, because he leaned close and whispered, "I have you, baby."

She nodded, the anxiety disappearing.

A man dressed in a gray suit approached. "Welcome back to Chasers, Carson," the bar manager said. "Several guests are waiting for you and Ms. Reynolds at your reserved tables in the back."

Without delay, the manager escorted them through the cluster of high-top tables filled with patrons, past the pool tables, and into the far corner of the room. Sadie relaxed more as soon as she spied Barbi and Erika and several Warriors sitting together.

"You invited Ty?"

"Of course," Carson said. "We're celebrating, right?"

"And Solomon?"

"He's a friend, too."

"And what about the rookie?" she asked.

"Donovan is turning out to be a great addition to the team."

"I'll look forward to spending some time with him."

Carson gazed at his new friend. "Not *too* much time."

Sadie laughed.

Barbi jumped up from her chair and gave Sadie a long hug. "I'm so happy to see you, girlie!"

Sadie returned the hug with equal affection. "Did you ever think I'd come home? It's surreal."

"Are you happy?" Barbi whispered.

"Yes." Sadie said as she pulled back a few inches to look at her best friend. "Take a trip to the ladies' room with me?"

"Try to stop me."

Once they were inside, Barbi checked underneath the stall doors to make sure they were alone before she spoke again. "You have a lot of explaining to do."

"I know. I'm so sorry I haven't called lately. Between Carson and my work..."

"How in God's name did he convince you to come back to Fairhope?"

"Stick and carrot."

"What?"

"He dangled something too tempting to resist in my face."

Barbi gave her a toothy smile. "Like what?"

"Two things. A second chance with him and a professional goldmine. "

"Aww." Barbi embraced her again. "You're not so tough, are you?"

Sadie lowered her head, staring at the ring Carson had just given her. "Does this answer your question?" She held her hand up.

"What the hell?" Barbi grabbed her wrist and squealed like the young hostess up front. "Are you engaged?"

"Almost."

"Wait. How does a girl get *almost engaged*?"

Sadie gave her the condensed version, how Carson didn't want to force her into making a hasty decision, but how he couldn't keep his feelings a secret anymore.

"I think I hate you, Sadie Reynolds. The diamond is flawless, girl. If you don't accept his marriage proposal, you better hand him over to me."

"You like Carson like that?"

"Um, yeah. I'd fuck him."

Sadie snorted uncontrollably. "You're endearingly offensive, you know. Thank you for letting me know you'd sleep with my boyfriend."

"You better get used to that kind of thing, Sadie. Seriously. He's young, talented, and rich. Every single girl between the ages of sixteen and sixty wants to fuck your boyfriend."

Not in the mood to think about that, she changed the topic. "I told him to ask me tomorrow."

Barbi's expression sobered. "And when he does?"

"I'll say yes."

The restroom door opened and Erika walked in. "Thanks for leaving me alone out there with all that testosterone."

"Oh, Erika." Sadie gave her a hug. "I'm sorry—there's so much to catch up on."

"Does this have anything to do with the grin plastered on Carson's face?"

"Everything to do with it," Barbi answered.

"Then I have all the time in the world," Erika offered, sitting down on the padded bench in front of the mirrored vanity.

CHAPTER TWENTY-EIGHT

Carson took a swig of beer, then set the frosty mug on the table. "Did you hear about Tampa Bay?" Carson asked Ty. "Eddie Gomez just signed a contract extension. If that's the best Tampa can do for a quarterback..."

"Eddie still has some game left in him," Ty said.

"He needs to save his brand of game for the green."

"Eddie golfs?"

"Religiously."

"Shit. The day I pick up a putter, shoot me," Ty said.

"I'll remember that twenty years from now when you retire and move to Florida."

Ty smirked. "I'll still be catching balls in twenty years. What about you?"

"Hopefully watching one of my kids graduate from high school."

Ty nearly choked on his beer. "Excuse me?"

"I asked Sadie to marry me."

"What? When?"

"Half asked," Carson corrected. "Before we came here. I finally did it. I don't want to lose her again."

"And what did she say?"

"To ask her again tomorrow."

Ty emptied his mug. And refilled it with beer from the pitcher on the table. "What kind of an answer is that?"

"I told her I didn't want to pressure her at all but that I wanted her to wear the ring."

"Sonofabitch..." Ty slapped him on the back. "Would it be too premature if I bought you a celebratory shot of tequila?"

"Of course not. But keep this between us for now. Just in case she says no." Carson grinned, knowing Sadie wouldn't.

Two minutes later a waitress delivered the drinks.

Ty raised his shot glass. "To you and Sadie getting hitched."

Carson clinked his shot glass against Ty's and swallowed down the tequila. "How about standing up as my best man?"

For the first time since they'd met four years ago, Tyrone Baxley was speechless. "I'd be honored. *If* she says yes."

They both laughed.

Sadie and her friends came back to the table. The grin on Sadie's face told Carson everything he needed to know. She'd told Barbi and Erika about the ring. It felt good seeing her laugh with her friends, especially at their old hangout. It never failed, after every home game in high school, half the school and the team would pack Chasers.

Ty nudged him. "You know these guys?"

Carson looked away from Sadie and turned around. His old teammates were standing together, waiting for him. "Harp!

Georgie!" Carson high-fived them. "Jesus, Miguel—it's been too long. And Jonathan."

"Ty, Solomon, and Donovan, come over here," Carson said.

They joined him.

"Meet my offensive line from high school." Carson made the introductions.

Over the next half hour, everyone invited to the dinner showed up, including Leonard, which was a happy surprise for Sadie. They ordered enough hot wings and beers to feed a small army, then the pizzas started coming.

A few hours later, Sadie nuzzled up to Carson as he draped his arm across her shoulders, comfortably seated in an oversized booth. "Okay, sweetheart?" he asked.

"I'm sad Leonard had to leave early. Otherwise, I'm great. I can't believe we're all here. Harp is married with two kids. Jonathan owns a successful real estate company. Georgie is working on his doctorate, and Miguel travels all over the world…"

"If you think about it," Carson started, "all of us ended up successful."

"And happy," she added.

"That, too." Carson kissed her forehead.

"Get a room!" Ty said from across the table.

"Or maybe we should just hit *Record* on our cell phones and make a sexy video to post," Sadie teased back.

"Been taking notes, girl?" Ty smiled.

"I would never do that."

The same attractive cocktail waitress that had been serving the drinks all evening passed by and Ty grinned at her, the way he always did when interested in getting laid.

"Ty?" Carson said.

"What?"

"Leave her alone."

"Just because you have a girlfriend doesn't mean I'm willing to settle down."

Sadie lips curved upward into a sexy smile. "Ouch."

That's when Carson noticed Jason standing across the bar staring at them.

"Fuck." He shot up from the bench. "I can't believe that asshole showed up here."

"Who are you talking about?" Sadie asked.

"Jason."

"Who's Jason?" Ty asked, standing up, too.

"A jealous prick that doesn't know when enough is enough."

"Carson." Sadie grabbed a fistful of his shirt. "Don't make a scene. We'll figure out how to deal with him."

Carson looked at her. "This is about respect, too, Sadie. And as long as he goes unchecked, that asshole isn't going to stop."

"Please, Carson…We're just starting to get used to the idea of me being here, starting new, living here again…" Sadie let go of his shirt and slipped out of the booth.

"What did he do?" Ty asked Sadie.

"Harassed me in high school for dating Carson…old news."

"No," Carson hissed. "We ran into him the other day and he posted insulting shit on Facebook about us. I sent him a clear message after, not to fuck with Sadie anymore." He couldn't hold back much longer; Jason needed to learn a lesson the hard way. Carson wouldn't let anyone hurt Sadie ever again.

"What's going on, bro?" Solomon approached the table.

Harp, Miguel, Jonathan, and Georgie came over, too. They'd been playing pool with Barbi and Erika.

Carson pointed at Jason.

"Oh, shit," Harp said. "Not good..."

Sadie's heart dropped into her stomach as Carson and the rest of the men headed for the other side of the bar. Every fear she ever had about returning to Fairhope came rushing back. She didn't want any negative attention. Didn't want to be the cause of Carson getting into trouble. Didn't want the town fixated on Sadie's father being the town drunk. Breaking up with Carson was the end result of all her fears, justified or not.

In a small place like Fairhope, the fruit didn't fall far from the tree. And she'd be ruined if she stayed. Her career... the life that she'd built.

Her whole body started to shake. Thank God Barbi noticed. Her best friend slipped behind her. "Sadie?"

"I-I need to go."

"No you don't, sweetie."

Sadie spun around. "I tried to talk Carson down. If he gets into a fight, if any of them do, Ty, Solomon, or Donovan, they might get cut from the team. And what about Jonathan, Miguel, Harp, and Georgie?"

"Let them take care of Jason."

"But all the hard work we've done..."

"Jason needs to get his ass kicked. No one I know would get mad at Carson or any of those guys for defending you, Sadie. This town let you down before, it's not going to happen again."

Tears rolled down Sadie's cheeks. "I don't want Carson to get into a fight over me, Barbi. Please, go talk to him."

"Stay here," Barbi said, "I'll be right back."

Sadie nodded and watched as Barbi walked across the room to Carson and whispered something in his ear. She desperately hoped Barbi could talk some sense into the man she loved, because Sadie felt like she was going to have a panic attack, something that hadn't happened in a long time.

She inhaled through her nose and exhaled through her mouth several times.

"Barbi is right," Erika said. "Everyone knows what Jason and his sister did to you. But no one said anything because it was easier to ignore it."

"Not you, too," Sadie said.

"Let me get you a drink."

"A shot of whiskey might help settle my nerves. Thank you." She made the mistake of taking a last look at Carson—just as he wrapped his big hand around Jason's throat.

CHAPTER TWENTY-NINE

Carson didn't give Jason time to react. He grabbed him by the throat, lifted him off his feet, and slammed him through the set of double doors and forced him outside. He blocked out the world around him—the only thing in his sight was the man who had hurt his girl.

"Motherfucking prick," he seethed, his fists itching for violence. He no longer cared about his reputation or football. He had enough money to live comfortably for three lifetimes. All that mattered was Sadie. "You get one shot at telling the truth. Why are you harassing Sadie Reynolds?"

Jason swallowed, breaking out in a sweat. He stared up at Carson—too frightened to talk.

Carson pushed him, and Jason stumbled back, smacking into someone standing behind them. Carson looked around, there were dozens of people gathered, many with their cell phones recording everything he was doing. Might as well make the end of his career count.

"Why?" he asked again, stalking closer to Jason.

Just as Carson drew his fist back, Ty stepped between them. "Listen to me," he said calmly. "Save those hands for the game, okay? I've got this."

Before Carson could protest, Donovan locked his arms around Carson's waist from behind, holding him back while Ty landed punch after punch on Jason's face. Once he collapsed in a bloody heap, he kicked him in the ribs. "Didn't your mama raise you better? The next time you want to fuck with someone—call me." Ty reached in his back pocket and pulled out a business card, the kind most of the players had printed up to give to women they wanted to sleep with. He shoved the edge of the card between Jason's lips, leaving him out cold on the ground.

"Goddamnit," Carson cursed at Donovan. "Let me go."

Donovan chuckled and let him loose. "Don't get your jock strap in a wad. Ty knows what he's doing."

"Wasn't his fight."

"Sure, it was. We need you to play, Carson. Ty knew better. If he wants to sacrifice himself for the team, let him do it."

Carson scrubbed his face, frustrated and angry—wanting a piece of Jason himself. But the man was still sprawled on the ground, people snapping pics of him. Social media was about to be inundated with video clips and pics that his coach would see.

Sadie…Damn it. He needed to get to Sadie.

As he turned around to go back inside the bar, she was there, looking devastated, her beautiful face streaked with tears.

"Sadie. Sweetheart…"

"I can't believe this happened," she said. "You and Ty are going to get fired, Carson."

Carson knew he should give her some space, but he made a promise once he'd reunited with her to never let things between them ever get out of control again.

The next afternoon in her hotel room, Sadie sat with Leonard on the balcony, trying to make sense of everything that had happened.

"Why?" she asked again and again. The videos and pics were damning—pretty much documenting the full confrontation between Carson and Jason, and Ty's violent beatdown.

"I'm sorry," Leonard said. "Wish I would have stayed."

"To do what?" She swallowed a mouthful of ice water. "Lose your job, too?"

"Carson and Ty deserve a chance to tell their sides of the story," Leonard said. "As for Charles..."

Sadie palmed a stray tear from her eye. "Our boss doesn't care, Lenny. I've been pulled off the project and have to fly to South Carolina today and out again tomorrow."

"Where is he sending you?"

"To Nebraska."

"For what?"

"There's a pharmaceutical convention in Lincoln and he wants me to represent the company at the services booth."

"You're not a goddamned intern, Sadie. You deserve better."

"I need this job."

Leonard shook his head. "What about Carson?"

Sadie gazed at the beautiful diamond ring on her finger. "I

can't handle talking to him right now. I need some time to think about what I'm going to do."

"You're wearing his engagement ring."

"I know." She felt guilty. And was the biggest emotional coward she'd ever known. Instead of facing her problems head-on, she'd shut Carson down, told him she couldn't deal with their personal issues until she settled her professional problems first.

"Are you breaking up with me, Kitty Kat?" he'd asked.

"Ask me tomorrow," she'd said.

Well, it was tomorrow, and she wouldn't take his calls or return his texts. She felt responsible for everything.

"I'm glad you're taking over the project," she said to Leonard, trying to sound positive.

"You know I'll do everything I can."

"I know."

"But Sadie…"

"Yes?" She met her friend's concerned gaze.

"There are better jobs out there."

She clicked her tongue. "No reputable firm will touch me for at least a year after the media shitstorm I just caused."

"You have a point. But we could branch off on our own, right? Hell, we did all the work with the Warriors. We could pitch the NFL ourselves and start a firm. I'm open to anything at this point."

"I appreciate it, Lenny." As much as she loved the idea of being Leonard's partner, for now she was stuck with Charles Longley and would likely get demoted and have her pay cut in half.

"Leslie is going to get my office," she said.

Leonard shook his head. "Over my dead body. Think about what I said about starting our own business, okay?"

"Did I ever tell you how much I love you, Leonard?" She kissed his cheek. "Thank you for standing by me."

"I didn't do anything, Sadie. I tried to get Charles to listen to reason, but he's got his head up his ass, swears we might lose the NFL opportunity if you stay here."

"Please help Carson and Ty straighten this out with the owner and their coach."

"I'll do everything I can. The police are investigating, talking possible assault charges against Ty."

"I know." Her shoulders sagged.

Her phone lit up again and vibrated. She had new text messages from Carson and Barbi.

Carson: *Please, baby. Come back. We need to talk about it.*

Barbi: *Don't blame, Carson. It's my fault. I told him to punch Jason.*

Sadie gulped, anguished and confused.

Carson: *Remember everything we promised each other? Don't run away again. Please. I love you.*

Barbi: *Don't blow it, Sadie. You've come so far. You and Carson are meant to be together. Please, please call me.*

For a moment, she almost convinced herself to dial Carson's number. Or Barbi's.

But she couldn't, not yet.

The hotel phone rang, and she rushed to pick it up.

"Hello?"

"Ms. Reynolds, your cab is here."

"Thank you. I'll be right down." She hung up.

"Your ride?" Leonard asked. He was leaning against the balcony door.

"Yes."

"Did you see the latest posts on Facebook?" he asked, scrolling through his smartphone.

"I don't want to know."

"You need to look, Sadie." He crossed the room and shoved his phone into her hands.

Sure enough, dozens of new posts had been made.

Carson Savage confronts bully that threatened his old high school girlfriend.

Ty Baxley beats up his best friend's romantic rival—saving Apollo's hands for the game…

Then the pics…

Sadie's face was plastered everywhere. *Sadie Reynolds is back. More beautiful than ever. More troubled than ever. More elusive than ever. Runaway sweetheart causes mayhem in Fairhope, Alabama. You thought she nearly cost Apollo his career before—this is the NFL we're dealing with now. Maybe the UFC is recruiting.*

The tags made her sick to her stomach, and she ran to the bathroom to throw up.

"You okay, Sadie?" Leonard called.

"I-I'm okay." She felt dizzy and exhausted suddenly, the whole world closing in around her.

This is why she had stayed away from Carson and Fairhope. She loved Carson so much it hurt. But she'd let him down again, just by being back in Alabama. She rinsed her mouth out with cold water before she returned to the main room.

"Don't go," Leonard said. "We can figure something else out."

Sadie shook her head and hugged him. "Maybe I can come back after I'm done in Nebraska."

Her bags were packed and waiting by the door. She picked them up and glanced back at Leonard, who looked like he'd just lost his best friend.

"Call me when you land, sweetheart," he said.

CHAPTER THIRTY

Thanks to the Warriors' loyal fans, Carson, Ty, Donovan, and Solomon had made it out of the bar unhindered. Ty ended up spending the night at Carson's apartment after Sadie called a cab back to Mobile. Barbi and Erika came by that afternoon to check on Carson and see how they could help.

"Kelly just texted," Barbi told Carson. "Jason is still at the hospital. He doesn't want to press charges even though he has a broken nose and two broken ribs."

Carson thanked her and looked at Ty. "Twitter and Facebook are on fire."

"Yeah." Ty scrolled through his cell. "Did you see the posts about Sadie, too?"

"Welcome to small-town Alabama," Erika offered.

"Jason knows he's busted," Barbi said. "And if I know anything, once this story circulates for a few days, he'll get chased out of Fairhope."

"Jesus Christ." Carson started pacing. "I want Jason's head on a fucking platter."

"Getting biblical on our asses?" Ty asked. "Street justice, bro. Bet the bastard disappears by tomorrow."

Even if he did, Carson planned on making his life a living hell. But for now, all he wanted was to talk to Sadie. "Sadie won't accept my calls or answer my texts."

"She's probably at the hotel. Maybe I should drive over..." Barbi started.

"No," Carson disagreed. His girl hated to be crowded. "All we can do is wait."

Barbi looked shocked. "You? Wait?"

"I promised to be a better man for her, Barbi."

"This isn't the right time. We need the old Carson to rear his ugly head," she said.

"What do you want me to do?" Carson asked, willing to try anything at this point. Concern was eating away at his gut. But goddamnit, he was a simple man, sworn to protect the ones he loved.

"Call the hotel," Ty directed.

Carson dialed the Royale. "Sadie Reynolds' room, please. This is Carson Savage."

There was a pause, and then Blake, the concierge, got on the phone. "Good evening, Mr. Savage."

"Blake—I'm glad you're still at work. Did Sadie Reynolds check out of the hotel today?"

Blake cleared his throat. "Two hours ago, I'm afraid."

"Did she leave any messages?"

"Only one," Blake sounded uncomfortable.

"For me?"

"Yes."

"What did she say?"

"She'll call as soon as she can."

Carson closed his eyes, grief blooming inside him. "Thank you, Blake. Good night."

"Good night, Mr. Savage."

"Well?" everyone asked in unison.

"She's gone."

"Where?" Ty pressed.

"Fuck if I know," Carson snapped.

"Wait!" Barbi said. "I have a text from her."

"What does it say?" Carson rushed to her side.

"Returning to South Carolina. Will call when I can."

"Don't worry," Ty said. "I have a plan."

"What?" Carson doubted Ty could come up with anything he hadn't already thought of.

"Remember my little Christmas present last year? The Gulfstream G550 I have part ownership in?"

"You have a private jet?" Barbi asked.

"Yes."

Barbi shook her head. "Unbelievable."

Ty grinned. "Your itinerary, Mr. Savage."

Carson glanced at the screen and then back at his best friend. "Thank you, Ty."

He grabbed his keys and wallet off the breakfast bar, climbed into his Jeep, and drove as fast as he could to the Mobile Regional Airport. Sadie wasn't going anywhere without him.

* * *

Sadie mindlessly perused the shelves in the magazine store in the Memphis airport. Her flight had been delayed out of Mobile. Now she was delayed in Memphis for more three hours, waiting for her connecting flight to South Carolina. Unfortunately, the queasiness that had started in the cab hadn't gotten any better. She'd already had a ginger ale and two bottled waters, hoping to settle her stomach.

It didn't surprise her, though. Stress always went straight to her stomach. Forced to resort to using an over-the-counter remedy, she checked the first aid section in the shop. Nothing stood out until she knelt to see her options on the bottom shelf, where she eyed pregnancy tests.

She picked one up and read the instructions on the back of the box. She'd missed her period, but didn't think anything of it. Traveling seemed to interfere with her regular cycle. She paid for the test and headed to the closest bathroom.

She locked herself inside the stall farthest from the door and opened the box, which contained two individually wrapped tests. After she finished peeing on the stick, she waited impatiently for the results. Two pink lines appeared in the result window, indicating she was pregnant. Sure she'd done something wrong, she quickly tore open the second foil packet and followed the instructions precisely.

Two minutes later, she received the same result. Whether she liked it or not, Sadie knew she was pregnant. She felt it— the subtle change in her body—her moodiness—how desperately she missed Carson.

Closing the lid to the toilet, she sat down, burying her

face in her hands, crying silently. What the hell was she going to do?

And what about Carson? She stared at the beautiful ring on her finger and remembered his declaration. *If we never get any further than this, I want you to have this ring, to wear it, to remember this moment by. To know how much I love you. That I'm ready to drop to my knees and beg you to marry me. I won't yet—not until you're ready. But I can't keep my feelings a secret any longer. You complete me, Sadie. You drive me crazy. And I'll be damned if I'll ever let you go again.*

He loved her. She loved him. And this tiny, precious spark of life inside her belly was the perfect expression of their love. But she'd left him, again. After promising she wouldn't. Drying her eyes with a big glob of toilet paper, she opened the stall door and stepped out. No one else seemed to be in the restroom. She walked to the closest sink and turned on the cold water, checking her face in the mirror. Considering what she'd been through, she didn't look too bad. Maybe a bit exhausted, but nothing a cold splash of water wouldn't cure.

She washed her hands and face, then smoothed her hair and applied some lip balm and blush. Then she walked back into the main part of the terminal to await the arrival of her connecting flight.

As she searched for a seat, someone called her name.

"Sadie?"

She whipped around, her heart filled with every sort of emotion. "Carson? What are you doing here? How did you know where to find me?"

He looked equally exhausted, like he'd been beaten down

too many times. "Funny what a pretty face and a couple hundred dollars gets you."

Sadie shook her head. "You used your good looks and money to bribe someone to find out about my flight?"

"Sure did, Kitty Kat."

"And now that you're here, what do you have to say for yourself?" Every fiber of her being wanted to run into his arms and whisper in his ear that he was going to be a father.

"Take the ring off, Sadie."

She couldn't believe it. He'd come all this way to take the ring back? She pulled it off and sadly offered it to him. It might as well have been her heart, because that's how it felt.

As she waited for an explanation, Carson simply fell to his knees in front of her. "I'm sorry, sweetheart. But the bastard deserves to suffer—to feel the same pain you endured for so long."

Sadie's hands shook as she reached for his face, cupping his cheek.

"I'm an imperfect man. Jealous. Ambitious. Protective. And so in love with you that, if you want me to, I'll get on the flight to South Carolina with you and never look back. I'll leave the Warriors and find a new team. Live wherever you want."

His words lit her body on fire. He'd finally reached that point where he would consider her career above his own. All she wanted was Carson. To marry him. To return to Fairhope and start a family. "Carson…"

"Wait, sweetheart. Let me finish. Okay?"

She nodded.

A small crowd of curious bystanders had started to gather around them. "Is that Carson Savage?" someone asked.

"Yes," a woman answered. "He sure is."

"I love you, Kitty Kat. I really do. And it hurts whenever we're apart." He covered his heart with his right hand. "Marry me, Sadie. Please."

Sadie couldn't block out the noise from the people, the muted gasps and the anticipation on their faces. Then she gazed at Carson, his complete disregard for himself, as he stayed on his knees on the hard tile floor for the whole world to see.

"It's tomorrow," she whispered. "So I can say yes."

He shot up, whooping like a teenager, picking her up and twirling her around. When he set her back on her feet, he kissed her silly. "Give me your hand, sweetheart."

After he slipped the ring back on her finger, the crowd applauded. Flashes went off and several people begged for his autograph. "Not tonight," he said gently. "I'm getting married."

"There's one thing," she started.

"What, sweetheart?"

"I don't want to leave Alabama. I don't want you to quit the team. I have options here. Good ones. You were right all this time. I've missed my friends. I've missed our town. I want to move home." The idea of starting that business with Leonard popped into her head. It would change everything for her—give her the professional freedom she'd always dreamed of having. "And Leonard and I could start our own company."

"You're amazing, Sadie. If you're sure, then nothing would make me happier." As he picked up her carry-on and started to escort her away from the gate, she stopped him. "I have something else to tell you, Carson."

He stopped and looked at her. "You didn't change your mind, did you, Kitty Kat?"

"No," she said, motioning for him to come closer.

He did.

Then she whispered in his ear, "I'm pregnant, Carson."

He dropped her bag and tugged her into his arms, kissing her again and again. That's when Sadie finally realized, home was wherever Carson was—and now that included their unborn child. Their future. The beginning of the new life she'd always wanted.

EPILOGUE

Three months later
Lansdale Field

As the clock ran out, signaling the end of the first half of the home game against the Patriots, the Warriors leading 27-17, Carson jogged to the center of the field for an interview with Patrick Schwartz, an accomplished sportscaster with ESPN.

The crowd clapped, and Carson shook Patrick's hand, holding his helmet in his other hand.

"You had a great season last year, Carson. But there's something special about the Warriors this year. I heard somewhere your new wife, Sadie, has something to do with that."

Carson grinned. "Yeah—it took seven years to convince her to marry me, Patrick. And anyone who knows her agrees it was worth the wait. She's amazing, and a great advocate for our team. We're expecting our first child in a few months."

"I'm sure I speak for all the Warriors fans out there, Carson.

Congratulations. Let's move to the reason for the halftime interview. A month ago, you and Sadie revealed a special program to get teenagers off the streets in Alabama."

"Hope House," Carson said. "A fully operational farm in southern Alabama. The property used to belong to my great-grandparents. And we wanted to find a way to honor the legacy of my mother's family. Together, my wife, Sadie, and my mother, Betty Savage, decided we should dedicate the farm to kids from Big Brothers Big Sisters—give them a safe haven while teaching them real-life skills. Regardless of the challenges they face, Hope House offers an environment of healing."

"It's an amazing story, Carson, and has caught international attention."

"Thanks, Patrick. We're proud of the thirteen kids already participating."

"Let's bring out your family, staff, and the kids. And two of your teammates, Tyrone Baxley and Donovan Quick, who have spearheaded fundraising for the farm."

The crowd clapped as Sadie, his mother, sisters, and the rest of his crew arrived on the field. Carson stared at Sadie, loving the tiny baby bump showing through her dress. Everything he loved was right there, and it made him ever thankful for the blessings in his life. He kissed Sadie and his mother, then smiled at his sisters.

"That's quite the crew, Carson," Patrick said.

"Couldn't do it without them."

"Sadie, do you have anything to add about the farm?" Patrick offered her the mic.

"Thanks, Patrick. We're having a barbecue at the farm in December, and everyone is invited. Please spread the word—our kids need you."

"Thanks, Sadie. I'm sure everyone in the stands will be there. Better not run out of lemonade."

Sadie smiled and stepped back.

"Now for the big surprise," Patrick said. "On behalf of ESPN and the Warriors, we're happy to present you with a check for one hundred and fifty thousand dollars."

Carson didn't know what to say. He motioned for Jasmine Komisar, a savvy recent graduate from Vermont he had hired to run the business side of the farm, to join him. Ty and Donovan stepped forward with a huge check made out to Hope House.

"For the kids," Ty said, staring into the camera and winking.

"Jack Menzies is proud of you, Carson," Patrick offered, "and wishes he could be here tonight."

Carson shifted on his feet, that boyish sheepishness returning for a moment. "Thanks, Jack," he said into the mic, then blew the owner of the Warriors a kiss. "Love you. Get well for all of us."

Jack had suffered a minor heart attack two weeks ago and was convalescing at home. But he'd made it clear how pleased he was with Sadie and had offered her a long-term contract with the Warriors and a recommendation for the NFL contract. Donovan and Ty offered Carson and Jasmine the check. "Thank you," she said to Patrick. "This money will help so many at-risk kids."

"A round of applause for Carson Savage and his family," Patrick encouraged the full stadium.

The crowd roared with support, giving them a standing ovation as they exited the field.

"I'm speechless," Sadie said, holding Carson's hand.

"You did this," he said. "Everything you touch turns to gold, Sadie. I love you." He kissed her on the lips tenderly, then looked at Ty and Solomon. "Thank you."

"Save your praise for the Super Bowl, baby, after I make the winning touchdown." Ty said.

"You're welcome," Donovan replied.

"Gotta go, sweetheart," Carson gave Sadie a last kiss. "See you after the game?"

"Both of us," she said, cupping her belly. "Don't forget, Leonard and I are looking at some office space tonight. We want to get the firm up and running by the end of the month now that we officially have the Warrior contract and possibly one for the NFL."

"You're amazing, Sadie. Never forget it." And if she did, Carson would keep reminding her.

Please keep reading for a
preview of the next book in
The Playbook series!

Tight End will be available in fall 2018.

CHAPTER ONE

Jasmine turned into the visitors parking lot of Chantam Hills gated community. She felt fortunate to have been included on the "approved" list for charitable organizations that were allowed to visit the exclusive neighborhood for scheduled fundraising. Today involved going door-to-door, handing out flyers for the spring event at Hope House, where she worked as the fundraising manager.

She checked her hair and makeup in her rearview mirror, fidgeting with her bangs a bit, then refreshed her pink lipstick before she grabbed her backpack and climbed out of her Subaru Forester and locked the door.

March in Alabama usually meant sixty degrees with sunshine. But the weather had been unpredictable all winter, and she buttoned her tweed jacket, hoping to block out some of the cold wind. She approached the security shack, pulling her wallet out of her bag before she knocked on the window.

A middle-aged guard slid the window open and smiled.

"Good morning," he said. "What can I help you with, ma'am?"

"My name is Jasmine Komisar and I work for Hope House."

He grabbed a clipboard. "Let me check the calendar."

"Thanks." She gazed around the neighborhood. Four white pavilions welcomed anyone who entered the neighborhood. Extensive gardens and woods surrounded the community, along with a ten-foot green security fence that she didn't like very much.

"You're all set, ma'am. Can I see your ID?"

Jasmine offered her driver's license and the guard jotted something down on the paper on the clipboard.

"Here." He slid the clipboard toward her. "If you could sign right there." He indicated a spot on the bottom of the page.

She read the fine print first. Reminders on how to conduct herself while canvassing the neighborhood. If homeowners had a red diamond hanging on their front doors, it meant they didn't want any solicitors. Finished reviewing the rules, she signed the paper.

The guard scanned the sheet, then offered her a badge to clip to her jacket. "I'll let the patrol unit know you're approved," he said. "And here." He held out a twenty-dollar bill.

"What's that for?"

"The kids." He grinned.

"That's very generous of you, Mister…"

"Gene," he said.

"Thank you so much, Gene." She fished a flyer out of her backpack. "Join us next month for the Hope House Spring Festival."

"Will Carson Savage be there?"

Carson was Jasmine's boss and friend. "Yes. Several of the Warriors will be there."

She gave Gene the flyer, then walked through the pedestrian gate.

Perfectly trimmed lawns, cobblestone walkways, triple-wide roads lined with ancient magnolia trees and rose gardens, expensive street lights every few feet, and white-brick mansions with wraparound porches welcomed her. There wasn't a bus stop in sight. It's not that Jasmine begrudged anyone their success, she didn't. And the people living in Chantam Hills were beyond successful. These were legacy families or plastic surgeons—politicians and Wall Street geniuses, the type of people she needed to keep Hope House going. She just wished they were more accessible, more hands-on when it came to helping the high-risk kids she worked with.

She ended up at the first intersection and checked the neighborhood map she'd printed at her office before she'd left. Should she take Marlon Avenue or Marilyn Street first? She rolled her eyes; the streets were cleverly named after Hollywood royalty. She chose Marlon, picturing Brando as he looked in *The Godfather*. That made her smile.

After the first four houses she'd already successfully collected three hundred dollars in checks. The last home on the cul-de-sac sat by itself, larger than the other houses, chalet style with beautiful diamond-paned windows on all three floors.

"Okay," she said out loud. "Work your magic, Jasmine."

Putting on her confident smile, she made her way to the entry and rang the doorbell. No one answered, so she waited a minute and pressed the bell again. This time a dog barked from inside—a big dog. The door opened, and a man wearing swim trunks with a beer in his hand smiled at her.

"Can I help you?" he asked.

Jasmine didn't know what to say, his ridiculously sculpted chest covered in fine black hair, tapered waistline, and six-pack—maybe eight—she'd have to count the muscles in his abdomen very slowly to be precise, had stolen her voice and ability to look him in the eyes.

She heard him laugh and clear his throat, then say, "What can I do for you, Jasmine Komisar?"

He looked familiar, but how did he know her name? She met his amused gaze and frowned more out of embarrassment than irritation. "How do you know my name?"

He pointed at the nametag clipped to her collar. "Says right there." Then he shook his head. "Wait. Hope House?"

"Oh. My. God." She wanted to run away. "Ty Baxley?"

"You're that little brat from Penn State Carson hired last year!"

"University of Pennsylvania," she corrected. "And if anyone is a brat…" Something moved behind Ty, and she looked over his shoulder.

Not one, but two women wearing bikinis joined them at the door.

"What's taking so long, baby?" one asked, locking her arms around him from behind.

"Thought you were bringing us another bottle of wine," the other complained.

Jasmine wanted to puke. Every stereotype associated with an overpaid NFL player had just been proven in thirty seconds at Ty's front door. That's when she remembered her list of addresses to avoid. She pulled her notebook out of her backpack and opened it. Crap. Ty's address was on the top of the list.

"What's that?" Ty asked, still looking entertained at her expense.

"Nothing for you to worry about." She closed the notebook, but before she could stash it, Ty plucked it from her hand.

"Let me take a peek." He thumbed through the pages. "No-go list?" He looked at her, then back at the paper. "Avoid 8887 Marlin Avenue, Tyrone Baxley, asshole."

As he read her notes, she lowered her head. No one was supposed to see that.

"You think I'm an asshole?"

"Well…" she started.

A vehicle stopped in front of the house and an armed security guard climbed out of the truck. "Everything okay, Mr. Baxley?"

Ty's eyebrows rose and he looked down at her. "Are you going to beat me up or something?"

"No."

"Just fine, Andrew." Ty waved at the guard.

"Really?" Jasmine snatched her notebook back. "You needed to ask me that before you dismissed the security guard?"

"Hey," Ty said. "Dynamite comes in little packages, right?"

"At least you confirmed my observation."

"What observation?"

"To avoid this house. Thanks for your time."

She turned to go, but Ty tugged on her jacket. "Wait a second."

"Come on Tyrone," the women whined.

"Ashley. Macie. Go ahead back to the hot tub." Ty shooed them away. "Sorry about the distractions."

"I have to go. I have a lot of ground to cover." Jasmine said.

"You're here to get donations for Hope House, right?"

"Yes."

"Come inside." He opened the door wide.

"In there?"

"Um, yeah."

This isn't what she'd expected, an invitation inside Tyrone Baxley's sex nest. "Okay." She stepped inside the marble-tiled entryway. A crystal chandelier hung overhead, and an antique oval table with a vase full of red roses was arranged against the far wall. Elegant taste. Not what she'd expected.

"Wait here, Jasmine." He disappeared down a hallway and returned a couple minutes later with his checkbook. "Here." He tore a check out and handed it to her.

She looked at the check. "Three thousand dollars?"

"Of course. For the kids."

He had her tongue-tied again. Was she wrong about him being an asshole? He'd certainly acted like one when she'd first met him. But if this was the kind of donation he gave, maybe she should take him off the no-go list. "Thank you so much."

"You're welcome." He winked at her. "The kids are lucky to have someone like you looking after them. Tell Carson I'll call him later."

"Okay." She started for the door.

"Hey, Jasmine."

"Yes?" She turned around.

"Have dinner with me."

Her gaze moved up his body, taking in every detail, stopping on his big brown eyes. "I can't do that." Then she ran out the door before Ty had a chance to change her mind.

ABOUT THE AUTHOR

Kara Sheridan was raised in Corpus Christi, Texas. She spent her childhood reading, writing, and playing soccer. After meeting her husband in New England, they moved to Alaska, where she studied environmental science. Kara then spent nearly a decade working as an environmental scientist, specializing in soil and water contamination and environmental assessments. Kara still lives in Anchorage, Alaska, and spends her days writing evocative contemporary and historical romance. When she's not reading, writing, or editing, she enjoys time with her husband, pets, and friends.